A
DARK
COUNTRY

A Novel

A
DARK
COUNTRY

Kirk Bogart

Wild ginger Press

A Dark Country
© 2015 Kirk Bogart
www.kirkbogart.com

ISBN: 978-1-943190-01-0

Wild Ginger Press | www.wildgingerpress.com

For my family.

PROLOGUE

A red-tailed hawk circled upward in the warm morning thermals far above the two men lying on the rocky ledge. The hawk hadn't noticed the two men, even with his vantage from the air, and from the ground—from any direction—they were invisible.

They lay flat on their bellies with their chests propped up against camouflage packs behind large scoped rifles that rested partially on the packs and partially on bipods attached at the muzzles. The bipods held the rifles steady, the feet seated firmly on the rocky earth. Brush covered their position, and the morning sun rose over the ridge at their backs. The sun's positioning was intentional; it illuminated the target below, and no reflection off the glass of their optics would betray their position.

The two men tensed suddenly at the faintly audible brushing of hardened cartilage on rock on the trail below them. The sound was only noise to the men; it wasn't identifiable, nor was anything visible. But their nerves held them fixed on the trail, waiting to see what or who was on their path. Then, they heard the sound of a bush bending under the weight of a body and whipping back as the body passed. The men turned their rifles toward the faint sound, and each man heard a metallic click disrupt the silence of the hot Mexican morning air as the other released the safety on his rifle. They were ready for action as soon as the source of the noise below them presented itself. The men waited anxiously, and one of them, the one responsible for their safety, wondered, How could anyone possibly know we're here?

They had been stationed on the rocky ledge ten yards above the trail they'd hiked in on since the evening before. One of the men watched over the other, and sometime during the darkness of the previous night, he was sure he'd heard the rattles of a diamondback faintly clicking as the snake slithered over the hard, uneven ground. It wasn't the buzzing rattle most people associate with a rattlesnake, but a more common sound none but a few men would recognize. This man, however, knew the noise, and he also knew that his companion, his client, would not. So the guide said nothing and the client rested easily through the dark hours, blissfully ignorant of the viper in the brush with them. But now, as they lay in the dirt with the scorpions and snakes, waiting for their opportunity, the kiss of the morning sun warmed their backs and lifted the curtain of night's darkness. At least they could see danger if it were upon them.

The men's breathing quickened under the tension, and the guide took a deep breath and let it out slowly. His breathing eased to a normal rate, and he closed his eyes for only a moment and listened. He strained to pick out a sound from the brushy trail below that would give up their stalker's position, but nothing came except a long silence. Anxiety built in the guide's chest as the silence grew longer. He nestled into the butt of the rifle he was lying with in a prone position and wished he had a shotgun or some other open-sighted, close-range weapon. But he didn't. He looked through the scope and over it at the same time, and there was still only silence. His finger pulled up tighter on the trigger, ready for whatever was about to step from the brush into the opening in the trail. Then he blinked.

In the instant it took for the shutters of his eyes to close and re-open, a scraggly coyote stepped from the brush and stood in the trail. He was ratty, skinny, and unlike the plush winter coyotes in the North Country. The men exhaled with relief and chuckled silently, instinctively holding it in so they wouldn't spook the animal. The dog looked directly at the two men hidden by their camouflage, which matched the brush they were tucked into. The guide felt the thermals hitting him in the face and knew the coyote couldn't smell them. The dog lifted his nose in the air for answers to his hunch that something lay hidden in the brush above him. He licked at the air with his tongue and then licked his nose, searching for some shred of scent that would answer his wild curiosity.

The guide looked askance at the animal while his client looked him directly in the eye. The coyote's eyes recognized what his nose could not: a man staring at him. He continued on his way, dragging an injured hind leg that scraped strangely over the rocky ground. A synapse closed in the guide's brain, connecting the sound of cartilage on rock and the claws on the coyote's bad leg. The dog disappeared into the brush where the trail was swallowed by dense growth as quickly as he had appeared.

"There he is," the guide said.

Both men turned and looked at the house, and then at the photos of their target, which lay on the ground between them. Then they took turns looking through a spotting scope and the scopes of their rifles at the Mexican man in the office of his house nine hundred yards away.

"That's definitely him," said the client.

The guide reached over and clicked the dials on the tactical scope of his client's rifle, adjusting it for yardage and decline.

"Wait for him to step in front of an open window. Then take him."

The Mexican man sat down at his desk with his phone to his ear. His conversation was serious but not heated. Most of his conversations were serious. He wore Barker Black ostrich-toed dress shoes, a starched Lorenzini dress shirt, a Rolex watch, a couple of gold rings, and a fine gold chain around his neck. A woman fifteen years or so younger than he was came into his office, kissed him on the cheek, and placed a cup of coffee on the large desk in front of him. He nodded at her with contrived affection and motioned for her to close the door behind her as she left the room. When she did, he got up and walked over to the built-in cabinets on the wall of his office. He picked up the television remote and turned on the set mounted to the wall in front of his desk. The office looked like the home office of any wealthy businessman.

The well-dressed Mexican man walked back to his desk, flipped through a couple of channels, and then laid the remote down on the desk. He walked to the cabinet, and, turning his back to the two men nine hundred yards away who were watching him through riflescopes, he took something off the shelf and looked at it for a moment. It was a framed photo of his four children in front of a Christmas tree. Two were in their twenties, and the other two were younger—elementary school age, and from his second, much younger wife.

In an instant, everything shattered. His spine, his sternum, and the glass frame in his hand. Something had hit him in the back with the weight of a sledgehammer, and the force was so tremendous that it blew him face-first into the cabinets. He bounced off and fell backward. A blinding bright light filled his head for a fleeting moment, and then he felt nothing under him—no legs, no control. He fell on his back with an empty, dull thud. For a fraction of a second, he saw the ceiling of his office, but just as quickly it faded to black. Then all movement and all thought ceased forever. All that was left was black.

ONE

There was no time now for mistakes.

Jack Duncan looked down from the window seat of the Gulfstream jet at the Mexican landscape thirty thousand feet below him as though it were a living map. He tried to make out the cities on the Mexican coast, including Mazatlán, where he had been only a couple of days earlier.

Duncan watched the tropical southern Pacific coast dry out as the jet flew north for Los Angeles. He could see the delineation between the murkier inshore water and the clean cerulean water where dorado, sailfish, and tuna lived. He admired Baja and coaxed old memories out of the dark storage room of his brain as he tried to pick out the places he'd been in the bleak, rugged mountains, where he'd guided sheep hunters. He'd had friends on the dry desert ground below, and in his mind he tried to see them but could only muster a time-faded image from twenty years earlier. They were as distant to him now as the feeling of youth—that time in his life when nothing had happened that long ago, and everything was fresh, and there was still plenty of life ahead in which to make a decision, or a mistake.

Looking down at the surface of the earth, he tried to reconcile the facts of his current life against those of his youth: the beauty from the window seat of a jet; and the greed, corruption, and violence he knew was on the ground at eye level as well as on the plane, and possibly even living inside him, as it lived inside all but a few men.

What Duncan couldn't see from his window seat was the funeral procession for a Mexican man that was at that very moment passing through Mazatlán toward the city cemetery. Most of the procession's onlookers appeared stoic, if not emotionless, aside from several kids and an old woman, probably the dead man's kin. There was a younger woman accompanying the children, but the little grief she showed seemed contrived, and the general mood that hung over the crowd was one of fear and relief rather than of mourning. The dead man in the fantastic, solid, silver-handled rosewood casket was a notorious drug cartel leader, a violent man who had stopped at nothing in building his illicit empire using torture, decapitation, and an entire repertoire of headline-grabbing savagery from the miscreant's handbook. And Jack Duncan had arranged his ride in that finely handcrafted box.

From his seat in the jet, Duncan could not see the procession, or the crying children, or the old lady, or the dead man, but he could picture the man's face. He had seen him through the spotting scope as the bullet hit him, and he let the image haunt him for a moment. He imagined the man in death, in the casket, pale and void, but the haunting was fleeting.

Duncan was enjoying some bourbon over ice along with the view. He felt relaxed momentarily but eager to see his family. He was flying to Los Angeles to catch a commercial flight to Alaska, where he would meet them. And he was going to let his wife, Erica, in on a secret during their annual trip to their cabin on the Kenai River.

It was a secret that had been gnawing at him for nearly two years. Life had not quite gone the way the Duncans had planned, and when the challenges arose, Jack Duncan had found himself entangled in a business he wanted no part of. He had been away from home so much that he was almost a stranger in Ennis, Montana, and even more regrettably, a stranger to his family.

As Duncan looked down from the jet window, he let his thoughts wander from the earth below him to his family and to the mountains of his youth.

Jack and Erica had grown up together in Ennis, a town not far removed from the Old West. They could both still remember the dirt streets from their childhood and the hitching rails that lined the businesses that fronted them. Ennis was isolated from the rest of the world, a country of its own. It wasn't far from Yellowstone National Park but not really on the way from anywhere. Everybody knew everybody and everybody else's business, and not much went on that would have ever made news beyond the local tavern and beauty salon.

Erica grew up on a large ranch on the bench south and west of town that overlooked the Madison River Valley. Her father had a large Black Angus operation. They fed the animals through the stark, frozen winters and grazed them on expansive summer Forest Service allotments leased in the Gravelly Range to the west and contiguous with the ranch. Like any kid who grew up on a ranch, Erica learned how to work: she was part of that grass and soil, and they were part of her.

Duncan, on the other hand, loved the river located out his front door and the Madison Range located out his back. By the time he graduated from high school, he personally knew every trout that lived behind every boulder from Indian Creek to Raynolds Pass Bridge. He knew the bighorn sheep, the elk, and the mule deer that lived in the rugged mountains whose base rose from the sagebrush in his backyard. He loved those mountains. They were his home and his sanctuary, and where he retreated to solitude. He was safe there.

He hunted the deer and the elk, he fished the high lakes, and he had backpacked and horsepacked the entire range. He'd often gone into the mountains with friends and his grandfather, but if he could not find a companion, he went alone. He loved those mountains and their inhabitants, but it was the bighorn sheep that traversed the steep and craggy slopes that most captivated him.

He hunted them with cameras in the summer, and in the winter he horsepacked feed in to them, not so much because they needed it, but to keep them from migrating down the valley and becoming infected by the diseases that were spreading from domestic animals and decimating wild sheep populations across the continent.

The year he turned seventeen, he decided to hunt one. He had tried for four years to draw a lottery tag to hunt a ram, but he realized he might live to be one hundred and never draw, so he formulated another plan. Instead, he pulled one of the only sheep tags available over the counter in the lower forty-eight states for a portion of his mountains twenty horse-miles to the north. Duncan probably would have been content to hunt in that area, but there was a large old ram that lived above his home that he had watched since he was a boy, and Duncan was sure that the ram's time was up.

The old Roman-nosed monarch carried a massive head of horns. Though they were broomed off on the tips, they still came all the way around to a full curl and showed eleven growth rings. Duncan had watched the old ram spar for breeding rights for eight years on a craggy slope he could see with a spotting scope from his living room, and for seven of those years, the old ram had won the brain-rattling battles and defended his rights to one band of ewes or another. The ewes would begin to arrive at this craggy spot, emerging from the deeper mountains in late September in advance of the big winter snows. Then, the rams would show up in early October when the rutting season began.

The craggy slope the sheep liked had avalanche chutes strewn with loose boulders and laced with rabbitbrush, stunted willows, and other brows. The steep, open, south-facing slopes adjacent to the chutes were carpeted with a dense growth of protein-rich grasses, and they were often blown clean of winter snow. The previous fall, Duncan's ram had lost in the rut, beaten into the snow and driven down the slope. The demeaning loss had sent the old ram into solitude. For the first time in nearly a decade, the old ram went without his ewes and spent the winter alone, grazing near the other sheep herds but never joining the bachelor groups he'd led through winter in years past. The old ram lingered through the spring, staying in low country long after the snow melted and lambing season began.

He seemed reluctant to return to the high country, as though he'd lost interest. Duncan knew the old ram was done. He had lived out his useful life and would not survive another year. Duncan decided he would kill the old ram, and when the old bruiser finally returned to the high peaks, Duncan followed him.

Duncan lived in the mountains that summer between stints guiding fly fishermen on the Madison and on several of the private spring creeks that fed it and were locked up by dude ranches. He watched the old ram and learned his feeding areas, his bedding areas, and the places he'd go for water. When the ram traded the slopes above one high mountain basin for another, Duncan would promptly find him and relearn his habits. This also gave him time to plan the state crime of harvesting this beautiful animal.

The chunk of ground the ram lived on was not open to sheep hunting by the state of Montana. However, the boundary of one of Montana's unlimited sheep units was about a dozen rough horse-miles to the northeast. The state sold an unlimited number of tags for the small area and had a quota of two rams. When the state wardens or biologists confirmed that two rams had been taken, they closed the hunt and notified the remaining hunters so no more sheep would be killed. Mountain sheep were highly valued commodities to the states and provinces with populations sufficient to hunt; the permit fees were high, and penalties for poaching one were far more costly than those for more common game animals like deer and elk.

Duncan did not care. He had no regard for the state or federal government. In fact, he despised the government even at that early age for one reason: Duncan's father had been killed in Vietnam a year after Duncan was conceived, and before his father had even laid eyes on him. As far as Jack Duncan was concerned, the US government had killed his father.

Duncan had studied the politics and history of this war despite the lack of curriculum on the subject in the public schools. No matter how hard he tried to justify that war, he wasn't able to, and no matter how hard he looked for the reason that he had grown up without a father, Duncan could not find one. All he saw were the deeper, darker financial motives of some powerful large businessmen and their back-pocket political whores. The government blamed it on a communist bullet, but Jack Duncan knew a different truth.

When it came to the old ram, he did what he felt was morally legal and devised a plan. Two days before that season's sheep hunt opened, Duncan arrived at the main trailhead leading into the open unit. Biologists and wardens were stationed at the trailheads to advise hunters on a number of items the state deemed important, to check the rams as they were harvested, and to notify hunters when the quota was met and the season closed. There were trucks and horse trailers in the parking area and hunters in ahead of him hoping to find and kill a ram quickly. Duncan had a similar intention, but his strategy was dramatically different.

Duncan pulled the well-used Ford flatbed pickup, a gift from his grandfather, into the parking area with his two black mules in a three-horse slant trailer he'd borrowed from Erica's father. The parking area was nothing more than a large open prairie at the foot of the dramatic Madison Range where a dirt two-track road left the highway. Duncan made a large sweeping turn with the truck and trailer and left it close to the exit, pointed toward the highway for an easy departure upon his return. He knew most of the state employees at the trailhead, as he had been working on volunteer projects to improve game habitats since elementary school. He watched them watching him as he got out of the truck, unloaded the two mules, and tied their leads to the loops on the side of the trailer. Duncan brushed the mules while the men approached him curiously, the two biologists in the lead and the old game warden swaggering along behind them.

"Where you headed, Jack?" one of the biologists asked.

"I'm gonna look for one of your rams," Duncan said as he threw the riding saddle over the back of one of the large black mules.

"You drew a tag?"

"Yessir, do you need to see it?"

"No."

"Who's goin' with you?" the second biologist asked.

Duncan looked at the man as he tightened the cinch on the puffed-up mule. He looked at one biologist, then at the other briefly, and then back at his task at hand, ignoring the question. He walked back to the tack room of the trailer and grabbed the crossbuck saddle from its position on the swing-out rack and returned to the second mule without saying a word. The two biologists milled around, looking for a sign of a parent or partner heading into the wild with the young Jack Duncan. There was nobody else around but the old warden, who was now standing next to the biologists.

"You aren't going into those mountains alone, are you?" one of them asked again.

"Why not?" Duncan replied, going about his business of cinching down the packsaddle while the men looked at each other with disapproval.

"That's some pretty wild country up there, son," the old warden said.

"I'm familiar with it," Duncan said, looking at the old lawman, who wore a sweat-stained Stetson that he'd reshaped with his own hands and a swooping white moustache that hung down, entirely covering his upper lip. He was not wearing a regular uniform, but a pair of old Wrangler jeans with his state-issued duty shirt. There was a badge pinned to the front of the khaki shirt and a holstered double-action revolver that hung low on his right hip from an old leather cartridge belt. Duncan was familiar with the man in passing. The old warden had been born in the 1920s and had grown up surrounded by the old men who had settled the West in their youth. Duncan respected him but had no use for his concern.

"You oughta have a partner in those hills, kid."

"You offerin' to go with me, sir?"

"I'm just saying there's all sorts of dangers can befall a fella in these mountains."

Duncan went about his chore of saddling the mules as though the men weren't there. He dragged the two pannier bags off the flatbed of the truck, handing one to the old warden.

"If you're that interested in my well-bein', would you mind droppin' one of these panniers onto the crossbuck for me?"

Even as a teenager, Duncan was a competent horseman and packer. He came from a long line of Montana cowboys, and the physical void left by the loss of his father had been well filled by his grandfather, uncles, and, to a significant extent, Erica's father, Roy Bergstrom.

Duncan had packed the panniers at home and weighed them with a pack scale, fine-tuning them with stones from his yard so they would balance perfectly on the mule. *I've spent more time in these mountains than those two biologists put together,* he thought, but kept it to himself.

"There's grizzlies up there, you know," one of the biologists added.

Duncan looked at the man over the saddle as though he were an idiot as he tightened the bridle around the mule's big black head and again said nothing. He untied the mule with the packsaddle, turned his head away from the trailer, and handed the lead to the old warden.

"Do you mind?" he asked.

The old warden nodded back at him and took the lead. He had read enough people to know he was not going to change the young man's mind, and there was no point in continuing the conversation.

Duncan led his riding mule away from the trailer. He grabbed the saddle horn with both hands and swung up into the saddle in one leaping motion. He slid his boots into the stirrups and urged the mule forward, taking the pack mule's lead from the old warden and showing him a faint, sly smile. The warden had seen that leap into the saddle many times in his life, and he had performed the same stunt when he was much younger. He might still be able to do it, but he was old enough now that he didn't need to try it.

"I don't want to go alone; I just don't have anybody to go with," Duncan said to the old warden.

The warden said nothing and continued to look at Duncan.

"My friends have school and football. My grandpa's got too much farm work this time of year, and I've got a sheep tag."

"I understand," the warden replied.

"I've got to go huntin.'"

"At least tell us where you're headed?" one of the biologists asked.

"Well, how the hell would I know that? I'm goin' to where the sheep are." Duncan looked again at the two biologists as though they were idiots and then back at the warden, who was smiling. "If you know where they are, tell me and I'll go there."

"Good luck, kid," the old warden said.

"Thank you."

Duncan pulled the mule's head around with the reins in his right hand and spurred him slightly, starting away from the three men at a trot. After he was fifty yards or so from the parking area, he slowed the mules to a walk. The three men watched Duncan, who looked small against the backdrop of the dramatic mountain range.

As he rode off, Duncan thought about the three men, and he knew they were standing there talking about him going into the mountains alone. He would have preferred a partner, but he did not want anybody else to know his story, nor did he want to implicate his friends. He knew they would ask where he intended to hunt, so he'd evaded their questioning and said very little.

The old warden wasn't the least suspicious, as any savvy hunter with a good idea of the location of a legal ram would be foolish to give it away, so the men were not at all alarmed by his vague response.

Duncan slipped sideways out of the saddle and looked back at the three state employees standing at the edge of the parking area, watching him ride off. Duncan waved, they waved back, and he turned his attention back to what was ahead of him.

Duncan rode the black mules into the mountains and headed for the most rugged part of the hunt unit. The mountain basin he was going into was marked by incredible rock spires and avalanche chutes and creek drainages that were impenetrable on horseback, and some even on foot. It was an area of the unit that did not get hunted much, located toward the southern boundary and nearest to the old ram that lived in his backyard. Duncan set up a simple decoy camp in a small grassy opening too small to be called a meadow in the middle of a stand of dark alpine fir.

The camp was nothing more than a dark-green tarp over a ridgeline stretched between two fir trees and lashed down to stakes at the corners. There was also a cache of canned food and horse grain hanging from a limb, out of reach of grizzlies. The camp was very well hidden and unlikely to be found, but it was there in case someone looked. It had taken Duncan only half the day to get into his hidden camp and set up, so he picketed the mules, which gave them ample opportunity to leave signs should the state require him to show the location of his kill and his hunt. While the mules fed on the abundant meadow grass, Duncan cooked a can of beans on a four-ounce titanium backpack stove fueled by a small can of propane. After eating the beans, he napped the rest of the afternoon in preparation for the long, dark ride ahead of him.

As the sun dropped closer to the western horizon, Duncan saddled the two black mules and rode off. He left the camp and climbed to the top of the steep ridge toward the southern boundary of the hunt area. At the top of the ridge, he glassed the country, waiting for the cover of darkness. When it was sufficiently dark, he led the mules on foot through a scree slide that spilled into a dark patch of timber, and then he rode down through the timber a quarter of a mile before contouring around the opposite ridge to sufficiently hide his tracks. It was a difficult, ankle-turning, brush-busting traverse, but once he reached the other side, the clear, warm, late-August night made for an easy ride.

The mules knew the trail, and their smooth, surefooted gait and confident night vision allowed Duncan to rock in the saddle, half sleeping, as they made their way north to the house of the old ram. At times, the trail wound around the west sides of the ridges and Duncan got glimpses of the Madison River and valley below. At about three in the morning, they got to the first vantage point from which he planned to glass for the big ram. There, he tied the mules in a thick patch of lodgepole pine and gave them some grain while he set up a spotting scope and eagerly awaited the sunrise.

When the sun started to come to the surface of the eastern horizon, its rays spilled over the ridge at Duncan's back and spread light on the jagged granite cathedral in front of him. As more light gathered in his optics, he began to find the sheep. A small band of lambs and ewes were below him a mile down the drainage toward his home, and a band of six adult rams fed across one of the grassy slopes above him. There was no sign of the old monarch, but Duncan was not concerned. He knew that if the old ram were not on this side of the mountain, he'd be on the other. The ram would be feeding or napping on or near one of three benches that stepped down below a very steep headwall where three small fingers of a larger creek originated on the face of the mountain. Duncan mounted his mule and led the second mule behind him, contouring his way down the drainage so he would not alarm the band of rams above him. This enabled him to come out on the other side of the ridge on roughly the same elevation as the three benches, if not slightly lower, in the cover of thick lodgepole pines.

Duncan tied the mules near the edge of an opening in the timber from which he could glass for the ram. Standing in the midst of his boot prints from many previous trips to that very spot earlier in the summer, he set up the scope and spotted the ram feeding on the middle bench. He was hoping the ram would be on the first bench and within an easy range of two hundred and fifty yards, but the ram was on the far side of the bench on the middle ridge. According to the old range finder he'd borrowed from his uncle, the ram was four hundred and sixty-eight yards away—still a feasible shot for Duncan, who spent lots of ammo practicing long-distance shooting in the open sage country.

There was a slight downdraft still lingering in the mountains, but it would not be enough to significantly affect the flight of a bullet at the distance Duncan was facing. He wadded up an oilskin rain slicker that had been tied to his saddlebags and placed it under the forearm of his Winchester Model 70 .270, the same rifle and caliber made famous by the late sheep hunter and author Jack O'Connor. Duncan had read all of O'Connor's stories of great sheep-hunting adventures when he was a younger kid. He loved the stories, and when it was time to select a rifle, he chose the .270 for the same reasons O'Connor had: it was light, accurate, and flat shooting. And now, on the side of a mountain, he was living out a sheep-hunting adventure of his own.

He fastened a crude silencer manufactured from steel pipe and spray foam to the muzzle of the rifle with rubber bushings and a hose clamp. Duncan knew the silencer was probably unnecessary, but it was an added measure of caution in the unlikely event that someone else was in those mountains. He lay down behind the rifle on top of the little rock outcropping, nestling his chest and torso into the earth flat and firm, and found the old ram in the crosshairs of the scope. Duncan was in no hurry. He tested the wind one more time, took a deep breath, and then let it out as he settled the crosshairs just over the top of the old ram's back, just behind the shoulder. Duncan held the aim high enough over the ram's back to account for the bullet drop at that great distance, as the rifle was sighted in for a three-hundred-yard zero. Still, Duncan waited. The ram fed with his head down, walking slowly across the grassy bench, and then he stopped looking up to chew a mouthful of grass. Duncan took another breath. He squeezed the trigger as the last of his exhaled breath left his lungs.

At the shot, which barely made a sound, the ram lunged forward two steps and stopped to look around. Then his legs turned wobbly and he tipped over dead. Duncan was exhilarated and grief-stricken at the same moment. His own knees became wobbly, and every ounce of blood seemed to race from his head at once. He worked the bolt slowly so the spent cartridge slid out of the chamber. He removed it with his fingers and placed it in the pocket of his light wool pants. He lay with his back to the ground, dizzy, staring up at the big blue sky with tears forming in the corners of his eyes, lost in that ironic moment of confused elation and regret that only a big game hunter knows.

The steep, rocky terrain prevented him from leading the mules to the bench where the old ram lay, so Duncan climbed to the bench with an old packboard on his back. He was lucky. The ram had died on the relatively flat bench instead of sliding down an avalanche chute or into some other terrible hole like sheep and other mountain game animals sometimes did.

He laid out a soft canvas tarp and pulled the ram onto it. Then, he methodically skinned the entire hide intact up to the base of the ram's skull, at which point he severed the head. He intended to have a taxidermist immortalize the ram in a full-body mount, which he planned to hang over his mother's living room windows, overlooking the mountains the ram had come from, at least until Duncan had a home of his own.

Duncan strapped the packboard to his back and made six trips back to the mules with meat, offal, and trophy. The animals were tied in a patch of timber several hundred yards down from the bench. He dumped the rocks out of the panniers and equally distributed the boned-out meat, weighing each bag and then adding and subtracting rocks until they were equal. He placed the offal and the skeletal remains in garbage bags, which he loaded into a large canvas duffel along with hide and head so they would be out of sight. He then hung the bags back on the crossbuck packsaddle with the duffel lashed to the top of the saddle and boxes.

Duncan had removed the rib cages intact and rubbed them with salt, pepper, and a powdered teriyaki sauce almost immediately upon starting the task of processing the ram, and he left them to brine draped over a fir bough in the shade near the mules. When all the processing and packing was complete, Duncan built a small fire in the thick timber where the mules were packed and tied. He was careful to use only the driest wood to keep the smoke down, which he calculated would dissipate in the timber and be carried up and away with the warm midmorning thermals, far from any possible human nose. He then broiled the ribs over the coals of the fire using green aspen branches cut from a nearby tree and strung between an oven of rocks that he stacked on either side of the fire. Duncan rested in the timber, turning the ribs until they were broiled to perfection.

Duncan had grown up eating elk, antelope, and deer, but he had never eaten sheep meat until this day, and he delighted in its mild flavor. He expected the old ram to be tough, like an old mulie buck, but it was not. The flavor was mild, not gamey, with a sweetness that was accented by the teriyaki marinade. He ran his skinning knife down between each rib bone, separating them into individual portions, and he ate the entire rack one rib at a time. In his hunter's heart, each bite was just meat, a prized commodity separated from the ram that had been living only hours before. With each bite, he took sustenance from the ram's sacrifice, and he ate with no regret. Duncan glanced at the ram's head lashed to the packs atop the mule, and sadness crept back in for a moment as he looked at the head, with its massive set of curled chocolate horns and its lifeless eyes staring up at the big blue Montana sky. *A hunter is more cognizant of mortality than the average person,* Duncan thought. *He is faced with it repeatedly.* And sitting in the stand of fir trees with a belly full of sheep meat, thinking of the story he would tell when he returned to the valley below, he realized that the stories of all living things had the same ending, if you followed them to the actual end.

Duncan split the other side of ribs and packed them, one in each of his saddlebags. After eating, he slept a couple of hours, rested a couple more, and waited for darkness before heading back to the legal unit and his decoy camp.

At the outset of the return trip, Duncan had to spur the black mules away from home. They knew the trail and wanted to take the short two-hour trip back to Duncan's home and to their pasture. This would have worked to Duncan's advantage in the event of a mishap: left without a rider, the mules would have taken the contraband back to his home instead of the trailhead and the state employees. But he spurred them on and rode into the darkness. He could have easily slept in his own bed, eaten a breakfast cooked by his mother in his kitchen, ridden up and killed the ram, and returned home all in the same day, but legally, that would not have worked. The state officially marked the horns of legally harvested bighorn sheep, and any ram skull lacking such a mark couldn't be mounted by a taxidermist. Duncan did not want to take the ram and then have to hide his beautiful horns in a closet. So he rode through the night, depending on the mules to get him back to the basin where his decoy camp was set.

Once they reached the basin, he rode the mules across a grassy slope down the ridge where the scree slide hid his trail, and then he dumped the offal and bones on the side of the ridge where sheep did occasionally graze. After the earth near the mock kill site was sufficiently trampled by mule hooves, he rode into his decoy camp just before daylight. He tied the mules to the high line and removed the pannier bags and duffel to rest the barely sweating beasts. He slept as long as he could into the morning, and then he built a fire, this time a large one, as he was unconcerned about smoke. He burned the garbage bag in which he'd transported the waste, ate the remaining rack of ribs, and napped the rest of the afternoon. No evidence remained of the real hunt, as he had buried the silencer in a timber patch along the trail in the night, and if there had been any questions by the state wardens, he could have led them back to this camp and to the gut pile he'd dumped on the hill above it.

In the middle of the afternoon, he saddled the mules and rode out of the mountains. It was dusk by the time he reached the trailhead, which lent to the authenticity of his story of having killed the ram that morning.

Duncan could see four men in the parking area waiting for hunters to emerge from the mountains. As he got closer, he recognized one of the original two biologists and a younger warden in a full uniform as well as two other men Duncan recognized but did not know well. He had hoped to see the old warden in his jeans and hand-shaped Stetson. The men studied Duncan as he approached on the mules.

The sun had just set, and the rocky peaks at his back framed him like the subject of an animated painting. He rocked slightly in the saddle at the cadence of the smooth gait of the mule, and the second animal came out from behind Duncan, revealing the prize lashed to the top of the packs on the crossbuck packsaddle. Duncan looked larger now than he had three days earlier when he was riding out at the start of his adventure against the same grand backdrop.

Duncan rode the mules up to the men and passed them with only the slightest grin on his face, which hardly showed the three days in the mountains. He was barely soiled, and the wispy growth of a young man's beard scarcely changed his face. To the older men there to greet him, he looked fierce and proud, like a warrior returning from a vision quest.

"You made it," the biologist said.

"There was never any doubt I would."

One of the other men stepped forward as though he would take the mule's lead, but Duncan turned his head away from the man. "The only doubt was if I would find a ram," Duncan added.

"Well, you surely did!" one of the men said.

"And a dandy at that," the biologist added.

"Let me tie them up," Duncan said. "Then we can unload the ram and you can do what you need to do with him."

"Sure, kid," the biologist said. And the small entourage followed Duncan and his mules to his truck and trailer. There was no one else for the men to tend to, as none of the other hunters had returned from the mountains. Duncan swung off the back of the mule and dropped to the ground. He tied his mount to the trailer, and then he led the packed mule to the bed of his truck, where the men helped him remove his meat, trophy, and panniers and place them on the flatbed. The men admired the great ram while they examined him.

"Where did you kill him?" the biologist asked.

"Secret Peak," Duncan said and smiled at the warden first, then at the other men.

The warden bristled a bit and said, "You have to tell us where you took the ram; it's the law."

"I know, I'm just kidding. I shot him at the head of Silver Tip Creek."

"Really? There haven't been many rams taken in that basin," the biologist said.

"No, I expect not. That's some pretty tough country."

"Yes, it is."

"Sometimes you gotta get off the beaten path," Duncan said and went back to stripping the rigging off the mules, letting the biologist examine the head and mark the horns to show it was a legitimate trophy.

"It's funny; he's really broomed off on the left side. Really distinct head of horns. I don't recall ever seeing him on any of the winter ranges," the biologist said.

"Yeah, I haven't seen him either," one of the other men said.

Duncan could feel the eyes of the warden on him, but he never looked up. He continued putting up the tack.

"I never saw him scouting, either," Duncan said as he led his mount into the trailer. "I figured he must've wandered up here out of Yellowstone."

The men agreed and all went back to their tasks—Duncan putting up the mules and the state employees finishing with their examination of the ram.

<hr />

Word soon spread around Ennis and the rest of Montana that a seventeen-year-old had killed a fine record-book ram in the unlimited Spanish Peaks hunt, and it was not long before Duncan became something of a celebrity among outdoorsmen in the Northwest.

Duncan tried to shy away from attention over killing the ram, not because he was ashamed, but because he didn't like the attention. He did not enjoy his celebrity. It made him slightly nervous, but only slightly, and as time passed, he became secretly proud, not so much of what he had accomplished, but of what he'd pulled off.

A number of regional newspapers covered the story, as did a couple of national sportsman's magazines, and Duncan was invited to the National Sheep Foundation's banquet in Reno as well as several Rocky Mountain Elk Foundation banquets in Montana, Idaho, and Wyoming, all of which he attended.

He was asked to speak at the banquet in Reno and to give an account of his hunt, which produced a ram that turned out to be one of the largest rams killed in Montana in a number of years. Duncan was cryptic in his delivery, as he did not want to lie to the gentlemen attending the mountain sheep functions, which were put on to raise incredible sums of money for the conservation of wild sheep.

He opened his speech by saying, "I was lucky, I guess." Then he went into the account of his fictionalized hunt at the head of Silver Tip Creek, never saying the name of the drainage out loud. He memorized and rehearsed every vague detail of the story so as to keep his lie straight for every recounting of the adventure. He got to the end quickly, culminating with a bit of cowboy wisdom from his grandfather.

"Grandpa always told me, 'It's better to be lucky than good,'" he told the crowd of wealthy middle-aged men. "But if you're good, you'll eventually get lucky."

The crowd liked his youth and Western charm and lauded him with laughter and applause.

"I reckon I was lucky that ol' ram wandered north out of the park, but I've always been lucky when it comes to killin' game," he said, finishing the uncomfortable presentation by looking out at all the faces in the crowd.

Duncan knew that although the average Kool-Aid-drinking urbanite pictured hunters as plaid-cloaked rednecks, there was a class

of outdoorsmen who spent more money on aviation gas for a weekend of pheasant hunting in South Dakota than the same urbanite
might spend on recreation in an entire year. Some of these sportsmen
also spent more money on a shotgun than their skeptics spent on a
car, and many of these wealthy gentlemen hunted sheep or wanted
to hunt sheep. Aside from the lucky few who drew lottery tags,
hunting mountain sheep was a pursuit for the wealthy. Such gentlemen were in attendance at the banquet, and Duncan made their
acquaintance.

His newfound notoriety, horsepacking skills, and the simple fact
he was a young man—not one of these gentleman exactly, but a
gentleman in his own right—enabled him to transform from a sometime fishing guide into a professional hunter. To some extent, Duncan had bypassed the usual career path of a hunting guide; most
guides started as packers and wranglers or cooks, or even with some
other lesser job, but Duncan did it all from the beginning. Outfitters
who hired him loved him, as he could do—and most often did—the
jobs of three men. He loved his work and the rugged desolation of
his workplace.

The years passed by quickly, and in the blink of an eye, his twenties were gone. Then his thirties came and left him. Now, in his
forties, Duncan found himself wondering how he could have kids
who were closer to college than diapers.

And Duncan's work had changed. Looking down from the window
of the jet he sat in, a jet owned by a wealthy gentleman, one of the
many gentlemen he had guided, he could see the places where it had

changed. He could see the mountains and the coast of Baja Sur. He could see the resorts on the beach and the hotels and the large homes that were spreading farther into the country.

He thought about how many more people there were in the world now than there were twenty years ago. He had a nervous feeling about how quickly time passed, and that if he were going to make something of himself, he had better hurry, as he was at least halfway to the end. But Duncan mostly thought about how dark and complicated his life had become. He had loved guiding, but he'd gotten most of the way out of it in his thirties. Now he was back in it in his forties, only much deeper. The game had changed. The stakes had elevated.

TWO

As the jet continued north, passing over Baja California Sur, Duncan thought about the rugged, arid country below, and about a man by the name of Joaquin Vasquez.

Duncan had met Señor Vasquez at that first Sheep Foundation convention all those years ago. They'd had an instant mutual fascination for each other, which grew into a friendship and business partnership. Señor Vasquez was at the banquet promoting his hunting concession in Baja Sur. He was also looking at hunting trips that would take him to other parts of the world in search of mountain sheep and other game.

Vasquez approached Duncan while he was sitting in the booth of a Montana outfitter he would be guiding hunts for in the coming fall. Duncan sat on a stool off to the side, answering questions when needed, but mostly listening to the men around him, respecting his place in the pecking order. He was only eighteen years old. Large mule deer, elk, and bighorn sheep mounts hung behind him on the back wall of the booth, along with photos of the outfitter's camps, pack strings, and successful hunters. The other eighty or so booths were filled much the same as his. Many were filled with outfitters from Africa, Asia, or New Zealand, and others were advertising their equipment. There were custom gun and knife makers, high-end optics manufacturers, and makers of a wide variety of camping and hunting equipment. It was a scene Duncan fit into very well.

"That was quite a ram you killed in Montana," Vasquez said.

"Thank you."

"I didn't realize Montana's unlimited hunts produced rams like that."

"They don't," Duncan said.

"Then where did you kill the big ram?"

Duncan paused and worried for a moment that he had slipped with his story. He looked at the fifty-something stranger and wondered if the man somehow knew he had killed the ram in an area that was technically closed to sheep hunting.

"I just got lucky," Duncan said in his typically modest manner. Duncan studied Vasquez. He was about Duncan's height, very tanned, with a well-trimmed moustache and dark-brown hair that was being taken over by gray. He wore a custom-tailored navy sport coat with khakis and a white starched shirt, and Duncan recognized a subtle Spanish accent.

"You are a modest young man."

"I guess so."

"Yet you know you could go out and do this again."

"Do what again?" Duncan said, feeling slightly nervous.

"Kill a fine ram in this unlimited hunt."

Duncan looked at the man and smiled.

"Excuse me, I've been so rude. My name is Vasquez—Joaquin Vasquez," the man said and extended his hand to shake Jack Duncan's.

"Yessir, I believe I could kill another ram in this unit," Duncan said as he shook Vasquez's hand firmly.

"How do you feel about hunting desert bighorns in Baja?" Vasquez asked him. Vasquez was fascinated by the young Duncan and his confident, cavalier, and quietly commanding presence. He was a young man, a kid actually, and yet he commanded respect from this crowd of wealthy middle-aged men, who hung on to his words as if he were much older and more experienced. Duncan had killed one of the sporting world's most coveted trophies in some of the most rugged wilderness—alone.

Vasquez possessed ample competence in the mountains as well and recognized this quality in Duncan. He propositioned the young man to guide desert sheep hunters from his hacienda in the mountains west of Loreto, Mexico. To Duncan, it seemed the opportunity of a lifetime, and he accepted the invitation.

He joined Señor Vasquez at his hacienda in Loreto the following winter, during the spring semester of his first year in college. The hacienda sat on the terminus of a ridge that poked a short distance out into the Sea of Cortez. This peninsula formed a small bay and separated a relatively busy beach from more private lands on the north side of the peninsula, where guests of the hacienda rode horses and hunted quail in relative seclusion. The hacienda sat elevated on this ridge where it met the Sea of Cortez. The big windows looked out to the south toward Puerto Escondido and down over the panga-boat-lined beach and blue water that lapped at its shore.

The four buildings on the grounds were done in traditional Spanish-style architecture with whitewashed stucco and columns along the front, arched at the top and with windows in between. The columns caught the end of the red Spanish-tile roof where it extended past the walls of the building to form covered patios. All four buildings were positioned around a courtyard to catch an easterly or southeasterly view of the sea. A driveway entered the center of the courtyard, but it only saw traffic when guests were delivered. The drive was paved in hand-set terra-cotta clay pavers and lined with tall coconut palms and well-manicured flowering plants. The same flora lined the perimeter of the grounds and set it off as an oasis against the otherwise tan, sunbaked landscape.

The terrain to the west of the hacienda was new and enticing to Jack Duncan. For two weeks, Vasquez personally accompanied Duncan around the hunting area, the Sierra de la Giganta Mountains, which hid the setting sun from the hacienda each evening. Señor Vasquez taught him everything about the dry country and the sheep that inhabited it. Sometimes they took jeeps or burros, and at other times they went on foot with backpacks, and they looked at dozens of beautiful desert bighorn rams while studying the terrain. After the initial two weeks, Vasquez had Mexican guides accompany the young gringo on his scouting missions. The Mexicans served more as bodyguards than as guides, but the young Duncan had no idea he was being protected. A friendship grew between Duncan and Vasquez, and a close working relationship developed, which would last several years.

Southern Baja was spectacularly different from any sheep country Duncan had seen, including even the Southwestern United States and Baja Norte. The mountains of southern Baja were much greener, with the desert tan of the north giving way to richer blackish-brown soil and much thicker subtropical vegetation farther south on the peninsula. Water was plentiful and well dispersed, which was another contrast to most sheep country, even in the mountains of the north. The rocky landscape was dominated by palo blanco and palo verde trees: brushlike trees that reached heights of twenty to forty feet and were named for their smooth, peeling white or green-blue bark. Also marking the terrain was an abundance of cacti, including the smaller prickly pear, the larger organ pipe that reached heights of ten feet, and the elephant tree: a semi-succulent with smallish branches, minimal leaves, and a fat trunk for storing water.

The bighorn sheep were unique as well, with their dark-chocolate-colored coats that appeared almost black on their legs and along the dorsal lines of their backs and necks. The desert rams' bodies appeared slight to Duncan compared to their burly cousins from the high altitudes of the north.

Duncan and Vasquez became close, not only in their work relationship but also as friends. Before long, they began calling each other "Jack," although in the presence of clients, Duncan still referred to him as "Señor Vasquez." He didn't do this by request, but out of respect for his friend and employer.

Duncan learned that Vasquez was a powerful man in Baja, California, involved in a number of business interests and politics in both Mexico and the States. He was the direct descendant of a member of the Spanish de Anza expedition of 1776, which established a mission as far north as what later became San Francisco. However, the most interesting fact of Joaquin Vasquez's ancestry was that he was the grandson of the only known child of an infamous *bandito pistolero* by the name of Tiburcio Vasquez.

Tiburcio Vasquez was born into a moderately successful and law-abiding Monterey, California, family in 1835, and he came of age in a time when the United States was in the process of taking what later became California, Arizona, and New Mexico from Old Mexico and Spain.

Tiburcio was a charismatic, literate outlaw. He played guitar and charmed his many lady admirers with his swarthy good looks and poetry. He was also quick to go to guns, and he developed a reputation as a daring robber and pistolero. In the end, his penchant for women was his demise. After surviving gunshot wounds on two occasions and several narrow gun-battling escapes from the law, Tiburcio Vasquez was captured by a sheriff in Los Angeles. He'd been turned in by the family who was hiding him, and they did so because he couldn't keep his hands off the women of the house. While in hiding, Tiburcio had impregnated a teenage member of the family, and the resulting baby boy was Joaquin Vasquez's grandfather.

This was where much of the seed money for the Vasquez fortune came from. Tiburcio was a saver, and his brother and niece, who were raising the baby, gained possession of most of the spoils from his robberies. After Tiburcio was hanged in Los Angles for his involvement in a robbery and shoot-out that claimed the lives of four Americans, including a sheriff, the family who had hidden and then betrayed the outlaw returned Tiburcio's matched pair of Navy Colt percussion revolvers to his surviving brother. The brother handed them over to the boy, Joaquin's grandfather, when he was old enough, and they were passed down the line to become one of Joaquin's most treasured possessions.

Joaquin kept the matched pair of pistols in a teak box with a sliding glass lid, where they rested in a rich burgundy bed of velvet. On the bottom of the butt frame of the pistols, which held polished ivory grips, was crudely engraved "T.V." The pistols were kept on display in a trophy room that doubled as a study, and Duncan and Vasquez often spent time in that room trading stories while Duncan admired the many exotic trophies that adorned the walls. There were many sheep and goats from around the globe, including a Tibetan argali ram and a bharal, or blue sheep, which were taken on a single extended six-week expedition to Asia. There were also two Kamchatka bighorns taken on the Russian peninsula as well as chamois, ibex, and tahr, all of the sheep from North America, and an extensive collection of African animals. And, unlike his father and grandfather, Señor Vasquez still occasionally fired the .36 caliber pistols.

Jack Duncan was fascinated by the cap-and-ball revolvers. He had devoured all the Old West history he could get his hands on when he was growing up. Duncan and Vasquez shared this love of Western history, and also a connection to Spain.

Duncan's father's family members were said to have been the first Texans to drive cattle from Texas to Montana, and the family had records dating back to the early 1700s in Florida, where they'd immigrated from Spain. From Florida, the Duncans moved west and lived in Louisiana, Mississippi, and then Texas. Some of them had lived in Old Mexico as well, including one of Duncan's great-great-grandfathers and an uncle, who were both involved in those first cattle drives from Texas to Montana.

The Texans established ranches in the Montana Territory near what would become the towns of Miles City, Glendive and Ekalaka, and eventually on the Rocky Mountain front near Augusta and Choteau. They kept their ranches in Texas for many years before the connections faded, and Duncan's grandfather had been born in Texas but grew up in Montana.

Over those first two weeks of scouting, Duncan and Vasquez only spent half the nights at the hacienda, and they passed all the others under the warm, clear desert sky. On that trip, they developed an intense friendship and bond born out of a shared passion for the mountains and for hunting, and also for the paternal void they filled for each other, as Vasquez had only daughters. His two daughters were as beautiful as any young women Duncan had ever seen, and this left him feeling awkward and small when he was in their presence.

At the end of the trip, they relaxed for several days hunting quail and fishing for yellowtail and sierra mackerel in the Sea of Cortez before Duncan was to begin taking clients into the mountains.

They launched a twenty-foot panga from a beach located a short ATV ride from the hacienda, spent the morning fishing, and caught a couple of modest ten-pound yellowtail. Afterward, the two sipped very smooth tequila in the shade of a covered patio outside Vasquez's trophy study and recounted their trip.

The tequila came from a distillery owned by Vasquez. His father had made a fortune smuggling booze into the United States during prohibition, and Duncan's grandfather had done the same, smuggling Canadian whiskey into the States. In the late afternoon, the lodge chef chopped the fresh yellowtail fillets into small cubes and marinated them in the juice of limes from trees in the courtyard and sea salt. He tossed the fish with tomatoes, onions, and serrano chilies from the hacienda garden, making the finest ceviche.

As a Montana boy, Duncan had never eaten ceviche, but he devoured this. His mouth watered with each mildly tart and salty bite, washed down with cold Dos Equis beer. When they were through eating, Vasquez removed his great-grandfather's pistols from their plush case, and the two walked up the arroyo behind the hacienda, where Vasquez had constructed a pistol and rifle range. It was used for his guests' entertainment as well as for checking riflescopes prior to a hunt. Vasquez loaded all six ports of each pistol's cylinders with a light load of black powder and a .36 caliber ball, and then he put caps on each of the cylinders' percussion nipples and handed a pistol to Duncan.

Duncan owned a pair of replicas of the same Colt revolver manufactured by an Italian company. He had fired them so frequently they'd begun to loosen, and he feared they had become dangerous. He'd put the revolvers away with the intention of having a gunsmith check them, so when Señor Vasquez handed him the pistol, it felt natural in his hand, and it pointed so comfortably that it felt like the end of his own arm. Aiming the revolver was like pointing his finger, and the round balls traveled wherever Duncan's mind and eye directed them each time the hammer snapped on the primer with a cloud of acrid white smoke.

The two friends stood side by side, firing until each hammer snapped on an empty chamber with no effect other than the sharp metallic click of the hammer meeting the dead primer on the nipple. There were six clean, round holes in the center ring of the target twenty-five yards in front of the men. Vasquez's target was good, with six holes in the black of the outside ring, but it was not nearly as precise as Duncan's. The elder Jack looked at the two targets as the smoke cleared, then removed them from the wood boards and returned to the firing station, impressed, to show them to the younger Jack. No words were exchanged, and they returned to the shade of the patio.

"These pistols are haunted by the ghosts of the men who died by them," Vasquez said, breaking the silence.

"Were there many?"

"Family history passed down from my father and grandfather says eight or so," Vasquez said, looking at young Duncan for a reaction, but there was none. "But they hanged my great-grandfather for the murder of four men in Los Angeles."

"Then the guns must have taken some lives."

"He denied murdering anyone right to the end."

"Who? Your great-grandfather?"

"Yes, he denied having ever murdered any man. He never faltered in his denial, even standing at the gallows."

"But you believe he murdered men with these pistols?"

"I believe he *killed* men with these pistols."

"What's the difference?"

"One man's act of war is another man's crime. And no two men share exactly the same morality."

"But the men whose souls haunt the pistols were innocent, right?"

"Why would you assume that?" Vasquez asked as he looked Jack Duncan in the eyes.

"Only the restless souls of the innocent haunt things."

"And the only innocent man is the one who looks back at you from the mirror."

Duncan looked at the pistols, which had been returned to their case, but felt nothing. He did not possess a shred of superstition. On the contrary, he believed he was the master of his destiny. He felt only the weight of the gun in his hand, which he thought to be a little heavier than the reproduction, and smoother in the action. The cocking of the hammer and the rotation of the cylinder were smoother, better machined, and had a greater precision and polish than his reproduction gun. He'd felt the recoil in his hand and then nothing.

———◆◇◆———

The next day, Duncan began his career guiding wealthy hunters on desert bighorn hunts on a seasonal migration from the high glacial peaks of Montana, Canada, and Alaska to the desert mountains of Baja Sur.

This work would define the next six years of his life. Their hunting continued even after the president of Mexico put a temporary moratorium on sheep hunting in '92 to study bighorn populations and to create a management plan. It was an arrangement unadvertised and sold only by connections, but Vasquez bought and paid for the three permits, as the clients needed legal documentation to return their trophies to their homes and taxidermists. He paid for the documentation by donating the cost of one hunt, about US$35,000, which funded the studies of the bighorn sheep on the peninsula.

The setup was ideal for a young outdoorsman like Jack Duncan, and it was only burdened by a couple of complications. One of which was college.

Duncan was an intelligent young man who had graduated from high school at the top of his class, a place he shared with his childhood love, Erica, but he was not content going to school in Montana, as Erica chose to do. He felt he needed to see more of the world than another small town in Montana. She tried to convince him to go to Montana State with her in Bozeman, but it was too much of the same for Duncan, too small and too insignificant in the scheme of the world, so he went instead to the University of Washington in Seattle.

Duncan had always sensed the condescension city people had for folks like him. He felt it from so many of his fishing clients as a teenager and from so many of the tourists who came to Montana in the summers. He wanted to see what the city was all about. He wanted to prove to himself that he could make it in the city. And he did, at least for a few years. The irony he found in the whole situation was that it was so much easier to live in the city, and while he felt most of those folks looked down their noses at "rednecks" like Duncan and his family, they could not survive in the wild, at least not without someone like him to babysit them. Duncan got along fine in the city; he just didn't like its crowded confinement.

College was also relatively easy for him, and the only complication was juggling his guiding schedule and getting into his classes. He would often fly to Seattle from an airport near his hunt location so he could spend a week or two registering for his classes and getting their syllabi, books, and materials, and then he would fly out to shepherd another city dweller on a hunt in some wild corner of the West. He studied remotely, borrowed his classmates' notes, and frequently returned to campus just long enough to take midterms and finals before he was off again.

For a few years, this worked well for Duncan, and while he was guiding and attending college in Seattle, Erica was working at earning a degree in veterinary medicine and running barrels on one of the fine quarter horses her father kept for her. The two sweethearts would connect in the summers and at Christmas, if only for a few brief days, when they would talk of their future together and then be off again in different directions. Duncan had always assured Erica that when they were through with school and ready to settle, he was going to marry her and build her a home. However, one day while he was sitting on a jet flying to Seattle from Loreto to schedule some classes so he could guide for two more weeks, it occurred to Duncan that school was interfering with his career.

He was already doing what he loved, and he was making great money. He was sitting in classes when he could be in the field with clients making even more money, and the men he took into the field and spent hours and days with in close quarters were far more educational than his professors. His clients were successful business leaders, while his instructors' knowledge, with only a few exceptions, was academic, derived from books and entirely lacking in the substance of experience. When the jet landed in Seattle, he drove to his apartment in the university district, boxed up the few things that meant anything to him, threw the rest in the apartment dumpster, and drove to his mother's home in Montana, which was still his home base at the time. He often returned to Ennis between trips, as it was home, and if for no other reason than to see Erica. However, on this trip home, he tracked down a rumor that she was seeing a young man in Bozeman. The rumor came as no surprise to him. Logically, Duncan knew it was somewhat inevitable that this would happen, but it still felt like a punch to the gut to hear.

His mother was slightly surprised when he walked in the front door of their home, but she had grown somewhat used to his irregular and unannounced visits.

"I wish you would've called," she said as she got up from her seat at the table, where she was correcting papers. "I would've fixed a nice dinner."

"It's OK, Mom, I'm going to Bozeman. I'll be back tomorrow."

"Why aren't you at school?" she asked.

"I'll go back next spring," he said.

"What are you talking about, next spring?"

"I've got other business to deal with."

"Your business is to finish school, damn it!"

"I will," he said, to get her off his back.

"Well at least stay with me for a while so we can catch up," she said as she hugged him and then held him for a moment. But only a moment, as that was all Duncan could hold still for.

"Don't worry, Mom," he said.

"Why are you going to Bozeman?"

"To see Erica."

"You know, I've heard she's been dating a boy from school," his mother said as gently as possible, searching her son's face for a hint that he might already know. Hoping he knew, in fact, as she hadn't wanted to give him the news.

Duncan paused as he rummaged through his duffel, which he'd set on the kitchen table, and then he continued as though she'd said nothing.

"Is that why you're going to Bozeman?" she pressed.

"I have business there, Mom," he said, and she let it rest.

She fixed him a sandwich and they visited for a couple of hours, and then as the shadows began to gather the darkness of the early December night, Duncan left for Bozeman. He sipped from a fifth of Canadian whiskey he kept under the front seat of his pickup, and before he got through the canyon carved by the Madison River below Ennis Lake, the snow began to fly. The dry white powder swirled in the wind and on the road, making white apparitional snakes on the pavement in front of him lit by the headlights. The white winter ceiling closed in, and the snow went from swirling and blowing over the road to covering it. It took three hours for him to reach Bozeman instead of the usual hour and a half.

He was half through with the bottle when he pulled up in front of Erica's house in town, a couple of blocks from the college. He'd been sitting for twenty minutes or so, working up the nerve to knock on the door, when he saw someone peek from behind the curtains to the right of the front door. He got out of the truck and walked through the freshly fallen snow to the sidewalk that led to the house.

Erica came out of the front door and down the walk to greet him, but he stayed behind the gate on the city sidewalk, and when she tried to come through it, he held it closed. Then there was a moment of awkward silence. She started to speak, but he interrupted.

"Is it true?"

"Yes, but…"

"That's all I wanted to know," Duncan said as he turned to walk back to his truck.

"That's it? You're just gonna leave? Just run off like you always do?"

Duncan glanced back at the house. Somebody, a young man, was watching out the front window.

"Is he in the house?"

"Should I tell you?" she said as she opened the gate and followed him.

"If he is, why don't you send him out?" Duncan said as he watched the young man peering from behind the curtain.

"And what would you do?"

Duncan grabbed Erica suddenly and pulled her close to him. She leaned back but put up no real resistance. Then he kissed her, and she kissed him back long and deep. The young man watched from the window. If the man was going to have his girl, Duncan wanted him to live with the picture of the two of them kissing in the swirling snow. He wanted the man to wonder whom she was thinking about when they made love.

Duncan let her go, and she stood for a moment, a little dazed.

"You're drunk!"

"So what?" he said, and then he climbed back into his truck and made tracks down the snow-covered, tree-lined street.

Erica stood in the quiet white night and watched Duncan's tail-lights disappear down her street. She wiped the tears from her eyes before she returned to the house.

Duncan headed for the closest bar and continued his drinking until a couple of college girls took him home. He intended on sleeping with at least one of them, but he drank himself to sleep instead. He woke on their couch at about daylight and headed home to Ennis.

After visiting his mother, Duncan flew back to Mexico from Bozeman, and he remained there for the balance of that winter and spring. He did not return north until nearly July, when a second complication convoluted his annual migration.

After finishing his guiding season in late March, Duncan remained at the hacienda, where he was Señor Vasquez's guest and had little responsibility. He spent his days exploring the mountains, scouting sheep, and learning new country. He quail hunted, sometimes with Vasquez and more often alone while Vasquez was away tending business, as the older man did not spend much time at the hacienda when sheep hunters weren't present. Other days, Duncan took the pangas out and chased yellowtail, mackerel, and juvenile tuna with a fly rod. He was becoming proficient enough at catching them on flies that he could keep the hacienda chefs in fresh fish for the guests.

Duncan was enjoying his extended vacation until the complication arrived in the strikingly beautiful form of Vasquez's first daughter, Marialena. The beautiful twenty-two-year-old Marialena had graduated from UCLA the previous spring and was spending the winter at the hacienda. Vasquez and his wife kept a home in Point Loma, where they spent most of their time away from the hacienda. This left Marialena and Duncan ample time to become acquainted.

Marialena had fine Spanish features: long chocolate-brown hair with just a hint of gold touched by the Baja sun, and hazel-green eyes offset by her smooth, tanned olive skin and swimmer's body. It was a body she used to torture young Duncan, as most of their time together was spent in or around the water. They swam in the hacienda pool or walked for hours on the beach, and Marialena began to accompany him on his panga trips with the fly rod. The only time she wore anything more than a very small bikini was when they dined together with the guests in the hacienda dining room. Duncan loved Erica, but she seemed to be living her own life, or at least he saw it that way, which allowed him to fall in love with this beautiful sun-kissed girl who was the daughter of his good friend and employer.

There was no way the two could physically avoid each other, and one day while they were drifting in the panga in search of whatever fish they might entice with one of the gaudy streamers Duncan tied in the shade on hot afternoons at the hacienda, the tension broke.

Marialena held the ten-weight Sage fly rod in her right hand and the line in her left, with the coils of it lying in the bottom of the panga at her feet. It wasn't her first time, but she was still learning the art of fly-casting.

"Would you show me again?" she asked, looking at him with her wanting green eyes.

Duncan had instructed and taught many people in the art and science of casting a fly. It was purely timing, like everything in life, and Duncan knew that teaching timing with words was as impossible as it would be to teach it with pictures, or even by physical example; timing was felt, not taught.

"Show you what again?" he asked. He thought he knew what she wanted. He knew what *he* wanted, and he hoped it was the same thing, so he looked deep into those eyes, searching for the answer to the question she wasn't actually asking.

"You know, that timing thing you showed me."

Duncan usually attempted to teach timing by standing behind his clients and having them grip the handle of the rod while he gripped both the client's hand and the rod handle, moving both their arm and the rod so they could feel the timing.

He used the same method with Marialena, and the only thing between them was the thin white string of her bikini top. He moved her hand and arm, moving the fly rod in perfect rhythm, allowing the line and fly to lie out straight behind them before he tugged the slack line with his left hand slightly to load the rod and complete the cast in front of them.

Marialena went limp in Duncan's arms and allowed him to lead them together. Their warm, sticky bodies quickly fell into a perfect rhythm, rocking forward and back with each false cast.

Duncan dropped the fly line with his left hand and gently placed it on Marialena's tight abdomen between her belly button and the top of her bikini bottom, pulling her midsection gently but firmly into his. His head was over her right shoulder, and his left cheek was now pressed into her right. They were laughing.

Their laughter was innocent, like the laughter of small children, but at the same time, it was wrought with the nervous anticipation of a first intimate encounter. And then the laughter ceased, and both of them closed their eyes, heightening all other senses until there was only their warm breath in each other's faces. With his chest pressed against her back, each of them could faintly feel the beating of the other's heart over the pounding of their own. Before their chests exploded with the anxiety of the moment, Marialena turned into Duncan, pushing her breasts into him. They kissed deeply, and then they made love in the bottom of the panga as the sound of the warm, gentle waves of the Sea of Cortez lapped at the side of the insignificant white boat.

From that day on, Marialena spent her nights in Duncan's bed in the quarters attached to the hacienda's well-manicured horse facilities. She would sneak out of her room in the main house and come to him, attempting to avoid the staff, as the two felt it best to keep their affair from Señor Vasquez. At night, they would lie in each other's arms, talking, laughing, and making love the way new lovers did. Despite their attempts to keep it from her parents, the Vasquezes became suspicious over the course of a single weeklong stay at the hacienda. It was hard to miss the way the two looked at each other or the casual contact their bodies made. Marialena's mother knew without a doubt what was going on, and she was undecided in the matter but leaning in favor of the relationship. Señor Vasquez, on the other hand, was not as accepting.

He questioned Duncan about it in late June during a phone conversation just before Duncan left the hacienda for mountain hunting in the north. Vasquez made the call from his home in California at dinnertime at the hacienda, as he knew he would catch Duncan near a phone. One of the waitstaff approached Duncan at the table where he was seated with Marialena and several guests.

"Señor Vasquez está en el teléphono," she whispered to Duncan.

Duncan followed her to a phone in the hacienda lobby, which lay off the hook. He put the phone to his ear.

"Hello, Jack," Duncan said.

"Good evening, Duncan," Vasquez said back. "Are you well?"

"Yessir, thank you," Duncan said, recognizing an uncomfortable tone from Vasquez.

"I won't beat around the bush, Jack. I'm going to get straight to the point of my call."

"Yessir."

"It's come to my attention that you are dating my daughter. Is this true?"

"Yes."

"Why would you not tell me?"

"We were waiting for the right moment," Duncan said, trying to read where Vasquez was headed with this conversation.

"You don't understand how these things work here."

"No, I don't."

"It's different with my family, with my culture." There was silence for a few moments, and then Vasquez asked, "Do you love her?"

Duncan's response was straightforward: "Sir, I care deeply for your daughter." He couldn't recall ever addressing a man by the title of "Sir" aside from his grandfathers and uncle.

"Don't fuck up one good thing for another," replied Vasquez. And then all that was left of their conversation was the humming of the dial tone in Duncan's ear.

———◆◇◆———

Marialena lobbied Duncan not to return to the mountains of the north. She wanted to walk barefoot in the sand with him every day, but while she pleaded her case, her father's words played over and over in Duncan's head.

He struggled to understand what the exact message in Vasquez's words was, but he could not. The words eventually faded from his thoughts, as he was occupied by carrying heavy packs in the mountains of Alaska and then Montana as the aspen leaves turned gold and rattled in the autumn breeze. In the short moments before sleep each night when he laid his bag out on the ground, the bunk of a cabin, or some other hard, cold place, his mind wandered off to Baja and he missed Marialena. At the same time, Erica was always with him. The anger and jealousy he had felt had faded to regret as he realized he'd let her slip away more than she'd wandered.

When the season was finished, Duncan slept hard from the exhaustion of the long days in the mountains. Then, winter arrived, and he headed south to the hacienda at Señor Vasquez's request.

Marialena was there when he arrived, but the situation was strained. Señor Vasquez was ever present and kept Duncan busy guiding quail hunters and taking guests out in the panga with their fly rods, and there were three sheep hunters scheduled for the season, the last of them set to arrive in late February.

The two did manage to sneak away from time to time in the panga or into town. On one occasion, Duncan and Marialena left the hacienda separately and flew from the airport in Loreto to Mazatlán, where they spent three days at a private resort on the mainland side of the Sea of Cortez. Duncan disliked Mazatlán, as it was too hectic compared to the more relaxed environment of Baja, but he enjoyed the private time with Marialena.

The handsome young couple stayed in the rooftop suite of the private resort, which was located on the beach strip near the El Cid and Costa de Oro resorts. Their room opened to a private mission-style courtyard with palm trees and numerous flowering plants, and its spectacular lanai was finished in travertine stone tiles that continued into the pool and surrounding deck. There was a beautiful stone waterfall that spilled water into the pool and a palapa-covered bar on the other end of the courtyard next to a hot tub. On the evening of their arrival, Duncan pulled the mattress off the king bed from the room and dragged it out to the edge of the lanai, where they spent their nights gazing at the stars.

Back at the hacienda, Marialena and Duncan often dined with the Vasquezes, but the conversations grew quiet. Eventually, if he wasn't obligated to dine with the clients, Duncan began taking his supper in his sleeping quarters with the horses. A distance had grown between the two Jacks, and it was ruining what he had with Marialena as well. When February arrived, Marialena left the hacienda for California with her mother, and Jack Duncan kept mostly to himself, working or fishing or scouting. With the women gone, the mood was more relaxed and normal when the two Jacks were together.

The third client, a man by the name of James Beck, was scheduled to arrive toward the end of February, so the Jacks spent time together looking for good rams for him.

James Beck was a man of wealth beyond imagination. He owned a huge media empire that included television companies, newspapers, and magazines. He also owned manufacturing companies around the world and a number of ranches in Montana, and he was known of and disliked by most Montanans, including Jack Duncan. Duncan had instantly disliked him and his thin, tightly manicured mustache that matched perfectly with the skin stretched tightly over the bone and muscle structures of his face. His sandy hair showed the graying of age, and his body possessed a metropolitan thinness that held neither fat nor significant muscle. Duncan was eager to get the hunt over with so that he could spend more time with Vasquez. He wanted to understand the distance that had grown between them and to win Vasquez over to the idea of his and Marialena's relationship.

The hunt went off as planned. Duncan guided Beck to a fine desert ram that he and Vasquez had found only a two-hour jeep ride into the tan mountains east of the hacienda.

Mexican sheep hunts customarily involved a relative entourage when compared to the one-on-one and one-on-two guided sheep hunts of the north. On this hunt, Duncan and Beck were accompanied by the three Mexican assistants who usually hunted with Duncan. When Beck killed his ram, Duncan skinned the animal for a full-body mount and packed the hide and head back to the first jeep ahead of his assistants, who would bone the meat out and pack it into the second jeep. Normally, the entourage remained together as they packed, and then they returned to the hacienda as a group, but on this occasion the Mexicans insisted that Duncan and Beck return first with the head so they could reach the hacienda by cocktail hour and dinner. It didn't seem suspicious until the smoke and dust of that day had settled. Duncan knew the Mexicans disliked Beck as much as the Montanans did, so the two Americans left in the jeep and headed down the dry, rutted, and dusty road.

The trip back began like many others: Beck rambled on about himself while Duncan feigned interest until they rounded a blind corner and came face-to-face with another jeep stopped in the middle of the two-track road and quartered toward them.

Two Mexican men covered in the brown dust of the mountains leaped from the jeep in a hurried fashion, while a third man remained behind the wheel. One of them was armed with an old double-action revolver of a make Duncan didn't recognize, and the other had a lever-action Winchester rifle. Duncan skidded the jeep to a halt, and he made a quick decision not to hit reverse, fearing a hasty retreat might result in a backward plunge off the mountain. It might also give the armed Mexicans the opportunity to shoot them if they were inclined to do so. Instead, Duncan skidded to a stop and quickly stepped from the jeep. He had a single-action Ruger revolver in his right hand, hidden slightly behind his hip and out of sight of the presumed Mexican banditos.

The Mexicans were excitedly yelling something in Spanish about a robbery. Duncan stayed close to the jeep to use it as cover. Vasquez had instructed him to deal with any criminal element he encountered in any manner he chose, lethal or otherwise; Vasquez or money would correct any incident that might occur.

The two armed Mexicans came at Duncan and Beck, rapidly closing the distance between them to about fifteen yards, the one with the revolver in the lead.

"Throw your wallet in the road," Duncan yelled to Beck.

"What the hell for?"

"Just do it, goddamnit!" Duncan demanded again.

Beck pulled his wallet from his back pocket, stood up slightly in the open jeep, and threw the black leather billfold toward the advancing Mexicans. A puff of dust rose when the wallet hit the dirt in front of the armed men.

Duncan was focused and clear. Time unraveled, slowing with every thought and motion. It was a subconscious but conditioned response. The second man held the rifle, although it wasn't cocked; his thumb was resting on the hammer, but his finger was not on the trigger. The lead man with the pistol was nervous and edgy, and his pistol was cocked with his finger on the trigger. His eyes momentarily left Duncan's to look at the wallet, and as he stooped to pick it up, his pistol dropped for a split second.

Duncan raised his own pistol deliberately, smoothly. He cocked the hammer and squeezed the trigger, all in one fluid action with no thought, his mind completely clear, his aim subconscious. At the report, a cloud of dust erupted from the dirty cotton shirt of the front bandito as the bullet hit his chest and entered right under his first rib. It pierced his heart, killing him instantly. In a fluid motion, Duncan swung the pistol on the second Mexican, who was clumsily struggling to cock and raise the rifle. Duncan's bullet found its mark, centered on the Mexican's chest, and again a puff of dust rose from the impact site as the man staggered backward and fell to the earth forever.

Beck had readied his own rifle, a .338 Lapua with which he was deadly accurate, as Duncan sent two rounds at the driver of the jeep in front of them. The man was now feverishly trying to turn the jeep for an escape. One of Duncan's rounds hit the man in the right thigh, and then Beck's big rifle roared and the windshield of the jeep exploded in a cloud of shimmering glass as it sped away from them. Then, another shot, and the man's head exploded, scattering brains like runny scrambled eggs all over the hood of the jeep. The vehicle veered to the left and plunged off the road, tumbling end over end into the brush at the bottom of the canyon until it was no longer visible from the road.

Duncan stood next to the driver's side front bumper. His cool demeanor was intact, but a weak, shaky feeling was starting to come over him as a wave of nausea filled his belly. The second Mexican writhed slowly for a few moments and then lay as still as the front man. Deep-red blood began to stream thickly in the dust. It rolled into a wheel rut and formed a puddle almost as dark and thick as used motor oil.

"Did you see that?" Beck cried, excited by the event that had just unfolded. "We nailed those sons-a-bitches!"

Duncan looked at Beck and then back at the dead men lying still in the road in front of them, one with his leg twisted up under his body, contorted, and both in unnatural postures.

"What a rush!" Beck said, still excited. "You were awesome."

Duncan was speechless as Beck clamored on with his nervous chatter. Duncan heard the sound, but he wasn't listening to the words. He was in his own head, trying to untie the tangled mess. The feeling was not unlike what he felt after killing a game animal, only the elation never came, and the sickness in his belly remained. He felt light-headed, almost as though he were out of his body looking down, and as the enormity of the situation slammed into him, he turned to Beck and yelled, "Shut up!"

"What?" Beck replied, stunned. He was unaccustomed to being spoken at with such command and authority.

"Just be quiet and help me deal with this."

Beck looked at Duncan with anger but said nothing. There was no rule book or unwritten law of etiquette to deal with their current situation.

"Let's drag the bodies off the road and roll them into the bottom of the arroyo," Duncan said.

Beck climbed from the jeep, and his nervous chatter ceased. The men finished the chore of rolling the dead Mexicans into the arroyo, and then they tossed the weapons down into the brush with their dead owners.

Duncan drove quietly out of the mountains while Beck yammered on about the excitement of their "kill," having forgotten about the spectacular desert sheep trophy that was in the jeep with them. Duncan was sickened by the ordeal, and he was growing increasingly nervous, although he didn't show it.

He pulled the jeep around the back of the hacienda near his quarters, the horse barn, and the cold room, where the Mexican staff hung game and processed the meat and trophies. Customarily, they would have returned up the beautiful terra-cotta-cobbled drive, which was lined with coconut palms and African tulip trees and made up the main entrance, but Duncan felt safer leaving the jeep hidden in the back, should anyone have seen what happened.

Beck calmly returned to his room, where he packed his bags and called his pilot to ready his jet, which was waiting at the airport in Loreto. Duncan hurriedly searched the grounds for Vasquez, whom he found sitting in his trophy room smoking a fine Cuban cigar. Vasquez sat quietly while Duncan, now calm, recited the events of the day in explicit detail. Vasquez listened stoically, neither upset nor surprised.

When Duncan was done recounting the violent events that had just played out in the mountains with Beck, Vasquez, who had been sitting back in his leather chair and listening, sat forward and said, "You were perfectly justified."

"Justified or not, I want to get the hell outta here, Jack."

"Relax, son. I'll have you on a private jet before midnight."

"It's hard."

"What's hard?"

"Relaxing."

Vasquez sat back in the chair again and blew white cigar smoke as he looked up at the ceiling of his study and then around the room, seeming to examine the trophies on the wall. "You've killed plenty of game, but this is different."

Duncan nodded in agreement but said nothing.

"It's safe to assume you've never killed a man before," Vasquez said, turning his attention back to Duncan.

"No, sir, I have not."

"You'll be fine," Vasquez said, and then rose from his chair and walked to a madrone credenza against the wall behind him. He poured two glasses of tequila from a decanter, returned to Duncan, and handed him one of the glasses. "Drink this; it'll help."

Duncan took the glass and drank the tequila. Vasquez poured more tequila from the decanter into Duncan's glass. "Where would you like to fly to?"

"Bozeman."

"I'll take care of it," Vasquez said, and then walked out of the room.

Standing in the study and watching Señor Vasquez walk out of the room, the thought began to occur to Duncan that perhaps Vasquez knew more about what had happened on the mountain with the Mexican robbers than he was letting on.

Duncan left for his quarters to gather his items. It was the last time the two men would see each other for two decades.

Duncan passed Beck while crossing the courtyard on his return to his quarters adjacent to the barn. Beck stopped Duncan and shook his hand.

"Thank you for killing those men today," Beck said to him.

"I don't want to talk about it, especially not in the open like this."

"Nonetheless, you probably saved my life today, and I'm grateful."

"I was just doin' my job."

"I'd like to fly you home. Or wherever else you want to go."

"Thanks, but Señor Vasquez has arranged my travel."

"You trust him?"

Duncan thought for a moment that he trusted Vasquez far more than the man in front of him, but he said only, "Yes, very much."

"Good luck, now," Beck said, and Duncan nodded to him as he turned to walk to his quarters.

Duncan paced nervously around the hacienda grounds while he waited for his ride to the airport. He also helped his Mexican guides finish the meat and hang it in the refrigerated room for aging before it was processed and shipped to wherever Beck requested. At nearly eleven o'clock, one of the Mexican guides picked up Duncan from his quarters and drove him to the airport in Loreto. They drove right onto the tarmac. As Duncan climbed the steps into the jet, he breathed in the warm night air as if he were going underwater and would need it to last for a while.

The shrill, spinning whine of the jet engines filled his ears, and his head spun with doubt and distrust. He wondered if those final warm breaths of Baja air would be his last. He knew the air in Montana would be too cold to breathe in deeply at that time of year, that there would be no yellowtail to chase, that the guides on his fly rod would ice up if he tried to fish at all. He thought of Marialena and he missed her already, knowing it was very likely he would never see her again. He was going home.

THREE

Now, twenty years later, Jack Duncan sat looking out the window of James Beck's Gulfstream bound for Los Angeles from Guatemala City. As they passed over the Mexican coast, he remembered how empty he'd felt back then, as though he'd been taken from his family. Vasquez had been much more than just a friend to him. There was a time when he'd thought he and Marialena would wed and they really would become family, but the following fall Vasquez never contacted Duncan, and Duncan did not contact him. And Marialena was gone from him, too, as the first person Duncan found when he returned hastily from Baja was Erica.

Duncan had stepped off the jet that night into the cold of Montana with a gray-white ceiling closing in on him. He could feel the snow in the air. He took a cab to downtown Bozeman, where he rented a room at a small hotel and showered in an attempt to wash Mexico off him. He couldn't sleep. He didn't want to be alone, but he wasn't ready to deal with anybody familiar. He felt no real guilt for shooting the three Mexicans, but the scene remained vivid, like a movie replaying in his head.

Duncan walked to a coffee shop on Main Street, where Bozeman was waking for the day. He sat down in a corner where he could see every patron who entered the room. He wanted to avoid any familiar faces and to process the events of the previous day.

But "familiar" walked right in. When Erica entered the shop that morning, he made no attempt to hide his face, and she approached him as though the meeting were preordained. The boyfriend was gone, and as with any true friends, time apart had changed nothing. They picked up immediately where they'd left off, the length of the intermission being immaterial. Erica skipped her classes that day, and they were together from that moment on.

He had wanted to tell her what had happened the day before, and he struggled with how to do so until "the day before" turned into weeks before, and the weeks turned to months. They were so in love, and he so wanted to protect her from anything dreadful that he didn't speak a word of it. Duncan possessed a rare ability in a human: to keep a secret. It wasn't dishonesty; he just saw no reason back then to heap his burdens onto her.

And as he flew to Los Angeles en route to meet his family in Alaska, he felt no regret, at least not about family.

Jack Duncan stood off to the side at the baggage claim, avoiding the center of the room. He leaned against a column, which shielded him from much of the airport, so he could study his family as they entered the Anchorage airport terminal.

They were a beautiful sight: a handsome boy and an adorable little girl who reminded Duncan of her mother. Erica possessed a natural beauty that didn't require makeup or heels to draw attention.

She looked as good in Levi's and a T-shirt as anything else she put on. She followed the two kids to the carousel from the plane as though she were herding them. Her blonde ponytail was pulled through the back of a cap, and it bounced with each step almost in rhythm with the little girl's ponytail as Erica kept the girl and boy lined out. The boy carried a small daypack with a fishing rod tube strapped to the outside. The little girl carried a brown teddy bear and a small purse over her shoulder and pulled a wheeled carry-on behind her. Duncan smiled at the purse, thinking about how kids were in such a hurry to be grown-ups.

In her teens and twenties, Erica had been a moderately successful barrel racing hopeful who had never quite made it to the big time. In Ennis, Montana, however, she was a star, and for a few years, most of the rodeo world knew her name and face. She'd garnered a few big-name sponsors, and she'd appeared in some ads for several Western clothing companies. Now in her early forties, she looked much the same, just slightly more mature and confident. Erica still maintained her very athletic, perfectly feminine body and the fire in her striking blue eyes that had earned her the nickname "Tiger" from her dad.

To Duncan she was perfect, at least on the outside. She had small scars on her chin and the right side of her jawbone where she'd had a dozen or so stitches when she was ten years old. She'd landed on her face after being thrown from a barrel horse that stepped into a hole. Erica hated the scar, and while it was hardly noticeable, it was the first thing she saw when she looked in the mirror. Duncan actually liked it. He thought it was a cute little scar, and he told her it made her even more interesting to look at.

As Duncan watched her that day in the airport, he still only saw the little girl he'd played with on the banks of the Madison River as a kid and the beautiful young woman he'd taken to the prom.

"Daddy!" yelled his little girl, Avery, when she saw her father step out from behind the column. Both kids dropped their bags. Avery ran to him, while the boy, Coulter, strolled up, trying to be more cool and controlled. Duncan dropped to a knee, and the kids nearly toppled him over in their enthusiasm as they embraced. Duncan felt a warmth and contentedness overcome him. He had not seen his children enough over the past couple of years, and it had been painful to be apart from them. The only time he really felt good was when they were together.

But for Erica, it was different. Duncan had been gone so much over the last couple of years she was becoming used to his absence. Having him home for short periods broke her routine and her discipline, and in a way it complicated her life. To her, he had become something of an interruption.

Duncan stood, removing himself from the kids' mauling embrace, and looked into Erica's blue eyes. He moved closer to her and wrapped his big hand and arm around her lower back, pulling the middle of her body tightly into his while staying locked on to her piercing eyes. But she pulled away slightly.

He pulled her closer yet and they kissed with a love that called to mind the anticipation of two thirteen-year-old kids kissing for the first time after loving each other nearly all of their young lives. To Duncan, it was as though they were the only two people in the airport. But Erica pulled away again.

"You can't do that," Erica said.

"Do what?"

"Kiss me like that."

"Like what?"

"Like everything's OK. Like you haven't been in and out of our lives for the last couple of years—here today, gone tomorrow, sometimes with no more than a text telling me that 'it will all make sense someday.'" Erica took a half step back and crossed her arms.

Duncan stood quietly and listened, knowing instinctively it was a good time to keep his mouth shut. She was using a normal tone, but he knew that if they were in private, it would have been elevated.

"Like we aren't broke and haven't lost it all. Like you can send us tickets for an exotic vacation and meet us here and life is all normal again."

Erica said the words that had been building in her for over a year now with an angry, desperate tone. She stood a step away from Duncan, rigid and prepared for the fight that had been brewing for a number of months, but then big tears welled up in her cobalt eyes, and she quickly pulled Duncan close to her and hugged him so he couldn't see her wipe them away. But he could feel it; he knew her every move. The kids were at her back, and they watched but politely stayed out of it.

She was a rancher's daughter. She embodied the toughness of the West—a toughness that was diminishing in value in American culture but remained alive where rugged people made their lives on the high plains and desolate mountain valleys.

Duncan could see the strain in Erica. He could see the strain of what being a mother—a good one who worked and was always there—could put on a woman. Erica was a woman who got up every morning to work out and make lunches, only to go straight on to work, manipulating her schedule to make every field trip and sporting event. She was a real mother who made dinner every night from real food, not from a box or can. A mom who fell asleep reading to her kids, and who was there always, without fail. And the only sign of wear that showed were faint circles under her eyes.

Mostly, Erica didn't want her kids to see her cry, and she regained her composure before she released him, taking a step back to look him up and down. She couldn't help but love what she was looking at. Jack Duncan was unassumingly handsome in a weathered but not worn-out sort of way. The dirty blond hair of his childhood had darkened to a distinguished brown, and only a few gray hairs showed in his moustache, with even fewer around his temples. He didn't quite reach six feet tall, but with cowboy boots, he made it. His blue eyes were sharp, clear, and striking, framed by his sun-darkened features. Those eyes pierced through to the soul, causing men to take notice and women to feel as though they were standing naked in front of him, as though he could see everything he was looking for.

"Let's get out of here," Duncan said, picking up her carry-on luggage. He could see it in her eyes. It was time to tell her the truth.

"I can't take this anymore," she said.

"Can this conversation wait?"

"No! It can't."

Erica stopped in the middle of the airport concourse, defiant, as though she might get back on the plane and return to Montana. The two kids watched as their parents squared off, unconcerned and well aware that nobody would be going anywhere until their mother had her wishes met.

"You can't just wire us money from banks in strange places and take us on these vacations," Erica said. "That doesn't make us a family. That doesn't make you a husband or a father. Your kids adore you, but they don't even know you. *I don't know you.* Damn it, Jack, I don't know who the hell you are anymore."

Duncan moved into her space, and she stood resolute until they were nearly touching again.

"Erica. Can't you just trust me that this won't go on forever? That we'll be together again, like a real family?"

"Jack, I gave you my heart—my whole heart! I've trusted you for thirty years. I've never doubted you. When we were separated in college, I knew you'd be back one day. Somehow, I just knew it. Even when you were gone hunting for months in Mexico or Canada or China or Russia or some other goddamned place."

"I wasn't hunting; I was working."

"Call it what you want, Jack. You were gone."

"Listen, I tried! I tried to do it normal. When you got pregnant with Coulter, I gave it up. I tried. I bought a truck and a trailer-load of tools. I sold out to live a 'normal' life."

"Sold out? That's bullshit!"

"Not you and the kids! You guys are the only thing I *didn't* settle on. You guys are everything to me. I know I've been gone, I know I haven't given you all the details—and believe me, there are many— but it's only because I couldn't. It's because I've tried to protect you."

"Protect me from what?" Erica demanded.

"We can't talk in an airport. Let's get to the cabin, and then I'll tell you everything. I've wanted to for a long time, but I just couldn't. I was waiting for the right moment—and here it is, I guess."

She conceded, and the mood relaxed a bit. The kids were excited to see their dad, and he was excited to see them. Duncan carried his little girl out of the airport, even though she was a bit grown up for it. They needed to be close. The boy barraged Duncan with "Hey, Dad!" and story after story of the contraptions he'd built and the sports he was playing and the schoolwork he was doing and the fishing trips he'd taken with Erica's father.

It was overwhelming to Duncan, and his chest hurt from missing them. He had never wanted to be away from his kids for a moment from the time they were born, and now he was away from them most of the time. At least he had been for the past couple of years. Having grown up without a father, Duncan had wanted a real family more than he wanted anything. So much so that when Coulter was born, he'd given up guiding, at least full time, and he'd traded his passion for a tool belt and learned the construction trades.

Duncan loved his wife and kids enough that he'd never really considered his career change a sacrifice. But he'd also never really considered construction his career. It was just a way to support his family, to build a little wealth to one day retire, and to still be home in time for dinner. That was important to Duncan. There had always been an empty seat at the table when he was growing up, and he hadn't wanted that for his kids.

Even before the kids came along, Duncan hated being gone for extended periods. From the time he'd returned from Baja on that private middle-of-the-night flight that had reunited him with his childhood sweetheart, he'd hated to be separated from Erica.

And twenty years later, as the four of them headed west on the Sterling Highway for their small cabin on the banks of the Kenai River, he struggled with exactly what to tell Erica about the predicament in which he'd involved himself.

They wound along the edge of Turnagain Arm, taking in everything late June in Alaska had to offer. The smoldering orange-yellow sun hung low in the sky to the northwest, just over the tops of the volcanoes that defined the Alaska Peninsula, and shimmered on the calm gray waters of the Cook Inlet. Out the left side of the rented Ford Explorer, the Chugach Mountains rose abruptly from the side of the highway separating them from the cold, salty water and the mud flat exposed by the cycle of the extreme tides. Glaciers receded in high valleys that appeared as only crevasses from that distance, as though they were trying to escape the madness that dwelled in the low country.

The mood was lighter, although the heaviness of the last couple of years hung over the two adults in the car. The kids were gregarious, wound up over seeing their dad and also by the sun lighting up what would have been a still-dark sky down below in the rest of the country. Instead, the early-morning sky was illuminated enough for any activity without requiring artificial light. The family wound through the green valleys that the Sterling Highway followed over Moose Pass, and then they headed down the Kenai River toward Soldotna. Duncan turned the SUV off the pavement at the driveway: a narrow two-track overgrown with grass between the tire ruts, really just a gap in the dark spruce trees, marked with a set of bleached moose antlers nailed to a tree.

He had been alternating his attention between the kids and the struggle in his head over his life: what he would do with it, and how he would keep Erica on his team. The ties between them were strained, as they were with most couples approaching midlife with a family, only more so for the Duncans than the average forty-something couple.

After they'd married, Duncan had begun to curb his guiding work. Eventually, he narrowed it down to a couple of bighorn sheep hunts in September and weekend and day elk hunts in November, plus occasional exotic destinations with clients with whom he'd built friendships and trust over the years. He spent most of his time working at and learning carpentry, masonry, concrete, and other construction trades, and business was booming.

The Rocky Mountain West had become the spot for the wealthy and the pseudo-rich to buy and build trophy homes, and while it provided incomes for the working descendants of the hard people who tamed the land, it watered down the culture. Duncan hated it on one hand and was entirely caught up in it on the other.

By the time the kids came along when the Duncans were in their early thirties, Jack had progressed to building spec and custom homes, and he was doing quite well.

Wanting to raise their kids in an environment like the one they grew up in, Duncan and Erica left Bozeman and headed back to Ennis. Erica quit her job at a veterinary hospital in Bozeman to raise their babies, and Duncan worked long, hard days building. While he often caught himself staring pensively at the mountains and recollecting the days he roamed them freely, he was content. Sated by his beautiful wife and two incredible kids, he mentally drifted off into a blissful complacence. At least until the bottom dropped out.

Duncan was building. Not just homes and small commercial properties, but a future for himself and his family: the American Dream, which turned out to be a brutal lie that he and every other middle-class American of his generation had been force-fed for decades. And while it was his generation's lie, it had been a reality for the generation before him. His parents' generation had pulled it off, as had his grandparents, to a lesser degree, but one day Duncan woke up and realized that for him, at least, it had all been a lie, and now it was all over.

He and Erica owned a number of properties. There was their home in the foothills between Ennis and Bozeman and a rental house on the beach in Oregon that they kept because it had a guest cottage they could use for a week or so each August, when the winds were calm and the Pacific air was moderate, unlike hot, dry Montana. Then there was the cabin on the Kenai in Alaska, which they owned outright, having purchased the lot with cash and built the cabin together over the course of three summers before the kids came. Duncan was still guiding, so they'd had the time. They also owned half of a concrete duplex they'd purchased with Duncan's cousin Brett, who was from Texas but had gone to Belize and Guatemala and married a girl from there whose family was very wealthy and connected. It was a beautiful little place on a lush tropical hill overlooking the Gulf of Honduras from Belize, and it had only cost them $25,000. It was located just a one-hundred-yard walk to a fantastic white-sand beach, where they kept a flats boat for fishing excursions.

The Duncans also owned nearly a dozen building lots around the Gallatin and Madison Rivers. These properties were investments in their minds, as for a period of several years Duncan had made reasonably good money building a couple of very high-end spec homes on the properties each summer. The Duncans had built a great life around hard work and a little thrift. They were not wealthy, at least not compared to the grandiose urbanites who flocked to the area surrounding Yellowstone and for whom Duncan was building trophy homes, but they were gaining. But the hard thing about money, Duncan had discovered, was that if it was not in your hand or in a mason jar, it wasn't always actually there.

The Duncans' money was in real estate, and they continued to roll it over and build on it. They were perhaps careless in that they hadn't diversified, but they had been set up enough to weather the usual five-year boom-and-bust cycles that had defined the American real estate market since the end of the Civil War. What they had not counted on was an economic downfall, more severe in some aspects than the Great Depression—an economic and political paradigm shift that found them too leveraged to get through unscathed. The more astute members of his parents' generation sold out at the peak and reaped huge returns, but the Duncans and their peers were still in the building phase of life. They couldn't sell; they had to keep rolling assets over so there would be something for retirement. Then, they got caught when the music stopped; they were overleveraged.

First the building stopped, which killed the cash flow. Duncan completed a spec home over the winter and put it on the market in the early spring of 2007, and it was still on the market the following winter. The interest payments on the vacant spec home were growing increasingly difficult to maintain, and there was interest building on the lots as well. As work slowed, cash became tighter, and with almost no building going on in Duncan's part of the world, he was scrambling to keep his four employees busy. They were fine young men, and three of them had young families of their own. When it got too tough, Duncan used the equity line on his own home to keep them working and paid. The few jobs he was getting did not pay what they would have a year or two earlier. He had carried his crew in this manner in past winters, and when the snow melted, the work had come back. Within a month or two, he had always paid the credit line off, but this time, a shift had occurred. Duncan completed twenty-three job estimates that spring for summer work and only got one under contract: a large custom home for a doctor from Connecticut. In early fall, after it was framed up and dried in, Duncan laid off the three skilled laborers he had and finished the house through the winter with the one kid on his crew. It was a difficult decision, but he had been going under trying to keep his crew paid, and he couldn't postpone the inevitable any longer. When that home was complete and Duncan realized he had underbid the job by a large margin, which he'd had to do to get the work, he realized he was through.

In the meantime, Erica had gone back to work at a veterinary clinic in Ennis owned by a family friend, but she worked for not much better than an assistant's pay, as that was all the small office could afford. She could have done better in Bozeman, but Duncan did not want her making the drive, and the kids were going to school in Ennis. Her working helped, but it did not completely fill the gaps, and they slowly fell further behind.

The only work Duncan could find was for a large agricultural fabrication company that built and maintained their facilities around Bozeman, Helena, and Billings. He was now making a third or a fourth in a day of what he had been making before, and it came at a much greater physical and emotional expense. He was now in his forties and doing work he had paid kids to do for a number of years; it was far less pay for much more work. It was defeat.

Those with the wealth were capitalizing on those who needed to work, and Duncan was growing bitter. He found himself short with his kids when they were doing nothing more than being kids. He was short with Erica. He hadn't picked up a fly rod other than to move it around in his office for three years. He hadn't killed an elk or chased sheep in any of the mountain places that gave him peace. He took his boy to chase grouse occasionally in the aspen and chokecherry draws near their home, but there was tedium in his senses. He found himself angry at his beloved black and chocolate Labs, who accompanied them on their bird-hunting trips. The winter duck hunts on the river had become a burden. The ducks seemed more trouble than they were worth to clean, and his garage had become such a wreck it was impossible to reach the woodstove to heat it up enough to clean birds.

Then his cell phone rang one day. It was the couple that rented the house on the Oregon coast, calling to say they were moving out, and Duncan fell off the edge. The house sat vacant for three months, and to rent it they had to lower the price by $400 per month. Everything they owned aside from the two places paid for in Alaska and Belize had become slow financial bleeds. A few years earlier, the Duncans were millionaires nearly twice on paper, and now they were bankrupt.

In an attempt to save some shred of their finances, Duncan came up with a plan for them to divorce on paper, and a lawyer friend helped them put the plan into play. Through the divorce, Duncan would end up with all the properties with loans on them, and Erica would get the cabin in Alaska and the house they lived in. It was upside down, but at least they could afford it, and they needed a place to live. Duncan would get all the properties that were sucking wounds, and he would let them go by declaring bankruptcy to avoid judgments if the situation called for him to do so.

The plan was reasonably good. Duncan would take all the heat and the hits to his credit, and Erica would be able to maintain hers with a little effort. This way, she would still have credit for them to function and would be in a position to start her own clinic or purchase the clinic from her aging employer at some point. The plan was as good as they could come up with, but it didn't solve Duncan's struggle within himself. It did not change the fact that Duncan still didn't make enough money, and that he'd had it all and then lost it. He began to regret not finishing college or going to law school, which was his original intention. But college or even law school wouldn't have changed his plight. He wouldn't live in the city, and what type of job would college buy him in the sagebrush of the Madison River Valley?

He couldn't live with the fact that he wasn't giving his family what they deserved, or at least what he perceived they deserved. And Erica, who loved him so much and always found the good in every day, didn't entirely understand a man's need to provide. Like so many men, his efforts to provide for his family had resulted in his increasing absence, which had created distance between him and Erica and the kids.

The time he spent with his family was not the quality time it had once been. He was only distantly present when they were together, and if he could have just stuck with his original plan to divorce on paper and let it all go, they would have eventually gained it all back in some form or another, although in no special hurry. But there was more to his plan than he shared with his wife, and the restless demons that caused tightness in Duncan's chest whenever he sat idle too long eventually caused him to make a phone call he didn't want to make.

On a soggy March day, as a light rain fell on the accumulated snow from winter and the mud began to show, Duncan called James Beck.

———◆◇———

These years later, as the Duncans emerged from the dark spruce- and fir-lined driveway at the cabin, Duncan knew it was time to tell Erica about the phone call he made on that first day of mud season back in 2010. He would also tell her about the man in the black

Escalade who'd visited him at their home in Bozeman the summer after Jack returned from Mexico in the middle of the night.

As Duncan and Erica unloaded their bags and packed them to the cabin, which was boarded up to keep the bears out, Duncan felt relieved at the thought that he would no longer harbor secrets from his wife.

Now, he would tell her the truth. He would tell her about the three Mexicans he'd killed on the mountain with the man who visited in the Escalade. He would tell her the rest as well.

The kids jumped out of the car and ran through the tall green bear grass that grew lush on the southwest-facing bank of the river, where there were openings for sunlight to draw the grass out of the dark, moderate soil. They ran to the boardwalk dock that paralleled the swift-flowing, milky turquoise waters that came from Kenai and Skilak Lakes and the glaciers of the Kenai Range before the lakes.

Duncan rigged fly rods for both kids, buckled them into life jackets, and lined them out on flipping flies for the abundant sockeye salmon that hugged the shore on their way up the river to their natal spawning grounds. The kids were excited, but for the adults there were chores to do: turn gas on for the cookstove; split and haul wood for the woodstove; and get the generator running for a shower or to run the freezer to pack fish to take back to Montana. Duncan began splitting wood for a fire in the stove, should the warm, sunny mid-seventies day turn into a cool night and morning. Meanwhile, Erica silently carried the wood to the covered deck on the river side of the house, which offered a perfect landing for watching the glacier-covered Kenai Range to the south. Duncan fired the generator to make sure it was running, but they would live by the light of propane lanterns and oil lamps.

Erica interrupted his work, impatient for enlightenment. She felt her life had been vague and lacking a goal for too long.

"The kids are busy fishing," she said. "Let's talk."

He looked at her adoringly and with the look of a little boy who would soon be in trouble. "Let's grab a chair and sit on the deck," he said.

They each grabbed a folding camp chair from the toolshed that housed some of their camp equipment, as luxurious camping was what they did when they visited the cabin. They walked through the bear grass and the tall, thin white daisies that carpeted the cabin yard. They unfolded the chairs. Duncan pulled the cork from a bottle of Chateau St. Jean cabernet and filled two glasses halfway while they both kept one eye on the kids, who were casting from the wood plank platform on the river's creamy emerald edge.

"You aren't gonna loosen me up with wine, you know. I'm not twenty-three anymore."

"You aren't," he said, smiling.

"*We* aren't," she said. Her expression was serious, and she sat back in her chair but remained upright, anxious for some answers.

"You'll always be twenty-three to me."

"Thanks," she said out loud, but the expression on her face said, *Shut up and get on with it.*

"The wine's more for me," he said. "Truth serum."

"Is it that hard to tell the truth?" she asked, slightly angered.

"No, it's not. It's just that there are things to talk about that I've put away so as not to think about them for a long time." He had been smiling teasingly, but he became serious and sat forward in his chair, sliding out to the edge and looking at her.

"Erica, would you kill or die for your children, or me?"

"What kind of question is that, Jack?"

"Just answer the question: would you kill or die for your children? Forget about me. What about the kids?"

"That's got no bearing on—"

"Answer the question," he said, interrupting her. "Just answer the question. It's got bearing on everything I'm about to tell you."

She relaxed in her chair a little and looked at the mountains, and then her eyes returned to him and looked deep into his own eyes, serious, resolute.

"What do you think the answer to that is, Jack?"

"I know what the answer is, but I want to hear you say it."

She was finely honed, and he was shrewd and calculated, though he never manipulated her. He never tried to control her, as it was not in his nature, nor was it in hers to allow it. He loved her for it. She was unbreakable, his only match, at least the only one he had found so far, and he was done looking.

"I would, under the right circumstance, and you know that. Why would you even ask?"

"I want you to remember that as I tell you this."

"Just get to the point, Jack! Just say it. Just say whatever it is you've been keeping from me."

"I'm trying, but I need you to understand this. I need you to understand why."

"Understand what, damn it? Just say it. Tell me whatever in the hell it is you haven't been."

"Just promise me you'll focus on the circumstances, not the actions."

"I always think, Jack."

"You're a woman, Erica. You always feel first, and then you think."

Erica's face flushed, and her cheeks turned pink from anger at Duncan's comment. "You're an ass," she said.

"You've said that before."

At that moment, the kids yelled as the boy hooked a bright sockeye, which stripped line off the reel, making a metallic buzz as it streaked across the river into the fast water. Both Duncans stood for a moment, realized all was well, and then watched as the fish liberated itself to continue on its spawning run. Their attention returned to each other and to their conversation, and the kids returned to flipping flies into the river.

"I don't know how to tell you this, so I'm just gonna say it: I've been running a secret outfitting service. I research, plan, and guide the ultimate hunt for a group of wealthy individuals. It's called the Hunt Club."

He paused, and Erica focused intently on his words.

"What's so exotic about that?" she asked.

Duncan squirmed a little in his camp chair. He looked away momentarily, gazing at the distant Kenai Mountains, and he promised himself he would hunt that range one day.

"I organize hunts for men to hunt other men," were his carefully chosen words, as though it were no different than hunting any other animal.

Erica sat back into her chair, expressionless. Duncan's words were spinning in her head like the garble of static from an old radio between stations. And her silence pressed him to speak.

"This is where I need you to think for a minute before you judge me. You said yourself you would kill or die for your kids."

The words began to show themselves more clearly in Erica's head. "Do you go on these hunts?" she asked, trying to clear them up completely.

"Yes, I guide them," he replied, and he searched her face for a hint of what she was thinking.

"So, you kill people for money?"

"I don't really do the killing."

Erica glared at him but still didn't give up much of what she was thinking. She was still processing the revelation.

"I've been pressed into this. I didn't want to do it, but I had to."

Erica was silent, but the thoughts in her head were loud. So loud her head began to hurt, and all she could think was that they should have gone through with the divorce for real. Then she looked at him and softened a little inside, but she stayed cold to him. She was angry.

"I wish I could go back to our old life, building, making money, being home for dinner with you and the kids, but it slipped away," Duncan said. "I want that back, and this seemed like a way to get it. In hindsight, it might've been better to go through with the divorce on paper and file for bankruptcy like everyone else, but I had an opportunity that was unique."

He seemed tired to her. He'd always been hard to keep up with, and he possessed an endless supply of energy, but as she looked at him sitting on the deck across from her, he looked a little lost. He'd had this look before when the economy was spiraling into recession, taking their livelihood with it, and when he'd taken the regular job, but this was different. Now he looked scared, and she'd never seen that before.

"Unique, Jack? You call killing people unique?"

"Bear with me, hon. You have to let me explain. These men aren't men; they're monsters. They need to be killed."

"And God gave you the authority to pass that judgment on these men?"

"No. James Beck did, but he only thinks he's God," Duncan mused.

"James Beck? What's he have to do with this?"

Most everybody in Montana knew or knew of James Beck. To them, he was nothing more than another wealthy Easterner who bought up large ranches and removed the cattle, replacing them with No Trespassing signs.

"I know you've got questions, and I'm sure you're shocked and angry, but let me explain from the beginning. If we start from the beginning, it'll make sense. And it does make sense. For you and me and the kids, it all makes sense."

"Killing people for money is a hard thing to make sense of, Jack Duncan."

"Let me explain that first."

"OK."

"All the targets are drug dealers, murderers, and butchers of in- nocent people. Each target is chosen based on a very simple question: Would the world be a better place without them? We gather dossiers on the individuals, which outline their careers, their families, their crimes against humanity—everything about them. Beck and I put them into the pool as worthy targets. They're monsters in a human form that the law or politicians have allowed to exist, can't catch, or, in some cases, have created or coddled. Beck picks the clients. He knows so many exceptionally wealthy people from all over the world that he's able to bring the hunters. My cousin Brett and his in-laws and all their ties provide most of the intel and logistical support. They've provided some of the targets, and with the exception of one, all the targets have been from south of the border. One was a Mus- lim warlord from Africa who executed genocide against his own people. He killed a thousand men, women, and children, execution style. Babies, Erica! Shot in the head so he could build a reservoir to water the crops that were making him a fortune because he controlled the food supply in his small country."

Erica was listening to his carefully chosen words, aghast, but without much expression. What she had known so far was that Duncan had managed to sell all their properties for what they needed to get out of them and get out from under the looming foreclosures without harm. He also paid off their house in Montana. They had been taking vacations that had seemed like real estate shopping trips to her, and this had all transpired in fewer than two years.

"Let me go back to how this all started. Do you remember the man who came to visit me one night while we were living in Bozeman and you were finishing school?"

"No, not really."

"You remember. He came to the house in a black Escalade and we spoke on the sidewalk. Starched shirt, fancy boots. He was outta place."

"I don't know. Maybe?"

Erica had indeed seen Duncan visiting with the strange man outside their house nearly twenty years earlier. Watching through the window of the house they rented near the college in Bozeman, she'd recognized his face as familiar but was unable to put a name to it. He did look out of place in Bozeman, wearing a dark sport coat and starched white shirt. Jack didn't invite the man in. Instead, he walked the man down the sidewalk to converse with him. The man was animated and obviously in charge, or at least he seemed to think he was. She had watched as Duncan gazed off to the distant mountains. He seemed uninterested in what the man was talking about, and his demeanor bordered on disrespectful. They spoke for ten minutes or so and then shook hands, and the gentleman returned to the backseat of the black-tint-windowed Escalade.

"Who was that?" Erica had asked when Duncan walked back into their little house.

"Just a man I guided awhile back."

"What did he want?"

"To talk about another hunt."

"He looks like he's got a lot of money."

"More than God himself."

"How much is that?"

"That was James Beck."

"*The* James Beck."

"Yes."

"He looked handsome from here."

"He looks like a dick."

"Because he's rich?"

"No, because he *is* a dick."

Erica laughed. "Are you gonna guide him again?"

"No."

"Why not?"

"Duncan looked at her and smiled. "You're precious," he said.

She laughed. "So why aren't you gonna guide him again?"

He looked at her and grinned. "Because he's a dick."

Erica only vaguely recalled the conversation as they sat in their deck chairs in Alaska two decades later.

"Yes. You said he was an old client," she said.

"Yes. And he *was* an old client. I'd guided him on a desert sheep hunt at the Vasquez place in Baja. Something happened on that trip, though. Something went wrong."

Erica was paying attention to his words and to his expression. His brow furrowed as he went into the story. He looked at the point of a stick he was turning in a knothole in one of the deck boards. Then he looked at the mountains and again at the stick and then back at her.

"Beck and I were returning from the mountains on a lonely road out of some wild parts of Baja," he said, starting the story.

Then he told her how he and Beck had been ambushed by the Mexican banditos, how he'd killed them and dragged the bodies off to the side of the road, and how they'd rolled them into the bottom of the brushy arroyo. He left out any gore and tried to make it gentle for her, even though he knew she was tougher than he was. *A man only has to witness childbirth once to know that without a doubt,* he thought.

"Do you remember finding me in that little coffee shop in downtown Bozeman?" he asked.

"Yes," she replied quietly, preoccupied with the mental digestion of information.

"I had just stepped off a private jet in the middle of that night. I hadn't slept. I had shot those three men less than a day before when you walked into that coffee shop…I wonder if it's still there?"

"It is."

"We should go sometime," he said, attempting to make everything normal. Other than to fly, Duncan had not been to Bozeman in a year; in fact, he had hardly been in Montana.

"Go on, Jack," she said softly as she watched the kids flip their flies into the emerald water.

"Beck was buzzed by the shooting and later told me he wished he'd played a bigger part in shooting the Mexicans. I just wished it'd never happened."

Erica rose from her chair, walked to the handrail at the edge of the deck, and looked out at the kids and to the glaciered mountain range in the distance. "I'm still listening," she said. But she was also thinking.

"I can't tell you I feel any guilt for doing it. If I hadn't pulled the trigger, I may not be here now. In fact, in the split second I had to make the decision, there was no indecision."

With her back to Duncan, Erica thought about how maybe they'd all be better off if he wasn't there right now. It was easier to have those thoughts when she wasn't looking at him.

"I was sure they were going to kidnap us, which could have ended badly. But I can tell you that occasionally their faces creep into my thoughts."

Duncan paused. He was still sitting at the edge of the chair. He looked at her and at the Kenai Mountains beyond her. He wondered which part of the grandeur before them she was looking at and, more importantly, what she was thinking.

"I looked at them, Erica," he continued. "I looked them in their hollow, empty eyes as we dragged them off the side of the road and rolled them into the canyon bottom. You know the look. That far-off, empty stare."

But Erica's mind had wandered from the conversation. She was thinking about the boy she had dated in college. She'd heard he'd taken over his family ranch near Kalispell, and that he'd sold a small section on the lake to a developer for several million dollars before the bottom fell out of the market. She'd heard he was still unmarried, and she couldn't help but think she might have made the wrong choice.

"I wondered what they did, and if they had families who would come looking for them. Were they poor and needed money? Did they have children who would hurt for something in their absence? But Beck was excited by it."

Duncan rose from his seat and joined her at the handrail, but not close; rather, he stood at a distance where they couldn't touch. She continued gazing at the Alaskan scenery.

"I know what you're thinking," Duncan said, interrupting her thoughts.

"I doubt it."

"You're thinking you shoulda married that kid in college from Kalispell."

She jumped on the inside, but she didn't show it other than to blush slightly at getting caught in her daydream. He was good at knowing what she was thinking. She felt a moment of guilt at being unfaithful, if only in her mind.

"No, Jack," she lied.

Duncan just looked at her and smiled.

"I don't think you can pick who you fall in love with," she said.

"Who did you fall in love with?"

"Don't be an asshole; you know I love you."

"Are you sure?"

"Most of the time."

What Jack did not tell Erica about was his affair with Marialena. He had always protected her from anything that would hurt her. He didn't tell because it did not matter, and he never asked about any boyfriends she might have had while they were apart in college. He did not tell her that he suspected that Señor Vasquez had sent the men into the mountains after him because of the relationship with his beautiful daughter. And twenty years later, that did not matter either.

The kids suddenly yelled again, and Avery squealed with delight as a chrome-bright sockeye salmon ran and pulsed on the end of her line while Coulter shouted instruction at her in an attempt to help her land the fish. The Duncans ran down the hundred or so feet of trail to the boardwalk fishing platform to help the kids land the fish. The girl horsed the six-pound fish to the bank with the heavy leader, and by the time they arrived, the boy had it in the net. Coulter produced a knife from the pocket of his jeans and cut the gills of the fish, which was still writhing in the net. Then, he left it in the water to wash the blood down the river as he was taught, so as not to attract brown bears into the yard. Duncan took the fish from the net and filleted it on a wood board that he rinsed in the river, and then the two adults returned to the sunny deck of the little log cabin. They would cook the rich deep-red fillets in a piece of foil on the camp barbecue on the deck with nothing more than a little sea salt—all that fresh sockeye needed to make the mouth water with every bite.

By the time the two grown Duncans had returned to the deck and put the fillets in an ice chest, Erica had had time to let Jack's words settle in. She was disturbed and angry, but she understood his need to fix things.

"Is there more, Jack?" she asked when they reached the deck.

"Not really. Other than the fact I really want no part of it any longer."

He moved closer to her down the deck railing until his arm brushed her shoulder.

"I'm not like Beck."

"How do you know that?" she asked without taking her attention off the kids and scenery.

"I don't enjoy any of it and really don't want the risks. Beck is a sociopath. He's got a list of broken marriages and a pile of kids who barely know what he looks like."

She turned and looked at him. She raised her eyebrows at him in disbelief, saying everything without a word passing her lips.

"OK," he said, and looked away from her and toward the milky jade water rushing swiftly past his children. "When I listen to my own words, I guess I sound a little like Beck. But I'm not."

She continued to look at him.

"I don't want to be away from you all. That's the difference. And we aren't divorced. At least not yet."

"You need to fix this, Jack, or you're gonna be."

"Gonna be what?"

"Divorced, Jack. I love you, but at some point, that's not enough."

He knew she meant it, and that he had to untangle the mess. "You know I'm not like him," he said, for lack of something better.

"I *think* you aren't, but I really don't know anymore."

"He views other people as tools or machines put on the earth to serve him, to make him money. Clean his house, fly his planes, or manage his ranches or whatever else he owns. He's an elitist."

"And you, Jack? Where do you fit into it all?"

"I don't fit into anything that has to do with him. He thinks I do. He thinks we're friends, but he doesn't have any friends. He's dead inside."

"I don't know," she said, and looked back at the kids fishing. "This is a lot to digest."

"He would cannibalize anyone in his life, and at the first opportunity I see, I will get out."

"Why can't you just tell him you're done and you want out?"

"It doesn't work like that with Beck. Nothing changes, nothing happens unless Beck says it does."

"So he owns you, then?"

"Nobody but you and the kids owns me."

"What does he see in you, then?"

"That I don't care how much money he has, and that under stress I killed three men who would have likely harmed him. He would have sold me to those men to save his own hide. He has no honor. Like I said, he's empty on the inside. He thinks I'd protect him. I really don't know what he sees in me for sure. It doesn't matter. The first chance I get, I'll get out."

"And when will that be?"

"I don't know, hon. I don't know."

"That's not good enough, Jack, the kids need you. You know what it's like growing up without a dad. I can't believe you'd allow it. How much money is enough? Is it greed? Are you becoming one of these men?"

"What about you? Do you need me?"

"Yes, of course," she said, but she looked away as the words came out of her mouth.

Duncan was suddenly flush with regret. He wished he could go back and tell Beck no. He knew the value of time, and that even Beck's money couldn't buy it. He was bitter. He had been angry that bankers would own his property. He had been angry that trust-fund babies from back East would take what he had worked hard for at a discount. His back had been against the wall, and under duress, he'd accepted Beck's offer to create the Hunt Club to fight off the financial wolves, only to find later that he'd made a deal with a financial devil. He would have already left Beck, but he knew Beck would not let him. Beck was a megalomaniac with a god complex that would make the average egomaniac blush with modesty.

"I'm the boy you took to the prom. The one you skinny-dipped with in the hot springs in the canyon. The one who rode thirteen miles in the middle of the night under a full summer moon and swam a sweaty gelding across the Madison to taste your lips. I haven't changed much; I'm a little older and stiffer in the morning, but I'm still that boy. I just have the responsibilities of a man. I give you my word, and you have to trust me, I'll get out as soon as I can. Beck won't just let me walk, but when the opportunity arises, I *will* get out. You have to trust me and be patient. I don't want this any more than you."

Erica watched the kids laughing, having put two more sockeye in the net, and the boy tying the second of the three to a rope stringer with a bowline—a knot Duncan had taught him—and sliding the third on through the gills. She looked across the rolling spruce-covered hills to the mountains again.

Duncan said nothing. He admired her rear view, which was at least as impressive as the scenery of Alaska beyond her. He said nothing of the money he had. He wanted her support, but he would not buy it.

Finally, she turned back toward him with tears in her fierce eyes. "I wish I could leave. It would be simple. But I can't. At least not yet."

"So you're in? You'll help me see this through?"

"I'm not in. I'm just not out," she said.

He put his arm around her waist. She stiffened and resisted a little. He held her firmly, and after a few moments she relented and leaned her head against him. Duncan pulled her into his embrace, looked into her eyes, and said nothing until he felt her begin to ease and relax, then he pulled her closer, and they kissed. But before the kiss became deeper than a peck, she turned her head away from him. This might have alarmed him, but she did this often. In fact, as far back as Duncan could remember, she hadn't been overly affectionate with him.

Grinning, he leaned slightly back to where she could see his boyish grin and said, "I haven't told you the good news yet."

"I'm not sure I want any more news from you, Jack Duncan."

"I have several million dollars saved in offshore bank accounts and a little stash of gold that I haven't weighed lately."

"You do?"

"Some of these vacations we've been on have been real estate shopping trips. I really don't know how this is going to end exactly, and I—or should I say, we—may need to disappear."

She looked at him now as they stood on the deck. The tightness and anger in her face had eased a little, and she almost smiled.

"I have documents for you and the kids, too," he said.

"I don't want to disappear, Jack. Montana is my home."

"But there's a big world out there, and we may need to leave our options open."

"And I'd like to see some more of it, but when I'm done, I want to go home."

She smiled at him. She smiled because it felt good to stand her ground. It felt good to know where her roots were, and that they ran five generations deep in the marginal and often frozen and rocky Western Montana soil. "I love you, but you got yourself into this, so you'll have to get yourself out."

Duncan glared at her. He was trapped, and he hated it. All that was left of his roots in Montana were her and the kids. His mother had retired and sold her place at the foot of the Madison Range to move to Scottsdale, Arizona, tired of the winters. His uncles and cousins had dispersed to California and Texas, and with the rest of his kin passed on, he was the last of the Duncans left in Montana. He even looked at his children as more his wife's family's than his own.

"Let's join the kids," she said, and walked down the steps from the deck. "I'd rather fish than fight, Jack." She held out her hand for him to join her.

The Duncans spent a month in Alaska, soaking up their time together. They fished, panned for gold, dug razor clams, and thoroughly enjoyed each other. They had no real electricity and no neighbors aside from the occasional moose that wandered through their wild yard and a lynx that visited a couple of times. They spotted brown bear tracks twice in mud near the river where the trail caught up with the fishing boardwalk. They were a family.

FOUR

Three thousand miles from the breathtaking wilderness of Alaska's Kenai Peninsula, a sandy-gray-haired man of medium height sat very alone at an inescapably large, cold marble table in the penthouse of an exclusive Manhattan high-rise.

The man seated at the table was studying the ghastly résumés of several likely candidates for his little club. When he looked up from the photos and paperwork and his laptop computer screen to survey the view of the world-famous New York nighttime skyline from his fashionable city home, he only saw the twinkling lights set against the blackness. Though an incredible mass of humanity was laid out in front of him, his thoughts never drifted deeper than the light.

The exterior wall of his apartment was glass, and most of the interior walls, designed and completed by the most elite decorators and contractors in the massive city, were painted sensual, dark tones in blends of grays, plums, and mauves, with an occasional lighter tone for contrast. Given the fact the man had enough money to decorate and furnish every home in New York, his apartment was relatively empty, and entirely void of a sense of home. And despite the fact the man had four ex-wives, five children, and two grandchildren, there was no evidence of them on the walls, or on the very expensive, polished precast-concrete bar, or atop the tigerwood end tables. Nothing on the fridge, either: no photos and no cards, almost as though the space were a rental.

The man seated at the table sipped Glenfarclas 1955 neat to prevent bruising the half-century-old Speyside scotch. His outward appearance registered as content, but that was only due to forty-plus years of high-level business experience, from which he'd learned to reveal to his adversaries nothing. Nearing seventy, he was still physically fit, but his only human relationships were those money bought. He had several "girlfriends" forty years his junior, but his emotional investment in them was so minimal that they were nothing more than monogamous whores. And they probably were not even monogamous. They lived luxurious lifestyles with no need of a career simply because they possessed the mightiest of all assets between their smooth, creamy thighs.

The man was James Beck, and he sat at his table for hours. His cell phone rang several times, and each time Beck looked at the phone for the caller but didn't answer, intent instead on studying the men who would make his list. It was his purpose. He had been so financially successful that he could buy no more satisfaction. His lethal game of cat and mouse—identifying, studying, tracking, stalking, and then killing men he considered evil—was now the only event in his life that charged him with adrenaline. There was nothing on the planet that could be purchased that he could not have in minutes or days. He could fly to Paris for crepes or Tokyo for sushi. He'd once purchased an entire island in the South Pacific and relocated the inhabitants so he could escape the civilization that had molded and defined him. And through his hunting of men, he felt that he was contributing, performing a community service.

Beck had scrapped so many companies, killed so many jobs, and ruined so many relationships with his own family, and he felt that he was now giving back. It never occurred to him that he might be a serial killer, though only of sorts, as his victims were themselves predators of the innocent. These were real criminals who brought drugs and violence to the world. He reconciled the crime with the service, and the delusion that he was protecting the common people of the world.

The spectacular irony from Duncan's point of view was that, other than the first one, Beck was not even killing them himself. Instead, he was manipulative enough to use other men to do the killing for him, and even to profit by it.

Duncan had only been to Beck's New York penthouse once, as he preferred to stay as far away from both New York and Beck as he possibly could. When Duncan had been there, he'd noticed the art. Beck had original French Impressionist pieces as well as high-end modern American art in most of the house, but in the den there was the slightest hint of Beck's outdoor interests: an original Charlie Russell oil painting and several original commissioned Ken Carlson pieces, all of which depicted mountain sheep of the world. What Duncan found most out of place, however, was a photo of Duncan with the large ram he had killed as a teenager in the peaks above his childhood home; it was the only ram to date that Duncan had actually taken with his own rifle.

The existence of this photo had seemed especially odd to Duncan, as he knew Beck had children Duncan's age and even grandchildren, yet there were no photos of them in the fine high-rise city home. In contrast, Jack and Erica's home was well kept by Erica when Duncan was away, but it was lived in. There were photos of the kids, and in every room there was art: some fine Western art and wildlife prints, but more finger paintings. There was a rainbow trout the boy had done with acrylics at the age of six that was so impressive to Duncan that he'd had it framed in Bozeman at a high-end art studio. There were photographs of family members both living and long since passed, some of them black-and-whites dating back to the original ancestors who had settled in Montana. There was life on the Duncans' walls and in their photos. It was a legacy, and it made a home.

Beck's place in the city made Duncan uncomfortable, but most locations other than a wall tent in a high mountain basin or his own home did that. On the single occasion he was there for two nights, he requested that Beck make him a reservation in a room at the Westin New York hotel, even though in a show of affection Beck had invited Duncan to stay with him. Beck honored Duncan's request, and Duncan left as soon as they were through with their dubious business of sorting through dossiers and planning a manhunt. He could've stayed with Beck and drank $10,000-a-bottle scotch, but he did not want to nurture a relationship with Beck, who felt contrary to this and thought of Duncan as a friend. Duncan preferred the $25-a-bottle Canadian whiskey at the Westin's bar, where he entertained himself by people watching if not watching people, looking for the ones he figured that Beck sent to keep track of him. Duncan kept a notebook where he wrote descriptions of suspicious characters, and he often took photos to catalog them in his phone so he could share them with Erica if needed.

Most of the two men's meetings occurred on Beck's Gulfstream or at the ostentatious log home Beck kept on one of the ranches he owned between Ennis and Bozeman on the banks of the Madison River. There were many game animal mounts from around the world on the walls of that grandiose three-story log monstrosity. Duncan was as comfortable in Beck's Montana home as he was anywhere with Beck, and when their business was done, Duncan would return to his wife and kids at his own home, but that was their connection: hunting, the mountains, and the exotic sheep that inhabited the highest, most desolate reaches of those mountains.

The only things that seemed to excite Beck aside from business deals were the animals and what they meant to him hanging on his wall, and chasing them in places where only a helicopter or a day on horseback could deposit a man. That was what drew them together, at least initially. The difference was that Beck lived to go to the mountains intermittently between financial engagements, whereas Duncan lived in the mountains and the mountains lived inside him. He preferred the day on horseback or on foot to the helicopter. He preferred driving over flying when time would allow, and he had twice driven to Baja from the Pacific Northwest during his college days. Duncan felt a disconnection from the land and the journey when he flew. Flying robbed the traveler of changes in geography and climate, which made the destination feel artificial or manufactured. Getting on a plane in Montana when the thermometer read twenty-seven degrees below zero and then stepping off in the tropics where it was humid and eighty-five left him feeling alienated from the journey.

By the time Duncan contacted Beck about helping him hunt men, a decade and a half had elapsed since the unlikely partners had disposed of the three Mexican bandits in the mountains outside Loreto, and Beck had propositioned Duncan on the sidewalk in Bozeman about starting the Hunt Club. While the memory of the shooting had faded from Duncan's mind, it was vivid in Beck's. Beck had been in his fifties at the time, and after sixteen more years, he still needed the adrenaline rush of the shooting. He had been eager to rekindle the plan he spoke to Duncan about on the sidewalk in Montana years earlier. Like many super-wealthy people, he needed something that was out of reach. He was overtaken by the human desire to want more, and when he finally had everything, he had to search for something to want. He simply could not buy the sensation, at least not outright. Duncan was impressed with Beck's vigor after a decade and a half, although it was aggravated by the waning agility of the aged working at holding on to youth. This was reflected in the men's very first Hunt Club expedition.

At that first hunt, Beck was the shooter. He wanted to feel the adrenaline rush he'd had years earlier, and Duncan felt it would be wise to have a practice hunt before adding a paying client to the mix. These men would be paying the exorbitant price of one million dollars plus all the expenses resulting from the hunt, so Duncan wanted to work out any possible issues. They chose the regions south of the US border as their area to operate. And for this first hunt, they would be in Guatemala. There was an abundance of law-breakers and an abundance of drug traffic, and logistically it was easy. Duncan's cousin Brett was well connected through his in-laws in Mexico, Central America, and South America, and he provided the infrastructure as well as most of the intelligence for the operations. His cousin's contacts were more than happy to help, as they were relatively law-abiding businessmen and vehemently opposed to drugs and their trafficking. They were also more than willing to provide targets whose elimination would be of some interest or gain to the family. Brett Duncan's name was never spoken aloud to Beck or to any of the clients, nor were the names of Brett's in-laws, the pilots, the rare assistants on the ground, or anyone else with even the slightest involvement. This anonymous arrangement worked bilaterally, as Beck was too public of a figure for his name to be mentioned even once. Duncan spoke to Brett or met him in person, always providing the buffer between Beck and the support team. Duncan was the only member of the team who had actual knowledge of all the parties. This put him in a precarious position, as he held the most power and at the same time had the least anonymity. Every effort was made to protect him, and he went by an alias attached to various sets of false identifications: passports, credit cards, and driver's licenses, which were growing in numbers and kept in a safe box buried in a secret location in Montana. Even the clients knew Duncan only by his alias, *El Cazador*.

It was Spanish for "the Hunter," and it was an alias given to him by the Guatemalans involved with the Hunt Club. Anyone who might inquire about Duncan was misdirected by the story that he was from Argentina, and a German descendent of a Nazi war criminal, a number of whom had fled to Central and South America in the final days of World War II.

Beck had proven himself a liability on that first hunt, but by then it was too late. Duncan was in, and there were already several additional targets chosen and clients arranged to shoot them. Duncan and his cousin had chosen some Colombian cocaine runners who were using a river and some of Brett's land on the Guatemalan Pacific coast one hundred and fifty miles south of the Mexican border to warehouse the drugs. Beck had protested slightly, as they wouldn't shoot the leader of the drug operation, but the two men who were responsible for moving the drugs. Brett provided enough of a violent criminal résumé on the two Colombians to assure Beck of the need to rid the earth of these two men. Beck was also promised that there was a Mexican on the other end involved with getting the drugs to the United States, and they were still trying to track him down as a target for a later date. But the need to eliminate these men was real, and it was an easy test of their system of extrication. If there were a problem, Duncan was familiar with the area, having spent time at the *salinas* fishing and surfing on the weekends twenty years earlier, when he spent three months in Antigua at a Spanish-language school to further his success as a guide in Baja.

Brett Duncan owned the salinas, a rustic facility for farming salt from the ocean that consisted of approximately one hundred acres right on the beach at the entrance to a major river that drained the steep, jungled, volcanic mountain range and caught the relentless subtropical rains rolling in off the warm Pacific. There were mangrove swamps and estuaries surrounded by fertile river delta plains where Brett's in-laws owned commercial farms with crops like sugarcane and pineapple. On the beach, his employees made sea salt from water pumped out of the Pacific Ocean and dried on large sheets of black plastic. The indigenous people who farmed the land and swept and sacked the salt lived on the edge of the beach in palm-thatch-roofed palapas they built from material that grew on the land.

Brett was fond of the families who lived on and worked the land, and he brought them clothes for their children and kitchen implements and dresses for their wives from the city when he came to the coast. He often fished with the men, who poled him through the lagoons for snook and pargo in dugout canoes made by hand from timber on the land. They took him out in pangas launched from the beach to check nets designed to harvest shrimp, fish, and crab, which they sold in markets for extra money, always sending him home with a bucketful of fresh seafood.

The men who worked the salinas had contacted him about airdrops of cocaine that had begun to take place regularly. Every couple of months, a plane would drop bundles shrink-wrapped in waterproof white plastic with foam on the inside to keep them afloat should the contraband land in the water. The men at the salinas were very concerned, as one man among them had gone missing. This was not entirely unusual in a country full of bull sharks, saltwater crocodiles, and men who liked to drink and partake in machete swordplay— Duncan recalled many one-armed Guatemalans with machetes slid into their belts—but the local farmers and fishermen believed the Colombians had played a part in the man's disappearance. The farmers had watched the Colombians at work, and they had taken note of the methods and details of the operation. Every couple of months, weather depending, the two Colombians would arrive and spend a day and a night in a palapa several miles up the muddy, slow-moving river, where a slough branched off into the jungle. The palapa was accessible only by water, and the two men would arrive via the ocean in a twenty-two-foot aluminum river-running sled. The sled was powered by a large inboard jet, and when they arrived, they came in on the surf full speed at high tide, running over the riffled water as it passed over the sandbar into the ocean, never slowing down until they reached the slough, which provided easy passage upriver to the palapa hidden in the jungle. The next day, a twin-engine King Air would pass low over the beach, circling once out over the Pacific and then flying once more very low just off the ground before dumping the white bundles onto the beach after passing over the river entrance. The jet sled would arrive immediately, and two men would beach the boat on the river side of the sand strip that separated the muddy river from the surf of the Pacific. They would gather the bundles, pile them into the boat, and disappear back up the river to the inaccessible palapa. Within a day or so, a fifty- to sixty-foot long-range fishing boat would arrive at night about a mile or so offshore, and the river sled would emerge from the jungle and bang its way through the waves, breaking on the beach as it ran out to the larger vessel to off-load the contraband. The two boats would then head north again until they evaporated into the haze of water vapors that hung heavily over the surface of the blue-gray water to deliver the drugs to US soil.

Brett and the local men who worked the salinas arranged for Beck and Duncan to intercept these men on one of their missions. Duncan and Brett had scouted the area, the palapa, the sand spit that separated the river and the ocean, and the river in between. They chose a spot approximately two hundred yards from where the Colombians beached the sled to pick up the drugs, and they dug a pit and piled sandbags in front of it just inside the edge of the jungle to provide cover for an escape if necessary. The trap was set, and a couple of months later, Duncan's phone rang.

It was his cousin on the other end, calling to tell him that the Colombians were overdue. Beck landed his jet in Bozeman long enough for Duncan to get on the plane, and then they flew to Guatemala City. There, a man named Feliciano, whose features looked more Spanish than Mayan, picked them up in a gray Suburban and drove them to the Pacific coast town of Puerto Quetzal. The private pilot was instructed to return to Los Angeles and to remain at Beck's Malibu beach home until he was contacted to pick them up, and to advise no one of his whereabouts. The entire journey took less than fifteen hours from the time Duncan's phone rang with his cousin on the other end to the moment when Feliciano pulled them up to the entrance of the Red Lion Hotel on the beach at Puerto Quetzal. They unloaded their luggage, which included two military .308 semi-auto sniper rifles topped with Swarovski tactical scopes. At that point, they would wait for the manager of the salt facility to call with word that the jet boat had slipped up into the river.

The waiting was painful for Duncan. He was away from his kids and lovely wife, and he had never sat still very well. He did not necessarily love the excitement or action of the hunts, either, but when they were on the move or waiting in position, they were one step closer to completing the mission and going home. And he was one step closer to having almost one million dollars deposited into an offshore bank of his selection.

On this particular hunt, the waiting was palatable due to the patterning of the targets and the familiarity of their routine. They knew that when the jet boat came into the river, the men would not emerge from the jungle until the following day, so Beck and Duncan spent their time well.

During the day, they chartered a forty-foot Bertram whose captain was local and spoke no English. They knew he would not recognize or have much interest in the two Americans who checked into the hotel with false documents and aliases. The remnants of Duncan's Spanish got them along well enough, and they spent their days chasing sailfish.

It was a vacation for them both. They'd leave at 7:00 a.m. from the small boat landing that was home to fewer than a dozen and a half boats, most of which were pangas the locals called "shark boats." There were also about five larger boats similar to their Bertram. The port was a river entrance with short jetties at the mouth where the river emptied into the open Pacific over a sandy beach and bar crossing that was rarely, if ever, dredged. When they approached the bar crossing each morning with its breaking white waves that spanned the entrance from tip to tip of each rock jetty, the captain would turn the large boat around, putting the bow into the current running out of the river and the stern toward the breaking waves of the Pacific. Then he'd troll the engine just slowly enough to hold their position in the river while the first mate counted the wave sets with a stopwatch and took notes on a small ringed pad. After ten or fifteen minutes, the mate would say, "Estamos listos." *We are ready.*

Then, from the flying bridge, the captain would say "Okayeee!" in his Spanish accent.

After a few more moments, the mate would yell, "Dale, dale, dale! Rápido!"

The captain would then turn the boat promptly and gun the motors, running across the perfectly flat bar between the wave sets. Duncan and Beck would look back in the wake and watch, impressed, as the waves would begin to break again immediately after their crossing as they ran from the greener inshore water to the clear blue offshore where the big game fish lived.

They trolled for hours, waiting for the satellite phone to ring and rarely seeing more than one other boat in a day. On the first day, they released four sailfish and one small striped marlin just under two hundred pounds. They also put about a dozen and a half dorado into the fish hold, bled, on ice. Several of the yellow and blue-green-spotted fish would go back to the hotel with them to be turned into ceviche or to be grilled fresh by the hotel chef. At the end of the first day, the captain apologized to them for "average" fishing and asked if they would like to try for an oversized tarpon in the river, but the Americans declined, feeling worn out by the oppressive humidity and heat and looking forward to an afternoon by the pool. But they did ask the captain to clear his schedule indefinitely, as they wished to fish with him every day until they were ready to finish their task. The captain agreed, as Beck tipped him well, and they sent him back to port with plenty of fish each day to sell on top of what they paid him.

In the afternoon, Duncan and Beck would sit by the beautiful pool under the coconut palms in and out of the water to temper the intense heat of early summer. Duncan enjoyed the local beer, Cerveza Gallo, with a wedge of lime pushed through the mouth of the bottle, as well as watching the pretty young women in their very small bikinis swimming in the pool and running jet skis up and down the river near the fishing marina. For a late afternoon snack, the chef would prepare ceviche with the dorado, after which he would prepare a meal of grilled dorado, once with a lime cream sauce and on another occasion in a sweet marinade and then topped with a mango-and-avocado chutney. The fish was always accompanied by a shrimp bisque of local origin, often served as a side to the ceviche.

On the third day, Duncan and Beck lucked into several yellowfin tuna—one in the one-hundred-and-twenty-pound range—which excited the men, including the captain, and a fine fifty-pound wahoo, one of the finest eating white-fleshed fish in the world. Beck called the hotel chef personally and insisted that he obtain wasabi and sushi rice, and then he taught the chef how to make sashimi and sushi in his kitchen at the hotel. They feasted in their rooms, not wishing to draw the attention of other guests. They were comfortable that the local staff not only would not recognize Beck but also truly had no real interest in the two Americans. This went on for nine days.

Duncan was anxious to get back to his family, but he did not call home on these trips, not wanting to leave any traceable trail to his whereabouts. Also, he was beginning to tire of Beck and his demands. Beck placed a strain on everyone around them, and a forty-foot boat was a small space to share with someone as marginally tolerable as he.

"Why don't you speed up?" Beck would say to the captain, who spoke very little English.

Duncan would translate the demands for the captain, though he tempered Beck's abruptness.

"Why don't we try a lure or different baits?" Beck would say when they had trolled for an extended period with no fish. Duncan thought about Beck and realized that Beck didn't know the process of anything intimately. He was a spoiled rich kid who'd grown into a spoiled rich man. He had always had somebody to do his work for him. He knew nothing of fishing, only of catching. And only of catching what a fisherman, the captain in this instance, coaxed to the hook for him.

Through a pair of binoculars, Duncan had spotted a marlin a half mile away over the glassy ocean. It was finning around a giant sea tortoise with an albatross perched on its back. They trolled around the tortoise in an attempt to coax the marlin to strike, but the satellite phone rang before they could bring the marlin up.

"Hello?" Duncan said.

"It's time," Brett said on the other end. "My wife's cousin will pick you up at your hotel."

"When?"

"He's already there waiting."

"I'll see you in a couple days, cuz."

"Just be careful."

"Always."

The captain was puzzled and slightly put off when Duncan told him to return to port immediately, but he accommodated the request. He wanted to hook the marlin for Beck, but Beck had his eyes on bigger game.

Their life sped up at this point, and Duncan could feel the anticipation and anxiety building in him like a bubble pushing up from his stomach into his chest. Its weight caused him to take short, quick breaths. Beck appeared unaffected. The hotel taxi was waiting for them at the marina when they returned, as Duncan had given them instructions to be there at least thirty minutes before the time the captain figured they'd arrive at port. The Suburban was parked in front of the hotel entrance with Feliciano sitting at the wheel. He rode the elevator to their rooms with them and helped them get their minimal bags and the rifles to the Suburban. Duncan checked them out of the hotel, paying with cash, and they began driving north toward the salinas.

They arrived at the small settlement, which had neither a name nor electricity and consisted of two palm-thatched buildings that were open on three sides. The buildings contained restaurants and saloons, and one had a dance hall where locals gathered at night to drink rum and beer and sing and dance. There were a couple of small *tiendas* and some chickens wandering about, scratching out an existence in the sandy dirt. Dirty children were running around in the low light of evening and kicking a soccer ball. Feliciano turned the

Suburban onto a two-track that disappeared into the jungle paralleling the ocean, from which they were separated by only a couple hundred yards and a sand ridge with palapas every one hundred yards or so. Some were inhabited, and others looked like rustic vacation huts.

The trail worked its way through coconut palms and banana trees and tall grass until it followed the edge of the lagoon where Duncan had fished for snook with his cousin years earlier. He also recalled killing a crocodile there one night with a spotlight. One of the salinas workers had held the light to blind the croc as they approached, and Duncan had shot it between the eyes with a .22 rifle while Brett harpooned the giant reptile between the shoulder blades. That night, they drank Cerveza Gallo while they danced around a fire with some of the men and women who lived on the beach and worked for his cousin. They'd butchered the croc, and the next day, they took five pounds of the meat from the tail to one of the two restaurants they had just passed. There, the old, mostly toothless woman who ran the kitchen coated the white chunks of meat in a light batter heavily infused with garlic and chilies, and then fried the meat in a giant steel wok over an open woodstove. Duncan had enjoyed the meal very much: sharing with the locals, the warm tone of the evening. The tone of this night felt very different.

They came out from the edge of the lagoon onto the top of the sand ridge, where they could see the burning orange sun smoldering into the surface of the Pacific as they pulled up to the warehouse where the salt was stored. Feliciano unloaded their bags, and the three men strung hammocks from the palm trunk posts that were buried along the edge of the concrete slab that served as the warehouse entrance. Feliciano then built an open fire on the slab, but he spoke very little and only to Duncan, and only in Spanish. Duncan had asked the hotel chef to prepare them some ceviche, and the driver had brought an ice chest from Brett that contained several more Cerveza Gallos, some black beans, tortillas, tamales, and a bottle of bourbon from an Argentine distillery that Duncan was not familiar with.

The air was heavy in the gathering darkness, and the men ate together but without many words. The Americans drank some bourbon on ice to calm their nerves—Beck with condescension, and Duncan enjoying each sip.

"So, is our plan in place?" Beck asked, looking at Feliciano, who deferred by looking to Duncan to answer, as everyone but Beck considered Duncan the leader. Duncan nodded at him to answer.

"Sí, pues," the man said, looking at Beck.

"Of course," Duncan translated. "Our man here has dug pits in the sand where we'll shoot from." Duncan nodded at Feliciano, recognizing his contribution. "They're a good distance from where the drug runners will beach their boat."

"How far?"

"I forgot my crystal ball, so I'll let you know when they beach the boat," Duncan said with more than a hint of sarcasm.

Beck looked at Duncan with aggravation, but before he could say anything, Duncan added, "About two hundred fifty to three hundred fifty based on where they've beached in the past."

"That should be safe?"

"Typically these guys are carrying small arms, .9 millimeters mostly. Pretty ineffective at that distance."

"Yeah," Beck agreed.

"Unless they get lucky and a stray bullet gets you," Duncan said, just to spoil Beck's comfort.

Feliciano was listening to their conversation and understanding bits and pieces. Duncan translated for him, and the man chuckled at the cavalier humor of being shot by "a lucky stray bullet."

Duncan and Feliciano visited for a moment, as Duncan remembered his face from many years earlier. He was married to a cousin of Brett's wife, and he and Duncan had met at several family gatherings while Duncan was going to language school in Antigua. The conversation was short, and the men retired to the hammocks early that night, knowing they would start early, before the sun rose again.

After sleeping very little, Duncan woke Beck and Feliciano, who had enjoyed a relatively sound sleep despite the sore back that came with a night in a hammock. Feliciano grabbed a pack with cold beans and tortillas and bottled water while Duncan grabbed the rifles they had assembled prior to falling asleep. Then they set off for the blind dug on the edge of the jungle a mile south down the beach.

Duncan searched the hole for snakes with the light of his cell phone, as the country was full of them, and when he gave the all clear, the three men climbed into the hole and readied themselves. They unfolded the bipods mounted to the barrels of the camouflage automatic rifles and positioned them over the sandbags in the direction of the location where Brett said the boat would be beached. Duncan readied a Leica range finder and laid it on a camouflage bandana to keep it out of the sand, and the men began their wait in the dark.

It was at least an hour before the faintest light began to spill over from a rising sun beyond the steep volcanic mountains that lined the Pacific. The three men waited silently, speaking of nothing beyond immediate concerns. The sun rose and they watched a man, one of the locals from the indigenous beach community, stalking the edge of a shallow lagoon across the river from them in the low light of morning. He was casting a throw net for a fish that only Duncan wondered the name of. His steps were painfully deliberate and slow so as not to cast a ripple or a shadow or send any alarm of his presence. To Duncan, the man was as perfect as a blue heron. He'd watched herons in Montana stalk the shallows of spring creeks, rivers, and lakes. Occasionally a movement would catch the predator's eye and the head would whip around and focus on a small trout or cisco, holding frozen like a statue, until suddenly the bird would thrust his head into the water and grab the small fish.

The man was a heron. Duncan watched him, feeling from that great distance what the man felt. He knew when the man focused on a school of fish; he felt the anticipation build before the man cast the net and returned to shore with it. There, he would remove fish so small the men in the hole could not make them out and put them in a fine mesh sack that hung from his belt. They watched him work the flat, sandy lagoon for a couple of hours until the sun was high enough in the sky that the men were beginning to feel damp from their own sweat and mosquitoes buzzed about them in their annoying fashion. Feliciano paid no attention to the fisherman, and Duncan assumed the man did not even notice the net-wielding heron. Beck saw him, but he thought nothing about him and made no comment.

As the sun climbed closer to its midmorning place in the sky, the fisherman slung the net over his shoulder and waded back to the dry sand, his cutoff jeans wet only at the fringed bottoms just above his knees. He sat on a log buried in the sand, smoked a cigarette, and relaxed in the glow of the sun, which was still tolerable for him. After the cigarette, he returned to the edge of the lagoon and began gutting the fish. The man suddenly turned his head to the southern sky, then picked up his net and sack of fish and started quickly toward the cover of the palms on the southern end of the lagoon. As he neared the tree line, his pace quickened to a slow jog, and before he disappeared into the shiny green of the beach jungle, the three men in the sand hole heard the drone of the King Air.

The plane did not appear to their eyes until it was barely visible above the tops of the coconut palms. It was flying parallel with the varied line where the calm surf rolled up the beach and stopped before sliding back down the dark sand into the Pacific. As the plane neared the river mouth, an open door became visible, and as it passed over the place where the river met the surf, white bundles about half the size of one-hundred-pound hay bales began falling from the side of the plane. The first one bounced on dry sand on their side of the river. An even dozen white packages fell, almost one on top of the other. They left the plane and landed scattered over a stretch of sand two football fields in length. The packages bounced as they hit the sand and then rolled end over end to rest in an erratic pattern up the beach between where the river paralleled the surf in its southwest-erly flow and where it turned at its terminus and emptied into the Pacific. As the drone of the twin propeller engines faded to the north and west, the muted roar of the jet boat filled the three men's ears as it came down the river, fitting perfectly into the scene they were expecting.

The only thoughts in Duncan's mind were of the fisherman run-ning for the cover of the palms and banana plants in an attempt to avoid the scene. Duncan felt clear in his head with an altruistic confidence that they were about to make things right for the fisher-man and for his fish-eating family.

It appeared that this first scene for the Hunt Club would come off like a well-rehearsed play, and to an extent it did, at least until the boat beached on the sand spit.

Two men stepped off its bow holding Uzi submachine guns while a third man, not part of the rehearsed play, stayed behind the wheel of the boat and held the bow on the sand without having to throw an anchor. Thoughts flashed through Duncan's mind at a white-hot speed. They had expected an anchored boat and two men armed with submachine guns. With the boat anchored and two men collecting the bundles of cocaine, the boat was to be retrieved from the shore and disposed of, taken by the salinas workers and used by the fishermen on the beach. The two men would have been easily dispatched while they were on the sand and had no chance of escape, but with a third man in the running boat, there was the risk of an escape, which put the locals as well as the hunters at risk.

"What's the range?" demanded Beck as he eyed the three Colombians through the tactical scope.

"It's two hundred thirty-seven yards to the boat, but don't shoot."

"Why not?" Beck demanded.

"There's a third man in the boat...no anchor. It's different; not what we were expecting."

"Nonsense."

As the words left Beck's lips, Duncan felt Beck's rifle discharge. The concussion blew sand up around them. The grass they were hiding behind blew away from the sandbags their rifles sat atop, cradled by folding bipods.

Through his naked eye looking over the scope, Duncan saw one of the two men on the sand spit drop his load and gun and fall face-forward into the sand. He saw this as his right eye found the eyepiece of his own scope. He acquired the remaining targets through it as he saw the yellow muzzle flash of the second man's submachine gun and then heard the bullets whizzing through the canopy above them. He instinctively eased the crosshairs to the left to level on the boat captain to prevent an escape, but not before he saw the second man fold as he felt the concussion of Beck's rifle a second time.

As with the robbers in Mexico, time slowed and Duncan was overtaken by a methodical clarity. The little .9mm machine gun went *pop, pop, pop,* but the bullets had no effect, as the Colombian reversed the motor and attempted to duck below the glass windshield. Duncan squeezed the trigger as his crosshair floated over the man's chest. The man lurched backward and fell dead into the bottom of the boat, and the popping of the small machine gun stopped. The boat continued in reverse captain-less, backing stern-first down the river and into the breaking waves that were beginning to rise.

"Empty your clip into the hull at the waterline!" Duncan ordered.

The two shooters raked the aluminum hull at the waterline with holes as the boat backed into the breakers, filling with seawater, rolling, and disappearing into the frothy brown water.

"Vamanos," said Feliciano.

The three men grabbed their empty cases and their packs and followed Feliciano, who seemed unaffected by the scene, through the tropical foliage. They made their way stealthily to a black Zodiac raft hidden under freshly cut palm fronds a half mile up the river. They slid the boat into the muddy water, started the Yamaha outboard, and motored quickly up the river for several miles, throwing the empty brass cases into the river but keeping the rifles, which they broke down and put into their packs.

The synthetic black raft seemed from another time or planet as it cruised up the river, passing dugout canoes and docks made with indigenous wood lashed together by handwoven hemp ropes. It was just such a dock they tied up to, and then they unloaded and followed Feliciano into the tall cane grass. They walked until they reached an opening, where a Cessna 206 sat waiting for the men.

The plane sat at the end of a dirt runway on one of the plantations owned by Brett's in-laws. The three men hurried to the plane but felt no immediate sense of danger. They loaded their gear and then themselves into the plane. Duncan took the front seat next to the pilot, whom he was delighted to see, and he nodded to him as he buckled in. Beck and Feliciano sat in the two rear seats.

Beck felt relieved to see an American behind the stick, and one that Duncan was obviously familiar with.

The flight was short and silent. The pilot was a friend of Duncan's: a rough but gentlemanly sort with whom Duncan had taken many bush flights into the wilds of the Yukon. He was a man who could land on a ridgetop, turning the plane on a one-hundred-and-eighty-degree dime while his passenger—many times Duncan—jumped out and chocked the tires so the plane, now pointed downhill, would not ghost fly itself off the side of the mountain. Then, the skilled pilot would launch the Super Cub, nearly free-falling off the face with less than half of the required runway on flat ground, and he would fly his cargo or passengers back to civilization.

The bush pilot, whom Duncan had arranged to pay outrageously for his services, had been instructed to speak nothing of their previous friendship, but Duncan didn't want to fly without him. He had picked up Duncan in all variety of bad places in the Canadian mountains, and he had executed his every move with flawless perfection. It was a fantastic bonus that he could fly private jet charters.

When the men landed at an airport at Puerto San José, south of

Puerto Quetzal, a small Raytheon jet sat fueled and waiting for the three Americans.

Feliciano shook hands with Duncan.

"Nos vemos. Vaya con dios, El Cazador," he said, and then nodded, first at the pilot and then at Beck, before turning to disappear into the airport as the three Americans climbed into the jet. Duncan showed Beck to a private space in the back of the jet where he could sleep if he chose, as he often did on his own jet. Duncan then called Beck's personal pilot, who was staying in the Malibu home, and instructed him to fly Beck's Gulfstream to the Houston airport the following day. Before Duncan left Beck on his own, he grabbed the self-appointed god by the arm and said, "If you ever disobey me again, it's over."

"You don't call the shots," Beck said. He tried to pull his arm from Duncan's grip, but he could not.

Duncan pulled Beck even closer with the death grip he held on his arm. Beck could not physically separate himself from the younger, much stronger man.

"I *do* call the shots in the field, do you understand that?" Duncan growled, now in Beck's face. Beck glared back at Duncan, saying nothing. "What if the driver had escaped in the boat?"

"But he didn't."

"Because I shot him, you fool! That wasn't part of the plan. I'm not a shooter, just the guide."

"Then why do you carry a gun?"

"'Cause sometimes people like me have to clean up after people like you."

"I'd have gotten the driver."

"If it happens again, we're through—got it?" Duncan said, giving

Beck's arm back with a shove.

Beck wondered for a while about the message and then slept while Duncan and the pilot recounted old times behind the closed cockpit door. They landed early that evening on a private runway on a large ranch Beck owned in Texas, located only a couple of hours out of Houston. The hunt complete, the men returned to their lives the next day.

Almost two years later, Beck sat at the marble table in his New York apartment, looking over the selection of violent men he'd gathered and recalling the manhunt in Guatemala. As he perused the paperwork, deciding which man would be hunted next, or at least presented to a wealthy hunter as an option, he felt a rush remembering his own hunt on the hot Guatemalan beach.

Beck studied the résumés, reading a chronological history of each potential target's exploits. The information had been gathered entirely by Brett and his extensive family connections. Brett had men in his employ who would go as far as to hire private investigators to compile histories on the bad men and present them to him, and he in turn would present them to Beck. This provided a couple of layers of buffering between Duncan, Beck, and the client. Duncan typically glanced at all the potential targets, but he just as typically left most of the decisions of this nature to Beck and his clients. That was Beck's domain.

After the first hunt in Guatemala, Duncan did not want Beck involved on the scene of the hunts, so Beck's main role was the selection process. He provided some travel and logistical support, and he stayed at a foreign base of operation while Duncan and the clients were in the field. Beck was a student, and he enjoyed the long hours he spent studying the résumés. He also enjoyed nurturing potential clients until he felt comfortable casting them a baited question to gauge interest in a manhunt and then finalizing their acceptance.

There was one résumé in the stack of eight before him that piqued Beck's interest and caused his cold heart to race just a bit. Shooting low-level drug runners who would never make the marquees had begun to bore the aging, already-bored man. It was not enough to hunt and dispose of these bad men, or to own a news network, more than half a dozen ranches, and a dozen companies that owned half a dozen companies apiece themselves. He wanted to see the dead men on the television screen when he turned on his news, or at least that was his excuse for escalating the notoriety of his chosen targets. And there was a person of interest in this stack of eight: a Mexican gentleman with a list of legitimate businesses in both the United States and Mexico, but a short list of dubious connections as well.

Beck picked up his cell phone, looked through the list of nearly a dozen missed calls on his caller ID with apathy, and speed-dialed Duncan.

FIVE

"Hello, Beck," Duncan said as he picked up the phone from his home in Montana.

"I've got one, Jack—one that you'll be interested in," Beck said.

"Yeah, Beck, we need to meet," Duncan said. "I have to discuss some of our projects—and that I need to move on. My family requires too much of my time these days, James, and I need to be at home with them."

"Oh, really? And what makes you think that's even an option, Jack?"

Duncan could feel the blood race to his head in an instant fit of anger. After his return from the Hunt Club's first mission in Guatemala, Duncan had resumed his life in Montana: taking odd construction jobs, guiding an occasional fly fisherman, and attending his son's basketball and soccer games and his daughter's gymnastics and dance events. He felt nothing from the hunt, or from any of the hunts that came after. He did, however, think of the man with the throw net and the keen focus with which he stalked the shallow lagoon every time he watched a heron or an egret working the small fish in the shallows of a Montana stream.

Several weeks would pass with no contact between the two men, and a sense of normalcy would creep back into Duncan's head, but then the phone would ring with Beck on the other line. Duncan would sense the excitement in Beck's voice, there would be a client and a target, and then the planning would begin. Duncan would travel to meet Beck, or sometimes Beck would come out to Montana, and Duncan's life would be on hold again for at least a couple of months. Duncan and Beck never spoke of any specific place on the phone, and they discussed other specifics only vaguely when they spoke on the phone. Every detail of the club's actions was handled face to face, and often in the outdoors, with Duncan working methodically to cover his back trail.

There had been four hunts since the first one with Beck, and Duncan was growing anxious and tired of the regimen. He'd already obtained what he needed from the Hunt Club: money. He had enough now to live out a quiet life peacefully with his family.

He was a wild, free man. He would not be owned by anyone, and the tone he read in Beck's response inspired rage. Duncan felt the murderous rage nearly overtake him to the point that he could have easily throttled Beck and snapped his neck if they'd been speaking in person and not by phone, but he controlled his emotions, as always.

"Yes, James, let's discuss your findings," Duncan replied calmly, even coldly, in reference to the "interesting target" Beck had mentioned.

"Good, Jack. I'm glad you're with me," Beck said, failing in his exasperating sociopathic ignorance to understand that he was dealing with a rare individual.

Jack Duncan came from a lineage of men who had left English-controlled Scotland after fighting for the relative freedom they found in Spain. His ancestors left Europe for the New World to land in what was now Florida, and they had slowly settled in the frontiers of the American South, working their way west until they found Texas. His great-grandfathers left Texas to explore the northern Rockies as free trappers, only to return to kin in Texas to tell stories of the open wildness of Montana, which inspired the first Duncans to leave the shrinking wilds of Texas to drive the first herds of cattle from the Lone Star State to the frontier of Montana.

Duncan had always thought of himself as a man who could not be purchased. He realized, however, while he was on the phone with Beck, that he'd been bought and paid for like a prize quarter horse or a whore. Beck owned him at the moment, but Duncan was bursting at Beck's shackles of indentured servitude, and he thought Beck a brilliant fool to believe he could own such an immutable soul.

Duncan responded with a calm, deviously seductive invitation: "The August hoppers are out thick. Come as soon as you can, and we'll float the Madison, or maybe the Missouri. I need to get some fly-fishing in before the snow flies. We'll work on your opportunities."

"That sounds great, Jack," Beck replied as affectionately as he was capable of. "I'm looking forward to fishing with you. We always have a time of it."

It was clear to Duncan when he got off that phone call with Beck that he was nothing more than one of the man's human tools. Jack Duncan and James Beck were nearly as opposite as two men could be, short of their shared love and interest for the outdoors. Beck possessed the common human trait of wanting more than he had, which was already a wealth beyond imagination. Duncan wanted less.

While his peers were living the banalities of middle-aged reality— kids' activities, abandoned sexuality, and a dreadfully boring daily job that never paid enough—Duncan was leaving it all every so many weeks or months to jet around the globe and fulfill the desires of men who had everything. For the first part of his adult life, this meant guiding them through fantastic mountain ranges to harvest the most elusive mountain sheep of North America, and to a smaller degree the world. Now, it meant guiding the slightest point of the economic bell curve of the same group of men through any variety of environs, be they urban or rural, to hunt the apex of apex predators.

Since the Duncans had returned home to Montana from their month in Alaska, Jack had resolved to simplify his life. He had no need for the thrill of chasing bad men or seeing the world; he had already seen it. For Duncan, there were a few inescapable truths of the world: parts were too hot and parts were too cold and some parts were both; some had snakes, some had large predators, some had both; people were people, and politicians were corrupt parasites running soon-to-fail systems of government. It didn't matter what the system was. Duncan's only wish was invisibility from everyone other than his family.

So Duncan had shut himself inside his office and made the call to Beck to tell him that he was done with the Hunt Club, but Beck would not have it.

If he could have changed the past, he would never have called Beck and started up the Hunt Club in the first place. He would not have sold his soul to a mortal devil. He would pound nails or mop floors or drive a school bus and have nothing more to pay attention to than his wife and children. He would have abandoned the complication, the secrets, and the near-paranoid sweeping of his back trail for the chance to watch every one of his children's sports practices and to hear every day's events recounted around the family table.

Duncan was livid; he knew that the Hunt Club was a game that

Beck would continue to play until he was too old and incapacitated or dead. It gave Beck what he really wanted, which was nearly omnipotent power. The money and all the things it could buy were not as important to Beck as the power it purchased: the decision of life and death, the ultimate mortal control. As long as Beck was alive, he would hold what the two unlikely partners had done together over Duncan. Aside from Brett and now Erica, nobody else with actual knowledge of the Hunt Club knew who Duncan was. And the only other humans with actual knowledge were the clients themselves, and they only knew his alias. Even his pilot friend who flew them in and out of harm's way did not know whom he was flying or why. He was smart enough to know they weren't flying humanitarian missions, but aside from that, he knew very little and was paid to forget about his questions.

Duncan was interrupted from his thoughts by the sound of a soft tapping on the solid pine door of his office.

Erica walked in. She noted the strain in Duncan's eyes and his fist clinched tightly around a pencil, resting like a hammer on his desk. His knuckles were white and his face was red.

"That didn't go well, I take it?"

It was more of a statement than a question. Erica walked around behind Duncan, hugging him from the side and resting her cheek on the top of his head in an increasingly rare show of affection.

"No," he said, wiping his face with the cupped palm of his hand as though to anoint himself with a solution to his predicament. "No, it did not."

The two embraced silently, each looking around the office. The room was a corner, and the exterior walls were coped two-by-six fir boards with log chinking in the joints, which gave the room the feeling of a cabin. Windows on each exterior wall looked across the lower Madison River Valley's cottonwood-lined creek bottoms and sage benches, all leading up to the abrupt and striking Tobacco Root Mountains.

For a room whose high ceilings climbed to a vault, the walls were relatively bare. The old ram he had taken as a kid lay bedded on its artificial rock outcropping and hung high on the vaulted side of the room. There were two elk racks with bleached skulls and a set of large mule deer antlers hanging on the fir-boarded exterior wall, the white skulls and lighter horns standing out against the fir boards.

On one of the interior white walls hung a grizzly rug from a bear Duncan had killed in Alaska on a guide trip after it returned to his base camp one too many times and exhibited no fear of men. A few larger photos hung in frames. Some were of exotic game and clients he had hunted with in his past, but mostly the photos were of his kids and the outings they had been on together. There were also paintings the kids had done for him and the kids' report cards from school on his walls. They were almost always exceptional, and even when they were less than perfect, their display built value. There was a belt buckle his daughter had won at a local rodeo barrel racing a pony, and newspaper clippings of Erica from her rodeo days sat in an album on a shelf along with Duncan's large collection of books.

"Don't worry; I'll talk to him again. He's comin' out so we can make arrangements for a client he's got booked for sometime in the fall."

"I just don't want you to go, Jack," Erica said. She let go of him but stood at his back for a moment before walking around to the front of the desk.

"I have to finish this hunt, but I'll tell him it's my last."

"Why can't you just tell him now? You said yourself you've got plenty of money."

"It's not money; it's not that simple."

"It is! Just say no."

Duncan could see the frustration in Erica's face as she stood in front of him.

"You don't understand."

"What don't I understand?" Erica asked, aggravated.

"Beck isn't gonna just let me walk. I'm a loose end. Somebody who's got something on him."

"We don't need the money. We need you here with us."

Erica took a step back away from Duncan's desk. She was angry. She had lived an uncomplicated, honest life, and now she was tangled up in her husband's mess. "I told you, I'm not going to put up with this crap. I love you, but I don't want this for my kids."

"I know, hon. I want to be here, believe me. I wish I could undo it all. I should've stayed working for the outfit in Bozeman. I screwed up—is that what you want to hear? I screwed up. I would take it all back just to stay home with you guys. All the money I have stashed in foreign banks and buried in mason jars means nothing if we aren't together."

"I don't want this for myself."

"I'll get out. I'll figure a way." Duncan looked into her blue eyes with confidence, trying to hide the anxiety building in his chest. "But I need time."

"How much?"

"I don't know. Enough to gain a bargaining chip? You know, some kind of leverage."

"Don't take your time," she said and walked out of his office.

Duncan waited till the following morning and called Beck again to schedule his trip out to Montana, but Beck did not answer. When he did not return the call within a couple of hours, Duncan began saddling horses.

His wife would have to return to work at the veterinary clinic in Ennis and he would have time with the children, but Duncan was determined that it would not be idle. He had work: odd construction jobs here and there, as he knew all the old Madison Valley families and many of the new ones, too. But the kids were still out of school for the summer, and he decided to indulge himself in time with them. And he needed time to think.

Erica was happy for them to go. It gave her a much-needed reprieve and some time allotted for herself. She wasn't worried; she had as much confidence in Duncan in the mountains as she did in herself in her own home. There were no cell phones or distractions of any kind that could skew him if he were on the valley floor, or any other low country on the globe. Her main concern was that Duncan would not get out of the Hunt Club soon enough. She knew Beck would call while he was gone, and that Duncan did not care. He wanted Beck to wait, and to simmer on the fact that he was momentarily out of control.

Duncan and the kids saddled three horses and fitted the fourth with a crossbuck and pannier bags, which hung from the packsaddle with no top packs. The rigging took less than an hour, simple and clean; no need for a large rig, as they were only going for two nights, or maybe three.

Duncan started down the driveway with kids in tow. He looked back at Erica, who was standing in the driveway to see them off. Then he looked at the kids, and all he could think was how much he had to lose. He handed Coulter the packhorse's lead and said, "I'll catch up with you in a sec."

He reined his horse around and trotted him back to Erica, who was still standing there watching them. He swung off his horse and kissed her.

"I love you," he said, then jumped back into the saddle and caught up with the kids. He guided them across the valley and sagebrush benches that led to the foot of the Tobacco Roots, where they would ride through an old friend's winter pasture to find an old family trailhead leading into the barren, rocky peaks of that range and the pastoral summer basin, which contained lush grass and alpine lakes.

The kids were solid riders by this age, and they had saddled their own horses while Duncan prepared the minimal camp equipment and food. Their rig consisted of a single polypropylene tarp of sixteen by twenty feet, a Dutch oven, a cast-iron skillet, a water filter and dromedary bag, a titanium stove, matches, a cookware set, miscellaneous spices, several sticks of butter, a bottle of olive oil, a pound of bacon, five pounds of potatoes and half that in onions, sleeping bags and mats, and fishing gear.

They reached the timber edge of the Tobacco Root where the sage of the low country met the green darkness just before nightfall, and they made camp at the foot of the mountains just before the sun began setting behind them.

The night was perfectly clear and dark but seemingly lit by the myriad stars that twinkled brilliantly against the darkened background of an infinite universe. They were barely through the flimsy barbed-wire fences of their rancher friend's ground and into the National

Forest Service land. There was no need for the tarp tent, only for enough wood to fire coals to cook potatoes with a few strips of bacon in them for the three campers.

"Can I help you cook, Daddy?" Avery asked.

"Certainly," Duncan said and handed her a knife and the cooler lid, which served as a cutting board for the potatoes and onions.

"Oh, great," Coulter said. "She'll burn the potatoes."

"If you complain, you cook the rest of the trip," Duncan said to the boy, and his daughter laughed.

Avery cooked the potatoes in the Dutch oven, and they ate them under the stars of the clear summer night.

"How many stars do you think we're looking at?" Avery asked.

"Billions, you idiot," Coulter said.

"Enough, boy. You don't need to talk to your sister that way."

Avery sneered at her brother across the dancing flames of the fire.

"More stars than we could put a number on, honey," Duncan said to his daughter.

"Infinity, right, Dad?" said Coulter.

"Yep, in an infinite universe. Do you understand infinity?" he asked Avery.

"Yeah, Dad. It's like never ending."

"You guys are smart," Duncan said, and his mind wandered back to Beck. He thought at first that this trip would be an escape from his troubles, but he realized as they were watching the fire that it would have to be a trip to sort through it all and calculate his way out. He wanted his uncomplicated life back—even the boredom of a real job if it meant more moments like this.

The kids shined as brilliantly as the stars and went on to barrage Duncan with all the questions their growing little minds could muster in a comparable volume. Duncan answered them, calmed and imbued with a patience provided by the physical and emotional warmth of the crackling fire and the closeness of his kids. After eating the potatoes and bacon and a can of beans they'd heated in the can on the edge of one of the rocks ringing the fire, they curled up in their bags on the upside-down saddle pads and Therm-a-Rest camp rolls. The saddles made a low barricade on their uphill side, and the dancing flames flickered reflections off the burnished leather.

"Lie between me and Dad, Avery, so we can protect you," Coulter said to his sister.

"Even though I'm a bad cook?" she asked.

"You're an all right cook," Coulter said.

"I know," she said, smiling, and took her place between them.

Duncan lay on one end with his beautiful little blonde girl slid up snug next to him, sandwiched between him and his son. The chocolate Lab bitch that had adopted the boy as her own pup curled up against him. His arm was over her just as they slept at home.

In the morning the posse swung into their mounts, eager for the day's fun. They slipped the horses into the morning darkness of the lodgepole timber and meandered up the trail until they reached the ridge, which they climbed up into the endless blue sky that defined Montana. Eventually, the ridge led to a pass that dropped them into a high mountain basin with a clear, babbling creek that flowed through an elk-infested mountain valley and a series of three beaver ponds full of brook trout. They rode up the valley paralleling the creek until they reached a bench one hundred feet or so above the lush, mosquito-infested valley floor, and they made camp in the sagebrush at the edge of the timber where there was ample firewood and they remained out of reach of most of the mosquitoes.

Duncan and the kids went to work quickly setting up the light bivouac-style camp. Duncan hobbled the horses so they could feed in the grassy meadow below the sage bench, where the kids were gathering firewood on the edge of the timber. The boy stripped the limbs of a four-inch-diameter pine at the base with the same small Swedish steel axe he had used to chop the tree down. The boy and his dad planted the lodgepole into a small hole they'd dug and threw a tarp over a rope they ran from it to a pine at the edge of the timber. The other end ran to a stake Coulter pounded into the ground ten feet to the side of the lodgepole to stretch the rope tight. They staked the back corners of the tarp to the ground with wood stakes the boy made by cutting and splitting the straight trunks of the smallish pines. Then they pulled about six feet of tarp over the rope and lashed the corners to stakes in the ground, completing their bivouac tent. They placed their food in a canvas game sack cinched with a built-in drawstring and hung from a tree, out of reach of bears. There was no real threat of grizzlies in the Tobacco Roots, but still no reason to let a black bear get away with their food. The Dutch oven and cast-iron skillet were arranged atop the stack of firewood, and Avery arranged the sleeping bags and sleep pads under the tent.

Camp set, they strung up the three fly rods that were in tubes tied at the back of the saddles, and they headed toward the upper lake. The three walked up the green valley, which was hemmed in on three sides by magnificent craggy peaks. They fished along the rocky shoreline of the lake instead of the swampy lower end and caught hungry brook trout and cutthroat. They all caught fish after fish on small wet flies. The pattern did not matter, as fish in these high mountain lakes with limited food sources generally ate anything put in front of them. The three Duncans laughed and shared in the excitement of catching fish, and when the warm August sun was high in the big Montana sky, they stripped down to their underwear and swam in the cold, clear waters of the lake. After Duncan had been cooled by the icy waters, he gutted the two dozen brook trout they had kept on a stringer while the kids played in the lake.

After playing and enjoying the sun, the three hiked back to camp and got ready for the evening while the horses fed down the valley next to the creek. Duncan and his daughter started a fire in front of the tarp tent while the boy continued to fish the creek for brilliantly colored trout with dark-purplish backs and vivid salmon-orange bellies. Duncan sliced potatoes and onions to fill the large Dutch oven, and his little girl brought rocks back to camp to form an oven in the coals, on which they rested the cast-iron skillet for frying the trout. Then she ran down the sagebrush bench to the grassy meadow with her fly rod and joined her brother.

Duncan leaned back against his saddle. He had dragged it out from the back of the tent for just that purpose, as they lacked the accouterments of a car camp or even those of a larger horse outfit. He watched his children fishing up and down the small stream, nearly hidden by the lush overhanging grass. Clouds of evening caddis flies danced above them in the waning light of the day. The sun had slipped behind the cathedral of peaks and was showing through the gaps, flooding into the mountain basin like spotlights. Tiny mayflies mingled with the caddis, and the two kids worked the water, catching fish every second or third drift. They laughed and taunted each other. Duncan could hear their voices, but not clearly enough to discern the words. Still, it did not matter. He could tell what they were saying by interpreting their body language.

The little girl fished ever closer to her brother in an attempt to get his attention. The boy would move away from her as she came near, and he would yell at her periodically in an attempt to make her keep her distance. The scene played out with classic sibling banter, and eventually the words were not enough for Avery. When she stripped in a six-inch brook trout she had brought to her little hand, she cocked her arm back and threw it at her brother. The airborne fish hit Coulter dead center in the back as he focused on his casting form. He dropped his rod and lit out across the meadow as she ran from him, knowing and hoping he would catch her. And when he did, he tackled her into the grass and wrestled her down, tickling her, beating on her not with malice or viciousness, but with just enough force so that she would laugh and cry out. It was more for the attention of her father than any other reason, but Duncan just watched.

He was content, yet at the same time a thin strain of sadness crept over him. He thought of his own father, who had missed all of this joy that was playing out in front of him by the creek because he had been sent by politicians to die in vain in a sweaty jungle that did not matter. Then his own sadness over having to leave again to guide one of Beck's cronies on a manhunt crept in. He was becoming scared, but only because he had too much to lose.

Duncan had come on the trip with the kids to spend time with them, and it was turning into an exercise to figure out how to spend even more time with them. He was more focused in the mountains with fewer distractions. He knew there was no way to get Beck off his mind, and he thought that in the high country he'd be able to sort through it in his head and figure out how to get away from Beck before he lost everything that mattered to him.

The children eventually made their way back to camp, from where Duncan had been watching them. The boy held a Y-shaped alder branch with brook trout slid onto one of its forks as the two kids climbed the spine of the low ridge to make their way back to their father. The chocolate Lab cast about in the sagebrush in advance of the kids in her genetically ordained search for game birds, but she always checked back with the boy and girl. When the dog spotted Duncan, she ran up to him as he sat watching from the edge of their spike camp. She greeted him with her wiggling wag, but she returned immediately to Coulter and Avery.

Duncan had been around and had owned Labs and cattle dogs, mostly border collies, since as early as he could remember. He loved both breeds. Although they were very different in their quirkiness and training, both were fiercely loyal and dutiful to their chosen humans. He remembered all his dogs fondly and how they'd all loved him to die for. He remembered his first chocolate, Sadie, a gift from his grandfather for his fourteenth birthday, and how she'd refused to retire, even after she'd aged into her teens. When Sadie was twelve and a half, Duncan took her out on opening day of duck season to hunt a side channel off the Jefferson River that was loaded with ducks because of the unseasonably cold and frozen early October. The shooting was good, and he and Erica were near their limits of mallards and teal when they almost lost the old girl.

A large flock of green-winged teal had settled in over the decoys, which were coursing about in the current where the eddy tailed out and picked up a little speed before dropping into a run. The two hunters dropped five teal with a short volley from their shotguns, and the old, graying brown dog jumped into the river to retrieve the small ducks, which were slowly drifting into faster water. Worried about the dog getting swept down the river, Duncan waded out and picked up some of the birds to assist her, knowing she would not be able to retrieve them all before the current took them downriver into some slow water that was frozen nearly all the way across. Duncan had four teal in hand, but he could not reach the fifth bird, as the river was too deep, and Sadie went for it. Duncan watched the dead bird gain speed as it drifted toward the faster water, and before the gray-muzzled Lab could get back to him with the teal in her mouth, she was swept down the river.

"Shit," Duncan hissed and ran for the dog.

"Get her, Jack—before she's swept under!" Erica yelled as she jumped from the blind to help.

The two of them ran down the willow-lined bank paralleling the dog, who still clutched the drake green-winged teal in her mouth. When the dog washed into the sheet of ice that covered the river nearly all the way across, she struggled to climb onto it. It was thick enough to hold her weight, and in her younger days she would have had the strength to pull her body up. Duncan had seen her do it before, but her day had come and gone. The current pulled her under the opaque ice sheet, and yet she held on to the bird. As Duncan ran down the bank parallel to the dog, he could see her face through the ice, her eyes wide with fright and the duck still in her mouth. She would not let it go.

She was only under the ice and water for seconds before Duncan found an opening in the willows and, without slowing down, launched himself into the air and landed on the ice, shattering it only feet from the old Lab. She popped up through the surface of the broken shards, relieved to have Duncan grab her, tuck her under his arm, and carry her to shore, where she shook off and proudly placed the drake teal in Duncan's hand.

It was her last real hunt. From then on, when Duncan left to hunt without her, she cried mournfully all morning, knowing where he was and what he was doing.

All his Labs had loved him like this until the current one. The small chocolate that had adopted his two children as her own was ambivalent about Duncan, and as he sat on the edge of camp watching the dog and the kids, he thought about why.

His grandfather John Duncan had always been surrounded by Labradors, shotguns, and bird hunting. The man bred Labs and hunted birds for the love of it. Ranching had only been his business, and when he was just shy of retirement age, he sold the family ranches and bought a small piece of property not far from where he and his family had ranched near the town of Miles City. The two-hundred-acre piece was large enough to accommodate his dogs and his horses, and it was adjacent to an endless piece of Bureau of Land Management land that nurtured a large population of Hungarian partridge and sharp-tailed grouse. It was also near some old friends' pheasant-infested farm ground. The sale of the ranch had angered some of the family and had caused a number of the cattlemen in the state to wonder about Duncan's grandfather, as the ranch had been in his family since it was established by Duncan's great-great-grandfather a year or so after the smoke cleared from Custer's blunder at the Little Bighorn. Duncan's grandfather had no interest in what anybody wondered about him. His wife was happy to be closer to town, and ranching was a hard life despite the romance that surrounded it.

Duncan spent as much time with his grandfather as possible as a child, and he worshipped the old man. He had been born in 1898 on the family's winter ranch in Fort Worth, Texas, a ranch that was later given to one of Duncan's great-uncles. The old man was Duncan's living connection to an Old West that he loved and studied as a boy. His grandfather was born to a man and woman of the generation that had tamed the Western frontier, and Duncan had heard their stories from his grandfather as well as the old man's own tales. When Duncan was about six, he began spending time in the summer with his grandparents in Miles City and traveling around the West, including Canada and Alaska, where he learned much of what he knew about horses and Labs. The old man trained both horses and Labs, and he often hunted partridge on horseback, having broken all his best mounts to shoot from. He would follow his roving pack of Labs through the wide, open prairie and into the sage and juniper breaks, in search of game birds. At least that was his excuse, and young Duncan accompanied him as often as he could.

The relationship filled a void for both Duncans: the younger of the two was in need of a father, and the older needed something to help slow the emotional bleed left by the loss of a beloved son. John Duncan often blamed himself for his son's death in Vietnam, as he himself had fought in the trenches of Europe in World War I and then had volunteered for the Air Force in World War II, where he had been a squadron leader and had flown air combat missions against the Japanese in the South Pacific. He felt that his own foolish patriotism was difficult to live up to for his son, and that it had inspired him to join a meaningless cause. But some men were just born warriors, and Duncan's father simply could not let a war go by without participating. John Duncan was proud of his son's bravery, but that did not stop him from discouraging such behavior in his grandson.

The loss of Duncan's father had been too much to bear for his grandmother, and when Duncan was nine, she'd passed away from what those who knew her well considered a heart broken by the loss of a child. The old man was stubborn and stayed alive, if for no other reason than to see that young Duncan had a man in his life.

The old man lived on, and when he began to slow down a bit in his eighties, he and young Duncan built a log cabin on Duncan's mother's property. For the next couple of years, he would fly back and forth using a dirt runway he had built on his property. He would land the Cessna on a gravel county road near Duncan's mother's house and taxi it down the road, leaving it in the field in front of the house. He had flown all over the West in this fashion since before the second war, landing on friends' ranches and on rural county roads all over Montana and never bothering to obtain a pilot's license. Folks knew him or knew of him and looked the other way, figuring he was exempt because he'd been a combat ace in the war. This worked until he was eighty-eight and a young deputy became incensed at having to wait for him to pass and turn into young Duncan's driveway. The deputy threatened to call the FAA, and the two agreed he would get a pilot's license, which of course the old man never did. It was easier and probably time anyway to quit flying, but he didn't quit before he had taught Duncan to fly and had given him the Cessna. At that time, the old man began spending most of his time close to Duncan and his mother.

Duncan's grandfather spent his days working with his Labs and horses or resting in the shade of the porch on his cabin in his starched button-down shirts and his dusty, hand-shaped gray Stetson. He'd sit in a wooden rocker and smoke a hand-rolled cigarette while he watched the sky on the western horizon, typically with a couple of Labs at his feet or coursing through the yard.

As Duncan sat on the edge of camp watching his own kids and waiting for them to return, he thought of his grandfather and his

Labs. This little Lab that loved his children so much was from his grandfather's original lines, and they were good. The old man hadn't been much of a field trial breeder and preferred hunting the dogs, but he did sell a number of dogs to the field trial community, with one of his pups winning a national championship title. Duncan remembered a line his grandfather had repeated to him throughout his childhood: "Every Labrador retriever deserves a little boy, even if it's just the one that still lives inside an old man."

Duncan thought about what his grandfather used to say and realized at once why the little Lab preferred his children's company over his: he had been gone so much of the last few years that the little brown dog didn't know him. And what she did know of him was different from what Duncan's Labs before her knew. The little boy in him was gone. The lightsome character who got down in the grass with them and played and wrestled had atrophied, and the man who was left was serious. Constantly in thought about how he would get out from his physical and financial woes. How to keep a roof over his family's head and new shoes on their feet. And, more recently, how to execute Beck's missions and come home safely. The only way to get any of it back was to get Beck out of his life.

Duncan and the children slept soundly under a big sky full of stars, and in the morning Duncan rousted them and sent them down to the creek for some fresh brookies to take home to their mom. Duncan rode up to the very head of the basin to the cathedral of peaks and scooped some glacier ice to pack the brook trout in a cooler bag for the ride home.

He was taking the tarp down when the kids reached the bench with a stringer full of trout and saw that their dad was at work breaking camp. Coulter protested, but Avery was happy to go see her mom, and they joined in the packing. It was less than an hour before the three were headed down the mountain.

Having gotten an earlier start for the trip home, there was no need to spend the night on the trail, so they rode on until they could see their home in the evening sun. As they got closer, they could see their mother and wife in the round pen, where she was working with a young gelding, one of her many. The horses began to whinny.

Duncan and the kids watched her working the Appaloosa around the pen at the end of a lunge, the young horse's majesty paling only next to Erica's graceful command and her own beauty. The kids watched their mother, entranced by the rocking in the saddle as they rode up the dirt road to the house and by the rhythm of their mother's dance with the liver-and-white-spotted pony. Duncan watched her because he never could take his eyes off her.

The horse wore a saddle but had never been ridden. Erica's way of breaking horses was more about training them, and it was entirely different from the old ways. Her method was much gentler on both horse and rider than Duncan's grandfather's method of breaking horses. She loved animals, and horses most of all. Erica's father always joked that if he had let her, she would have brought her barrel racing horse into the house with her at night when the two were done riding. Her father had purchased the horse for her in the spring of '79, and when she was a pigtailed nine-year-old, she had rigged an electric fence in their yard with her mother's help so that the big bay quarter horse she loved and ran barrels with could pasture outside her bedroom window.

Her father had estimated that the four-year-old horse would run barrels as fast as any girl or woman could ride him, and if his little girl was going to race, she might as well win. And win she did, until her beautiful, blue-eyed face was on Wrangler and Stetson ads and she was appearing in national championship rodeos. But when she was home, the bay horse stood affectionately at her bedroom window, his head inside the wood-clad double-hung window while Erica talked to him and fed him carrots and assorted greens from her mother's garden.

Erica loved the animals, but she was a ranch girl. She was in command of them and understood their utility and place in the world. It was always her job to care for the orphaned and injured calves in the spring. She bottle-fed them and doctored them until they were capable of taking care of themselves and could return to the herd. Often, these orphans that were kept out and fed and not given hormones or antibiotics wound up on the family grill, so she gave them food names like "Wellington" or "Quarter Pounder." When the processor came out to the ranch to kill and butcher them, she did not protest. At least not out loud.

Duncan watched her as she brought the horse in close and finished the training as the three approached. The four met at the hitching rail in front of the tack room off the barn.

"Hey, Mom! I caught more fish than Coulter."

"You did not!"

"Yes, I did."

"We brought you some fresh brookies," Coulter said.

"They're in a cooler bag in the packsaddle."

"Thank you," Erica said, looking at both of the kids, then at her husband.

"I caught most of them," Coulter said.

"I did," said Avery and smiled at her mother.

"There's venison stew in the pot on the stove top. It's probably still warm, and if not, you can heat it, and there's a salad in the fridge," she told the kids. She knew Duncan and knew he'd be home a day early to deal with Beck. "Your dad and I will put the horses up. Get in and get cleaned up so you can tell me about your adventures."

Normally she made the kids put up the horses and tack, but she wanted a few minutes alone with Duncan. The kids raced off to the house and then disappeared in the warm wood-and-stone house with the little chocolate Lab at their heels the whole way.

Duncan and Erica kissed and began removing the bridles, then the saddles and blankets. Duncan said nothing, but he was in thought constantly, working through the predicament in his head. Erica was used to men and their silences, having spent her life with cowboys of one variety or another. She knew consciously that it was nothing personal, but she would still only take so much of it.

"Your phone rang several times while you were gone," she said, breaking the silence. "It was Beck."

"I'm sure it was," Duncan replied. "He'll want to set a date to come out to discuss our next trip. And he wants to fish."

They finished putting up the saddles and let the animals into the pasture nearest the barn. They talked and held hands after turning the animals out and lived in the moment. Erica dreaded him leaving again and feared it; he dreaded being gone, but he was ambivalent about what he was doing. Maybe even numb to it.

He was not scared about going or of what he did on the trips; he just didn't want to leave his home. He had lived his life traveling the West and then the world, and he loved it. He hated the day-to-day monotony of a real job, of building, of any work that required he go to the same place every day. He liked change. But now that he was a father, he wanted to be home. He was tired of the risks he was taking and most of all the people with whom he was entangled. He wanted time with his kids, and he wanted to sleep in his own bed with his wife.

They walked together up to the house. The sun was lower and at their backs. Their home looked warm. They could hear the kids messing with one another from the kitchen, laughing and needling while they ate the venison stew their mother had made them. The windows were open in the warm August evening, and the noise of the children was comforting to their parents, especially Jack Duncan, who had missed a lot of these moments.

Erica was eager to hear the kids' tales of their trip into the mountains with their father. She loved her kids; they were her whole life. When they were born, everything else took second seat, and like everything else she had done in her life, she went about raising them with her complete devotion.

When they decided to have the kids, she had cut back on barrel racing, or at least on her traveling. She limited herself to the local clubs and rodeos, which were more of a social outlet than anything. Even her career as a vet took second seat to her job as a mother. But she still took care of Duncan. She had loved him since she was a child, and she always would. She knew him completely, and had never tried to change him. Maybe, to some extent, his being gone had actually been good, but she was ready to have him home.

They stopped on the porch, sat on the top step, and looked back across the valley to the west and the last few moments of evening.

"It's time to build our house," he said.

"What? That's outta the blue."

"Not really; we've got the money now."

"But you've always liked to keep your own space."

"I just think it'd be good for you and the kids, and I guess I'm just a little bit older. I see things a little differently now, I guess."

"That's exciting," she said. "Can I tell the kids?"

"Sure," he said. She got up, and he watched her as she walked into the house.

They'd discussed the plan for a number of years, and Duncan had the site marked out and blueprints drawn for the two-story house that he and Erica had spent several years designing. For a while, they thought that it would never happen, but Duncan had the cash now and Erica's folks had invited them to build on the ranch many years earlier. Duncan *had* liked to keep his space, and while Erica was in favor of the idea, as she had always enjoyed her parents and liked the idea of being close to help with the ranching activities, she never pushed it on him. However, his involvement in the Hunt Club made him contemplate all the possibilities. The people he was involved with were infinitely perfidious, with the exception of his cousin and his pilot, so he felt his family was more secure living close to his in-laws. Life would also be easier for Erica if she had her mom and dad close by to help, both of whom were in good health and still worked the ranch.

Erica's father, Roy, was a rancher. He had graduated from law school at twenty-five and worked for a law firm in Helena until he was thirty, but he could not live in the city. He never could get used to the artificial city streetlights, and he could not sleep without the sound of cows out his window. So he took his young wife and moved back to the open skies of his family's ranch. Whereas Duncan's grandfather had farmed and ranched as a profession, Roy Bergstrom ranched because if he did not, he would cease to exist.

The Bergstrom ranch, which overlooked the Upper Madison River at the foot of the Gravelly Range, had been in Erica's family since about the late 1860s, when two brothers more or less settled in the area. They had wandered off the Antietam battlefield grief stricken by the loss of a brother and cousin and shell shocked by the record-setting loss of life they'd participated in. The green fields were littered with the mangled dead and dying, and as the brothers wandered through them, confused and unwilling to fight any longer, they slipped into the nearest woods and started out for the West.

They were young, well armed by the federal government, and battle hardened. Because they were technically AWOL, they never intended to return to the East. They made their way instead to Missouri and then on to the Dakota Territory, where they hunted buffalo in the spring. Eventually, they traveled west to the Yellowstone area at about the time of the Alder Gulch gold discovery near the modern-day sites of Virginia City and Nevada City, a short distance north and west of the present-day ranch. The two brothers headed for the gold site, and, already accustomed to frontier life, they settled in Virginia City. They mined gold in the summer, built a small cabin, and trapped and hunted the Madison and Upper Missouri River region. The two brothers liked the Upper Madison, if for no other reason than that there were not many white inhabitants, and most of the Indians of the region were of one of the several bands of Bannock or Shoshone who were relatively peaceful.

One of the brothers married at an old age and produced a son, Erica's great-grandfather. The ranch was then handed down the line until her father became its steward. Duncan loved the ranch, and he appreciated Erica's frontiersman ancestors' selection of a home site, as it was obviously selected for its defensible attributes, sitting high on a plateau on the bench overlooking the Madison River Valley. Basalt cliffs protected it on three sides, which left only one approach that exposed trespassers and guests from over one thousand yards away. The men chose the site before the Plains Indian Wars were over, and the fierce Blackfeet and Crow still passed through the area on occasion.

Now, Duncan felt it was best to move his family there, as he did not know what was coming for him, or who. He only knew that the man he was working with could not be trusted, and that Beck would stop at nothing to get what he wanted. His wife would be happy there, as would the kids, and Duncan could help his father-in-law with the ranch. He could quit his odd jobs, and he wouldn't have to guide if he didn't want to. He could live off the money he'd stashed, and nobody would question it, as he'd be working on the ranch.

That night, Duncan and Erica went over his plan and the blueprints, and Duncan began calling friends who would help him construct the home. He had cash, plenty of it, and he knew that he would be too busy to build all of it on his own in time to get it dried in before the snow flew in three months. He also called Beck.

"Where have you been?" Beck asked when he answered Duncan's call.

"On a trip," Duncan said.

"What trip?" Beck said.

"What difference does it make to you? I was on a trip with my kids."

"Just wondering why you didn't answer my calls."

"I was busy."

"But we've got things to do."

"And I've got kids who I like to spend time with," Duncan said as he thought about Beck and the kids he'd sired but paid no attention to.

"Oh."

"So what's up?"

"We need to plan our fishing trip so we can discuss our next projects," Beck said. He sensed Duncan pulling away from him. "We're still fishing, right?"

Beck felt he owned Duncan, as he did every other man and woman who was unfortunate enough to work for him, and despite the fact that Duncan had made reference to being done with the Hunt Club, Beck refused to hear it. He went on speaking of plans for the next two targets and their coming meeting. He requested—or, more accurately, insisted—that Duncan take him down the canyon section of the Teton River two hours south of Ennis, on the Idaho-Wyoming border.

"Sure, I'll be around. Just give me a day or two's notice when you're coming."

"OK, I'll get back to you."

After the call, Duncan found Erica, who was excited about the plan to relocate to her family's ranch. She called her mother, and she and Duncan drove out to the ranch the next day with the kids while they made plans to sell their current home.

Once they were at the ranch, Erica and her mother went their way and Duncan and Roy walked out to the site Duncan had already staked off so the two men could talk. Duncan had decided that he would come clean with his father-in-law about the Hunt Club.

SIX

Roy Bergstrom was an intelligently fierce man. He was the strong, silent sort, but when he did speak, his words carried a sledge-like weight. He loved his daughters and his grandchildren, and though he never said it aloud, he loved Duncan as well.

He had always empathized with Duncan when he was a boy for his lack of a father in his life, and he filled in where he could when Duncan's grandfather could not. The Bergstroms often included young Jack on their family vacations, and Roy taught him all of what he knew about horses and ranching. As a young boy, Roy also took Duncan on a number of big game hunts. As he got older, Duncan took Bergstrom up the aspen draws to shoot grouse with his bird dogs, an activity that Bergstrom grew to love. Occasionally, he also joined Duncan on the river with a fly rod.

Duncan had heard it said that no man had ever been born who was good enough for any father's daughter. Now, whenever he looked into his little girl's big blue eyes, he saw not only her but also her mother, whom he loved deeply. And he saw the little girl he'd fallen in love with in the rugged beauty of the Madison Valley. Now that he was in his forties, he understood this paternal protectiveness painfully well, and for the first time, he felt like a man, if for no other reason than that he cared more for his own family than for himself.

Duncan realized now why his father-in-law had held him so close. He'd kept him close enough to make sure that he was good enough, or at least as good as a boy courting his daughter could be, and while Duncan had grown into a fine man, he still felt young in the company of his wife's father.

After he moved his family from the city back to the ranch when Erica was still a girl, Roy Bergstrom had continued to practice some law, but mostly he focused on taking over the largest burdens of the ranch from his own father. He studied modern ranching to grow the ranch with the times.

For a man who had spent most of his time with horses and cows in an empty corner of the Rocky Mountain West, he developed impressive connections all over the country and even overseas. He'd sold well-bred horses in countries all over the world, including Russia, China, and Saudi Arabia.

Once, when he was a teenager, Bergstrom had asked Duncan to join him taking a man on an elk-hunting pack trip into the Gravelly Range above the ranch. The man was the private pilot of a wealthy individual to whom Bergstrom had sold some blooded horses and for whom he'd done some legal work. He liked the pilot, and they had flown together on a number of business trips, so Bergstrom invited him on a hunt when the pilot expressed a desire to hunt elk, an animal not available to him in his home state of Michigan.

One night, Bergstrom left the pilot in Duncan's young but capable care while he rode seven or eight tough miles to scout a distant mountain basin. Duncan and the pilot finished the day without an elk and returned to camp in the dark. They started a fire on the clear fall night, over which Duncan broiled steaks and Dutch-oven po-tatoes.

"Your dad is something else," the pilot said.

Duncan looked across the fire at the man who was sitting in a canvas camp chair and thought about correcting his assumption, but instead he let it pass.

"Oh yeah, how's that?"

"Your dad can do just about anything, and he's good at it, to boot."

Again Duncan didn't correct the pilot.

Bergstrom had addressed young Duncan as "son" on several oc-casions, and the pilot, not knowing either Duncan or Bergstrom intimately, made the assumption Bergstrom was Duncan's father. Duncan never corrected him.

The pilot was quite enamored with Bergstrom and told Duncan a story about a flight across the Caribbean Sea during which Berg-strom had taken the controls of the jet and brought it down to within a few hundred or so feet of the water. There they flew for fifteen minutes, "just for fun," as Bergstrom had put it. They were returning from delivering several high-dollar horses to a client's winter house on Martinique, and after traveling for nearly fifteen minutes barely above the surface of the sea, one of the half-dozen men who were along to help with the horse delivery poked his head into the cabin in wonder; he had looked out the window and seen the blue water so close. Bergstrom instructed him to return to his seat, as they were just having some fun. The man did.

The pilot said, "At that point, I had an interesting thought about your dad."

"What's that?" asked Duncan, outwardly unmoved by the "dad" reference.

"Well, it occurred to me that if this plane was to go down in the middle of the ocean, your dad would likely be the sole survivor."

"And why do you say that?"

"Well, I realized while sitting next to him smoking across the blue Caribbean that if that plane went down, Roy would take the whole event in his usual stride. He'd skin the rest of the crew and build a raft out of our hides, and he'd eat the flesh to stay alive for months until found by a fishing vessel or merchant ship. He would build fishhooks from the items in our pockets and make line by weaving the threads of our clothes. He's like a modern mountain man."

Duncan laughed quietly at the image of Bergstrom floating alone on the sea, and at what this middle-aged pilot from Michigan would have thought of his grandfather landing planes on county roads and pastures all over the West for fifty years.

When the trip was over, the pilot had his elk, which Duncan had helped him kill, and while Bergstrom was driving the man back to Bozeman to catch a commercial flight back to Michigan, he complimented Bergstrom on what a fine son he had. "Jack is incredibly capable for a teenager," the pilot said.

"Yeah, he's pretty handy with horses and knows his way around the mountains."

"How's he the rest of the time?"

"Good. Does well in school, polite, he's a good kid."

"You must be proud," the pilot said.

"How's that?" Bergstrom asked, looking out of the corner of his eye at the pilot seated next to him in the passenger side of the pickup.

"To have such a fine son—you must be proud."

"He's not my son."

"Well then, who is he?"

"He's my oldest daughter's friend."

"Really? I assumed he was your son."

"Why's that?" Bergstrom asked.

"You treated him like he was your own. And when I was talking to him, I referred to you as his dad, and he never corrected me."

"The boy lost his father, so we've sorta filled in where we could."

Bergstrom thought about young Jack and about hearing that he'd never corrected the pilot in his assumption of their paternal relationship. He was proud of Duncan, and he'd have been proud to have a son like him.

On the dried-out mesa one hundred yards from the main ranch house where the Bergstroms lived, Duncan and his father-in-law examined the site where Duncan would build his new home. Duncan had picked it because any vehicles would have to pass through the front yard of the main ranch house before they reached his own yard. This gave him an added feeling of security for his family.

Duncan had to tell Roy of his dilemma. He wanted the man to help him watch out for his family. He knew Roy would anyway, but Duncan felt that the man needed to know the details. He knew he could trust this one and only man because their interests were the same, but he was still nervous. On a small, hidden level, he'd always sought Roy's approval, and he was worried that telling him might change the friendship they'd always enjoyed. Duncan scratched at the dusty soil with his boot and looked at the mountains.

"There's something I have to tell you," Duncan said.

"What's that?"

"I've tried to think of a way to sugarcoat it, but you'd see through it, so I'm just gonna tell you." Duncan knew Roy was hard enough to handle the concept of the Hunt Club, but at the same time, he knew that on some minute level it was wrong. At least in terms of his family life.

"Go on," Bergstrom said and looked at Duncan.

"I have become a man-hunter."

"A what?"

"I guide super-wealthy men on manhunts."

Bergstrom said nothing. He showed no reaction to what he was hearing, at least not on the outside. He looked at the mountains and at Duncan's boot, which scratched nervously at the ground. "Go on," he finally said.

"My clients have killed five intended targets," Duncan said.

He went on to tell Bergstrom of the people he and his clients had killed. Duncan told him of the horrible crimes their targets had committed and of the violence they were responsible for. He did this to justify the rest of what he was telling this man, who was the closest thing to a father he would ever have. He even told him about the three Mexicans he had shot with Beck in self-defense, almost as a confession, but also to set the stage for the story behind the inception of the Hunt Club. Bergstrom listened quietly, which unnerved Duncan. Aside from telling Erica, he had kept this endeavor completely secret until now. He went on to explain how he had been in financial ruin, and that he'd needed the money to keep his family going, and that while he had only intended to go two or three times, Beck was unwilling to let him quit.

Bergstrom was a smart man, and while Duncan never asked him for anything or shared his financial problems with him, he knew that

Duncan and Erica had had some trouble when the economy nose-dived. He pondered the words he was hearing from Duncan, and there was a long silence.

"Who would've thought a little ol' redneck kid from bumfuck nowhere, Montana, could change the world?" Bergstrom asked, breaking the long silence.

"I'd hardly say I've changed the world."

"Well you've rid the earth of some of America's most prolific drug runners and outlaws."

"If there is one thing I've seen in all of this, it's that there seems to be no limit to the evil men do, and for every son of a bitch whose ticket we punch, there's several more to take his place."

"Well that should be good job security," Bergstrom said, teetering between admiration for and disappointment in what Duncan had told him. The disappointment came only from the fact Duncan was doing this while married to his daughter and raising his grandchildren. He had no moral dilemma with what he was hearing.

"So you understand why I'm doing this?"

"I understand this is the dumbest thing you've ever done," Bergstrom said. "And that's saying a lot, 'cause I knew you when you were a teenager."

The two men looked at the mountains beyond the stakes in the ground, and at the pink string that outlined the footprint of the foundation that would become the Duncans' home. They were both quiet for a few moments. "Why did you tell me this?" Bergstrom asked. "Wouldn't it be safer for you to tell no one?"

"Yes, but I'm more concerned about Erica and the kids' safety. I told you because you're the only man in the world who loves them as much as I do. You're the only person I trust as much as Erica."

"And what about her—does she know?"

"Yes."

"What does she think about this?"

"She was angry that I waited to tell her until after I had gotten into it, and she wants me out of it."

"And you, Jack?"

Duncan looked very seriously at his father-in-law and said, "I wish I would have told her up front because she would've talked me out of it. But I had my back to the wall. The construction business was in the tank and I was losing everything I'd worked hard for. I felt trapped. I had nothing to fall back on."

"I understand, Jack."

"You do?"

"I understand having your back against the wall," Bergstrom said and paused, looking at Duncan and then back to the mountains. "I didn't say I think it's a good idea."

"But you knew the money trouble I was in?"

"Of course, Jack, why do you think Barb and I offered for you guys to live here on the ranch? I knew you wouldn't make it working for someone else. You've done your own thing for too long. It just isn't in your makeup."

"I guess I should've asked you for help."

"You didn't have to ask; I offered."

"It's hard to take help sometimes."

"You aren't the first man to let pride put him in a fix."

The men paused from the conversation and continued to look things over.

"Besides, it sounds like you are doing it your own way again with this Hunt Club."

"But I'm still somebody's bitch—just a better-paid bitch."

"Everybody's somebody's bitch, Jack."

"You aren't."

"Sure I am, at least at times, and all the time when I was your age. It's just the way the world works. Besides, my hunch is you are calling most of the shots."

"If I were calling the shots, I'd quit. I don't want any part of this shit anymore. I'm not greedy. I've got enough to start another business or invest, enough to live on. I'm not like Beck. I just want to be here in Montana, and at our cabin in Alaska, you know what I mean? Hunt and fish a little, ride with the girls, and tuck my kids in every night after dinner. Just the simple life."

Bergstrom chuckled softly, smiled at his son-in-law, and said, "Who are you trying to kid? Simple—you? The man who's traveled the world in everything from a Super Cub to private Gulfstreams hunting the most exotic game in the world? For Christ's sake, Jack, you've been to Mongolia, Tibet, Africa, Patagonia, and places I can't pronounce, and you want simple?"

"Yes! Yes, I do. I just want to raise my family. Life goes by so fast, and I'm missing too much of what's important to me. I guess it just took me a while to see it."

"So, again, Jack, why'd you tell me if you've told no one but Erica?"

"Because Beck's a son of a bitch. He won't let me out of the Hunt Club, and I don't trust him. He's had me followed—for what reason, I don't know. The dipshits who follow me aren't especially sneaky and they're outta their element here, but I wanted you to know so you could look out for Erica and the kids. You need to know what I'm dealing with, and if something happens to me, they're best off here with you and Barb."

"Nothing is going to happen to you."

"You don't know that."

"I know it because you can't let it," Bergstrom said firmly. "But you'd better be careful. You're leaving tracks in a dark country."

"I know."

"By the sounds of it, you've been livin' on the edge of the shadows for quite a while."

"Doesn't everybody?"

Bergstrom paused for a moment, lost in thought. "No. Most folks have a dark side, but they avoid it."

"It's not easy living on both sides at the same time."

"You can't. At least not forever. Not if you're gonna raise your family."

"I know," Duncan said. He looked at the dirt at his boot tips, then back at the mountains, and he nodded as though he were accepting Bergstrom's words as an order.

"I'll help you any way I can; you know that," Bergstrom added.

"Beck's an evil son of a bitch ruled by money and a sociopathic lust for power. He won't let me just walk away."

"You don't think so?"

"Not a chance. He's as bad as the men he picks to shoot, only the crimes he commits are legal. He's no better than the African warlord we killed; he just has to be more crafty within our democratic legal system."

The hunt for the warlord came back to Duncan in vivid detail as he recounted the story to Bergstrom. In the version he told his father-in-law, he omitted most of the trip's details and focused on the cause and justification for what he had been doing. But in his own mind, it played out in color like the rerun of a show he'd seen many times before.

This particular African warlord had come to Beck's attention because one of Beck's companies sold the warlord forty million dollars' worth of farm equipment at the time he was killing his own people to make way for the farms. At the same time, Beck was operating a plant in Ohio that was emitting carcinogens into the air that were suspected of causing an incredible cancer cluster downwind. Beck had knowingly manipulated the research with studies he bought and paid for as well as with a variety of political gifts, contributions, and bribes that had kept the factory operating even to the present day. In that decade, there were more recorded cancer deaths connected with the pollutants coming from his plant than the warlord had killed in the valley he flooded with a reservoir for irrigation. And the hypocrisy ran even deeper. Beck waited, of course, for the forty million to clear the bank before they hunted down the African. They shot him to death while he lay in a recliner at the side of a private Honduran resort pool, surrounded by prostitutes and bodyguards. It had been less than a year since the mission, and it was still fresh in Duncan's head.

There were no innocents in this program. The client who had actually pulled the trigger was a Saudi oil baron who spent most of his time in Texas on a ranch that shared a border with a sitting US congressman. They drank together at least monthly, even though it was against both of their religions. Duncan had disliked the man from the time they boarded Beck's Gulfstream for the flight to Guatemala, which was the staging area for intercepting the target on Roatán.

After Beck retired to his room in the back of the plane, Duncan sat down with the Saudi in the lounge area and looked him over. The man wore a sport coat and slacks and a keffiyeh held on by a little circlet of rope around his head called an agal. He was young compared to the other Hunt Club clients, about the same age as Duncan, and pompous in the way of royalty, which Duncan refused to recognize. As an American, Duncan didn't acknowledge royalty or that it even existed. When Duncan looked at him, he couldn't help but think of the news footage of Yasser Arafat he'd seen when he was younger, except that this man, while dark in complexion and hair, had much finer features.

After listening to the man for a while, Duncan said, "Lose the headgear when we get to Guatemala City. I don't want to see it again till we fly home."

"Excuse me?" the man asked. "This is my traditional dress; I won't just take it off."

"Flying around the world shooting people for fun is hardly a traditional sport. Traditions don't mean shit here."

"But I wear this everywhere I go!"

"Here's the deal," Duncan said, leaning over the table between them and putting his hand down in front of the man. "I've got two objectives with this trip. Number one is getting us home safely. Number two is getting you a shot at your intended target. I won't jeopardize number one for number two. And if you wear that thing on your head in this country, we'll stick out like a fat tick on a gnat's ass."

The man sat back in his seat and glared at Duncan for a moment.

"I'll have the pilot turn this plane around right now if you'd like."

"No," the Saudi said with reluctance. "I'll take it off."

"Thank you," Duncan said. "I'll see you when we land." He got up from the table and walked to a seat in the corner of the plane where he would be left alone.

The men landed in Guatemala City late in the afternoon, where Duncan arranged a taxi to take them to the hotel—Barceló Guatemala City—where they would stay one night before departing for Roatán.

They checked in, and Duncan headed off to his room alone and enjoyed the respite from the wealthy Saudi's verbal diarrhea. He looked out the window of his room, where he saw the volcanic peaks that surrounded the city and wondered if one of them was Pacaya. He had seen the volcano erupt when he'd been there in the nineties, but it had been long enough that he couldn't remember the geography in detail. As he looked out the window, he called Beck.

"Yes," Beck said when he answered the phone in his room.

"I'm going to meet my cousin, to work out the details."

"OK."

"You can babysit your friend tonight," Duncan said as he looked out the hotel window and admired the view of the volcanic cone backlit by the sun's last light of the day. "I've already had enough of him."

"You don't like him, huh?"

"What's to like? I wouldn't leave the hotel—eat dinner at the restaurant here," Duncan added quickly, before Beck could answer.

Then Duncan called his cousin.

"I'm here," he said when Brett answered the phone.

"I'll send Feliciano to pick you up," Brett said. "He'll be with you again."

"Sounds good."

Feliciano met Duncan in the lobby, and the two men drove to

Brett Duncan's home, which sat up in the hills above the mass of humanity and the black smog that hung over the city. It was dark when they arrived, which Duncan regretted, as he enjoyed watching the variety of tropical birds that lived in the lush mountains around Brett's home. Brett and his wife greeted Duncan on the cobblestone entry in front of their home. The two men shook hands and hugged, and then Duncan hugged his cousin's wife.

"You and Feliciano have gotten reacquainted?" Brett asked.

"Yes, he's a good man."

"He is."

Duncan handed Brett a box that contained an assortment of wine from Oregon, Washington, and Napa Valley, all reds. The four went in and were greeted by Brett's teenage children, and they had a nice meal, which the Duncans' live-in maid had prepared for them. After dinner, the men enjoyed a drink in Brett's office, where they discussed the mission. After going over the details of the excursion, Feliciano returned Duncan to his hotel.

The December morning dawned dry, with a fresh breeze that partially cleared the usual black air that hung over Guatemala City. The mountain peaks were shrouded in clouds, and it was cool at the city's high altitude. Duncan and Beck had breakfast with their client in the hotel restaurant, and Feliciano was there at seven a.m., as promised. Duncan and the client left with him in a diesel Toyota pickup, and Beck flew back to the States for a few days. He would return to meet them at the end of their trip.

Duncan met Feliciano at the truck with their light bags and some fishing gear while Beck and the client said their partings in the lobby.

"This one is a piece of work," Duncan said.

"Muslim trash?" asked Feliciano, a devout Catholic.

"Something like that."

"Wonderful."

"I think the African will be easy. Not shooting our client will be the challenge."

They loaded into the Toyota and started off for Puerto Barrios. The trip from the capital city to the Gulf of Honduras was uneventful, with their documentation checked at only one military checkpoint. Duncan always felt a slight tension in giving the authorities his phony passports, but they were waved through, and they made it to their destination in the usual four hours.

The three men pulled up to a hotel on the beach just north of Puerto Barrios on Amatique Bay. The hotel was beige stucco with a palm-thatched roof, and it was surrounded by tall palms. Feliciano got out and talked to a man, presumably the owner, and then returned to the Toyota and pulled it through a gate where it would be hidden behind mission walls. They grabbed their bags and walked across a manicured lawn toward the calm water where a floating dock met the light-sand beach. The place seemed nearly deserted except for an iguana, which ran across the grass and sand in front of them and disappeared into thick green foliage on the edge of the lawn. They threw their backpacks into the boat, a thirty-foot Grady-White with twin Yamaha outboards, and they departed for Roatán as quickly as they'd arrived.

Seven hours later, after banging their way across the Caribbean's three- to four-foot waves, they completed the one-hundred-and-fifty-mile trip, arriving at Roatán. They slipped over the reef and through an opening on flat clear-blue water between the tip of a palm-covered island and a rocky peninsula into the calm waters of a lagoon where they had rented a resort cabana. The cabanas were built on piers out over the clear water and had individual dock access. They checked into their cabana and settled into the small tropical cabin for the night.

In the morning, the three men visited the private bungalow where the African would be staying as well as the surrounding area, looking for a clear shooting lane. They had another reservation at a three-story hotel that Feliciano had already scouted, and after some study, he checked Duncan into the room. Then the waiting began, as the African wasn't scheduled to arrive for two more days.

They fished the first two days in the Grady-White boat outside the reef a few miles offshore where the shelf dropped off to deep water. This authenticated their cover of being on a sporting trip with Feliciano as their guide. The client protested, as he lacked the sea legs of the other two men and felt sickened if the waves came up, but Duncan made him go anyway. He said it was necessary for their cover, but the truth was Duncan enjoyed watching the arrogant man suffer with seasickness. And he did not trust the man to be left alone. The trips were generally short, and they returned to the cabana shortly after midday with wahoo both days and grouper on the second.

They spent the first two afternoons passing the time leisurely, drinking Port Royal beer in the shade of the cabana and feeding the small reef fish that liked the water shaded by their room. They ate dinner at the resort restaurant, which specialized in preparing their catch of the day, but they mingled very little with the other tourists. They spent most of their evenings sipping a local liquor made from the fruit of the hog plum tree, which Feliciano had introduced them to, and reading to avoid much attention.

The morning of their third day was the scheduled date of the target's arrival, so Duncan and the client moved into the room in the resort from which they would shoot the man. It was hot and very humid, but a gentle breeze blew off the water and up the slight hill their hotel sat on. When the breeze touched their skin and clothing, which was damp with perspiration, it cooled them and the air was pleasant. But in the room, which was closed up when they entered it, the air was still, thick, and brutally hot.

Duncan walked straight to the sliding door of the balcony and opened it.

"Turn the fan on," he said to the Saudi, who then flipped the switch on the wall. The fan came on, and in a few moments, the curtains, which were drawn open from the balcony door, began to flutter from the ocean breeze and the wind from the fan. Both men noticed the movement.

"Maybe we should close the door," the Saudi said.

Duncan just looked at him like an idiot, and then looked back out the window to the house their target would be staying in.

"Those curtains fluttering in the wind might draw attention to us," the Saudi added. "Maybe we should tie them up."

"At six hundred yards?" Duncan asked. "Every room in this hotel has the door open and the fan running. We'd be the only ones with our curtains tied up not blowing in the breeze."

Duncan went back to looking out the open door, and the Saudi set his pack on one of the beds and settled into the room. Duncan looked down and across the slight canyon to the spectacular home where their target would be staying. He admired the view: the shiny, green, broad-leafed tropical foliage; the flowering trees; the occasional pine; and the coconut palms that lined the white-sand beach where it met the clear blue water. *If only I were enjoying myself*, he thought.

Then he began to wonder about the men who paid him to guide

them on manhunts. *Did they enjoy shooting other men?* he wondered. Most men hunted for the enjoyment of the hunt, but this was different. He thought about it more and came to the conclusion that most of his Hunt Club clients would not pull the trigger if he were not watching over them. More than a guide, he was the peer pressure, the silent push past the reluctance of pulling the trigger on another man. He would have let them back out if they wanted, but none ever did. And aside from Beck and now the Saudi, the other clients were actually very serious and somber about the situation. They didn't appear to be having fun, yet they paid a small fortune to go. For Duncan, it was business; it was not supposed to be fun.

The Saudi eagerly put together a rifle and pushed cartridges into a clip. "What do you think?" he asked, interrupting Duncan's thoughts and his focus on a hummingbird hovering in front of him. The brilliant little bird moved from one to another of the purple flowers that spilled over and hung from a pot on the balcony.

"I think we should get the room ready so we can shoot this asshole and get out of here," was Duncan's response.

They arranged the room in preparation for the shot. They had a relatively clean line of sight at the pool area of the private rental house, which came with all variety of servants and staff. They arranged and rearranged the furniture until they had the line they needed.

The baluster on the balcony blocked a clear shot from the desk in the room, so Duncan pulled the dresser out from the wall and placed the hotel desk on top of it. It wasn't very stable, but it gained them the elevation needed to shoot over the balcony balustrade. They placed a cushion from a futon on top of the desk for comfort in case the shooter had to lie prone for an extended period while waiting for a clear shot. The shooting platform was arranged at the back of the room, and the shot would be made through the open sliding door with all the other windows closed to muffle the already-suppressed report of the rifle.

After arranging the room, Duncan and the Saudi went back to waiting. Manhunting was a game of biding time until the right opportunity—one that allowed for a clean shot and a safe, undetected escape for the shooters—presented itself. This was the worst part for Duncan. He hated waiting. And it was especially difficult with clients like the Saudi. He sipped the hog plum liquor that Feliciano had given him in the bathroom out of sight from the Saudi and napped while they waited. Evening came, but the African didn't.

The two men met Feliciano for dinner at the resort restaurant down on the water, where he waited for the shooters with the Grady-White ready. After eating, the shooters returned to their room, and Feliciano went for information on the African. In the morning, he knocked on the room door and informed Duncan and the Saudi that the African was running two days late.

"Shit," Duncan said, and he thought for a moment about fishing again. It was risky to move the rifles around, and it was risky to leave them in the room unattended. It was way too risky to leave the Saudi alone anywhere, so he decided they would just wait in the room. And after two more long days, the target arrived.

The entourage spilled onto the pool area of the exclusive private resort. One minute, the pool was empty, and the next, there were humans milling around as though they were a rolling party, moving from one place to another. There were resort servants serving drinks, and a half dozen or more prostitutes in swimwear scant enough to barely qualify as clothing of any kind milling about. There were an equal number of large black men who looked uptight enough that they had to be the warlord's bodyguards. There were also several others Duncan couldn't place in the order of things who milled about the large African man, performing one variety of service for him or another.

Duncan watched the scene through a spotting scope while the Saudi watched through the scope of the rifle.

"Don't shoot an innocent," Duncan said as he examined the target. "There's a lot of people to sort through down there."

"Not really."

Duncan looked at him, slightly confused, trying to hide the fact that he hated the man he was looking at.

"Just infidels and whores," the Saudi said.

The two men studied the photos they carried of the African and agreed that the man lying by the pool across from them was, without a doubt, the intended target. Duncan gave the Saudi the clear to fire.

When the rifle went off, Duncan stood next to the Saudi at the makeshift shooting table in the back of the hotel room. They were six hundred yards away from the pool, and he shot a .338 Winchester with a suppressor. Between the shots, Duncan remembered hearing the Saudi laugh.

But what Duncan remembered most vividly were the moments between the impact of the first shot and the prostitutes and bodyguards reacting. There was no noise to register the bullet, which blew through the large black man's chest and sprayed blood all over the sandstone-colored concrete pool deck. Before the situation had registered, another bodyguard dropped dead, a large bullet having passed through his upper chest as well. When the situation did register with the prostitutes, they scattered, and yet another bodyguard dropped as the remainder drew handguns and searched the surroundings for a shooter. At that point, the client's magazine was empty, and Duncan grabbed the gun, both to break it down for removal and to stop the shooting.

"Why the bodyguards?" Duncan asked the client as they quickly broke down the shooting positions and prepared to leave.

"They're all just infidels to me," was the Saudi's response.

Duncan nearly laughed out loud at the irony. He later learned that the African Muslim came from a rival faction of their shared religion, at which point he did laugh out loud.

When Duncan had finished recounting the story of the Saudi and his warlord kill, he and Bergstrom stood silently, looking at the Montana landscape. After a long pause, Duncan asked, "How has the world become so corrupt and perverse in such a short time?"

"It hasn't."

Duncan looked at Bergstrom for a moment while his father-in-law stared off at the mountains. After a few moments, Duncan looked back at the same mountains. "You don't think it's corrupt and perverse?"

"I think it's plenty corrupt and perverse. What I meant was it didn't get that way anytime recent." He paused and looked at Duncan. "I reckon it's been that way all along."

"You think?"

"Look at history."

"Yeah, I guess you're right."

"Sure I am."

"Does that make you feel any better?"

"Being right?"

"No, knowing the world's been shit all along."

Bergstrom thought about the question for a moment and said, "You know, I never gave it much thought, but now that you mention it, yes. I guess it does give me a little peace about the whole deal being a mess."

"Beck will be here in two days and I'll take him down to the Tetons. He wants to float the Teton River in the canyon section," Duncan said, turning the conversation back.

"You mean above where the dam broke in the seventies?" asked Bergstrom.

"Yeah, I guided it some when I was young. I don't like it much at all. It's hot and full of rattlesnakes and large rapids. When I guided there, we used regular McKenzie-style drift boats and it was dangerous, but we'll take a raft."

"He's a real pain in the ass, isn't he?" Bergstrom asked.

"I'll try to talk my way out of his stupid game, but I don't see it. He just doesn't go along with anything anybody else wants unless it's his idea to begin with. But whether he lets me or not, I'm getting out."

Both men knew what this meant, but no further words were spoken. The conversation changed to the subject of the house as Erica and her mother, Barb, walked across the dry, sun-bleached grass of the mesa from the main ranch house to the new home site.

In the morning, Duncan would start digging the hole for the basement with a track hoe Bergstrom kept on the ranch. He told his family that he had to leave for an overnight trip in two days, but that he would lay out the foundation. He had some of the men he had worked with in the past lined up to start forming up the footings while he was away with Beck, guiding him on the Teton and lobbying for his own freedom. They would pour the footings the day after he returned, and then they would put up the basement forms. He was excited to work with his old friends again and happy that he could pay them out of pocket—no loans, no banks, no realtors. Given the slowness of the building industry, he was able to line up all the subcontractors, his friends, and schedule them tight, as he was trying to get the house done so his family would be living in it around Thanksgiving.

The next two days went by quickly, although they were sixteen-hour workdays. Duncan got the holes dug and the strings up for the footings, and then he hooked up his raft trailer.

Beck had called the night before, and Duncan was exceptionally brief, instructing Beck to meet him at his house at 6:00 a.m. so they could arrive at the Teton by around nine.

The morning was a typical August morning. It was dry even at sunup, which was nearly an hour before the scheduled meeting. Erica stirred, but Duncan insisted that she stay in bed, as there was no need for her to get up. He had enough food packed for an overnight trip, and the weather was going to be warm, with no thunderstorms forecast. He would bring a couple of cots to keep them up off the ground. The Teton Canyon—or Narrows, as it was known locally—was full of rattlesnakes, but mostly on the warmer, sunbaked north side of the river, so they would camp on the south. He included a couple of tarps and several telescoping poles and ropes should the weather forecasts be wrong.

The two men exchanged pleasantries while loading Beck's personal gear into the boat, but there were few other words. Beck had arrived alone, which was rare. The only time Duncan ever saw him alone was when the two met to discuss the Hunt Club and their outings, which Duncan thought was incredibly ironic, as Beck found no other person in the world nearly as interesting as he found himself. Once they were in the car, however, the conversation heated up. At least Beck heated up, while Duncan mostly just listened quietly. Duncan wondered if Beck would bring up the subject of his leaving the Hunt Club, which he had brought up with Beck one of the last times they'd spoken, the evening before Duncan took the kids fishing in the Tobacco Roots.

"You're gonna be excited about the next target," Beck said.

"Hmm," Duncan mumbled under his breath, thinking it fitting that Beck was telling him how he would feel. Duncan looked out the window and let Beck talk.

The morning air was cooler than it would be all day, but it was still warm. Duncan drove up the Madison River toward Quake Lake, then turned south toward Raynolds Pass and the Idaho border. They stopped in Last Chance, where they had a quick breakfast of hash browns and eggs and purchased their Idaho fishing licenses. The morning was clear but a little hazy from the typical fires that burned in the Central Idaho wilderness complexes. Clouds of small trico mayflies danced over the Henry's Fork of the Snake River and dotted Duncan's windshield. Other than the company, it was a fine summer morning.

"This one's a piece of work, Jack."

"Aren't they all?"

"This guy is a real abuser."

Duncan said nothing and continued looking out the window.

"He trades in human flesh," Beck said.

"A slave trader?" Duncan asked, slightly more interested.

"Yes, he sells women and girls as prostitutes."

"Really?" Duncan said, almost as though it surprised him.

"Yeah, and for the most part the girls are kidnapped."

"Hmm," Duncan mumbled again under his breath.

"You're gonna enjoy killing this one."

Duncan took his eyes off the road and looked at Beck for a moment. "I don't enjoy killing any of them."

"Sure you do. I've been there—it's a rush."

Duncan looked back at the road.

"You're a lot like me, Jack, and I know you get a rush out of it."

"I don't enjoy killing anybody," Duncan said, and he wondered for just a second if he were, in some small way, like Beck. *Did he enjoy it? Just a little?* Then he just listened quietly as Beck went on.

This time the target was an American citizen. This caused Duncan some anxiety at first, but as Beck went on about his dubious credentials, Duncan began to want to kill the guy himself. The man, Ivan Libor, was involved with an assortment of criminal activities, including extortion, drugs, and a number of businesses that laundered the revenues for his dissolute pursuits. What captured Duncan's attention, however, was the man's involvement in the slave trade. In fact, the whole concept of slavery caught him off guard. In the United States, slavery had been made out to be an antique relic of history by popular media and perhaps public education. It was a subject that made white people feel guilty about being white. The Hunt Club's new target, however, dealt in slaves from a variety of origins. They were largely Anglo girls from Russia, but Ivan Libor was not prejudiced, and he peddled a variety of teenage girls and young women from around the world. They were taken primarily from Russia, but also from Thailand, India, Central America, and Taiwan, and then sold in the Middle East, India, and Russia as well as in the

States, Mexico, and Central and South America. The girls were either duped by false promises or straight-up kidnapped.

Duncan was certainly not naive. He had seen a lot of the world for a man from Ennis, Montana, but he had not given much thought to the subject of slavery. He was raised on the Golden Rule, and he had always treated his employees or any person he had business with very fairly, although he perhaps took freedom a little for granted, like many Americans did. What he learned about Ivan the Terrible—the name the Hunt Club attached to this target—and his dirty business of brokering human flesh momentarily sucked Duncan back in. This wasn't an accident.

Beck knew Duncan would be appalled by the monster and his sex-slave trade, and that Duncan would be drawn back into the club because of it. He was sure Duncan would not be able to pass on an opportunity to rid the earth of a monster who sold teenage girls into sexual slavery to brothels, pimps, and wealthy individuals around the world.

Duncan quietly drove his diesel pickup with the raft in tow. He was thinking about his own wife and daughter. He was thinking about the fact that Beck was attempting to draw him back in. He was also thinking about the fact that Beck was wrong about him, and he was thinking about the timing of broaching the subject of his leaving the Hunt Club again. Duncan knew he could not affect the slave trade; killing one man would not end it. There would always be another thug to fill in. But if he got out, he could spend his time with his own family. He knew he could make a difference at home.

It was shortly after nine in the morning when Duncan turned off the highway and onto a gravel two-track road that disappeared into the eye of a rimrock and sage coulee. The tops of most of the ridges were covered with an amber carpet of rolling barley fields on the verge of harvest. Mixed in with the sea of grain were occasional green-furrowed seed potato fields. As the road neared the rim of the major canyon formed by the Teton River and Bitch Creek, which drained the Teton Valley and the north end of the famous Teton Range, the flora transformed back to its native grasses, sagebrush, and junipers, with an occasional thick stand of aspen.

The point of the ridge where Duncan would leave his truck and from where the men would embark on their trip down the Teton Narrows offered a spectacular view on a clear day. Looking to the southeast, the men were confronted with the Teton Range and a direct shot at the Grand, the second-tallest peak in Wyoming, as well as the basin formed by this range and the Snake River Range. The fur trappers and early explorers had a number of names for the Grand, but one of the most common was "Pilot Rock," as on a clear day it could be seen from up to one hundred and fifty miles in all directions, and the men used it for navigation. To the east and northeast, Duncan and Beck saw the southwest corner of Yellowstone Park and the beginning of the Island Park Caldera. To the north was the Centennial Range, the only mountain range in the Rockies that ran east to west. It was the Continental Divide as well as the border between Idaho and Montana, and it was punctuated on the east end by Sawtell Peak, beyond which lay Duncan's home country.

Most people would do no more than admire the scenery from the canyon rim, but a scant few hardy fly-fishing guides drilled and fastened carabiners to the nearly vertical rock face and belayed boats down the face of a mountain to fish a treacherously pristine piece of water. The water had remained relatively unfished compared with the famous blue-ribbon rivers like the Henry's Fork, the South Fork of the Snake, and the Madison, all of which overflowed most of the summer with dudes who looked like they'd stepped out of an Orvis fly-fishing catalog.

Duncan and Beck readied their equipment, including the raft. Most of it went into two custom-made plastic crates to be slid down the chute of a trail to the river's edge two-thirds of a mile below them. Duncan carried what was left of their gear in a pack on his back as they lowered the outfit by ropes through the carabiners fixed to the exposed granite and attached to cables around the bases of juniper trees.

Once they reached the bottom, they assembled the rowing plat-form, inflated the raft, and launched the boat into the Teton, which was low and clear this far into summer. The trip down the face had been easy; they encountered only one rattlesnake, which Duncan shot with a .44 revolver he carried on his hip. They would not even have seen that one if Duncan had not been looking for snakes.

Once they reached the river, there was really no way out but the take out at the old dam site a dozen miles downstream. You could climb out of the canyon in places, but even in the lighter terrain, it would be difficult. Following the river's edge by foot was impossible in much of the canyon. It was for these reasons that Duncan waited to bring up the subject of his leaving the Hunt Club; to some extent, Duncan had Beck captive once they were in the bottom of the canyon.

The first section of the float was still in its native state, unaffect-ed by the Teton Canyon Dam and its failure in 1976. Large boulder runs and a couple of nasty rapids defined this section of river, but from Spring Hollow down to the old dam site, the river was scarred by man. The reservoir had been nearly full in June of that year at the peak runoff season when it broke. As the water dropped nearly instantly, it piled boulders, timber, and debris at intermittent locations down the canyon. Where the debris collected, the river was partially dammed, which formed a lake above it and a large rapid where the water dropped off the boulder and log piles and into the top of the next lake.

The Yellowstone cutthroat trout that lived there ate ravenously when the midmorning sun hit the water, and little finesse was needed to catch them; large dry flies on heavy tippets were the requisite tackle, and this day would be no exception.

Duncan and Beck pushed the raft off into the low but swift current of the upper Teton Narrows. Beck false casted about thirty-five feet of line and began to lay the large elk-hair stonefly pattern into the current seams where hungry trout lay waiting for the feed that collects in them. On the second or third drift, Beck's fly disappeared in a violent splashing swirl, and his line went tight as the long graphite rod bent and bobbed under the pressure of the bulldogging trout. Beck smiled his sly smile, and Duncan tried to ignore him.

Duncan looked up the steep canyon walls toward the rim and at the light-blue sky above and beyond the line of the horizon, which appeared close at the bottom of the canyon but seemed to keep moving out of reach as one hiked to the top. From the bottom of the canyon, a man got the feeling of being disconnected from the rest of the world. The bottom of that canyon felt like it was on another planet, uninterrupted by humans. Few had even seen it, and most of those who had had only seen a small part of it. Duncan imagined that the upper section did not look much different than it had when mountain men discovered it or when Shoshone Indians hunted sheep on its steep slopes. No sheep lived there now—they'd been evicted by humans—and during the summer, only an occasional moose was seen in the river bottom. Duncan remembered a day when he was guiding on the river and a cow moose with a calf charged his drift boat, coming out into the river with her ears laid almost flat against the back of her head. His clients were terrified, and they were at the top of a rapid, which meant they had to walk around so Duncan could safely negotiate the drop. He had to produce the .44 from his bag and fire several shots over her head to send her on her way with her calf. It had taken a lot of coaxing to get the two potbellied, middle-aged dudes to leave the debatable safety of his drift boat.

Duncan and Beck floated the first section in virtual silence. Duncan was deep in thoughts that had nothing to do with the dozens of green-backed, golden-sided cutthroat Beck was bringing to the raft and releasing. Duncan was not slowing the boat down much with the oars, and they made it to Spring Hollow in a few short hours, which was necessary if they were to make it to the camping spot by early afternoon. He knew there would likely be guides ahead of them from a local lodge, as this was the only real access until their take out at the dam site, and the fishing would slow a little for the time being as the river wasn't big enough to tolerate much pressure.

The first rapid below this access was a large one that washed out into the face of a vertical rock cliff that rose two hundred feet straight out of the river. When Duncan guided, he let the clients out to walk around this rapid, as it was a big drop with a tight gap between the Volkswagen-sized boulders that formed it. The gap was so tight that the oars had to be shipped into the locks to pass between the rocks and then returned to the water immediately when clear. This allowed the rower to get a stroke or two in to kick the stern left and miss a rock that showed through the surface just enough to look like the glossy back of a whale and could catch the bottom of the boat. Removing the weight of the clients from a drift boat made executing this maneuver less difficult. However, today Duncan decided he would take his client down the drop with him. He was in a raft, and rafts were forgiving, typically flowing over and bouncing off rocks.

When the raft flushed out of the bottom of the rapid, Duncan caught the eddy and floated out of the main flow of the river and up onto a gravel beach, where they got out and stretched their legs. The beach was surrounded by boulders left from the dam break, and downstream on their side of the river were vertical cliffs of granite. There was little flora aside from grass and an occasional juniper or sagebrush on this side of river, but the other side had dark patches of green timber on the shadiest northeast-facing slopes. The deep-green conifers started just below the rim and ran down to where the surface of the failed reservoir had reached up the canyon walls before escaping. The floodwaters had stripped everything off as they flushed down the canyon when the dam broke. It was at this spot that Duncan brought up the subject of his leaving.

Duncan got back into the boat while Beck looked up at the canyon rims and at the sky. Duncan took the oars and backed the boat into the eddy, holding in the dead water about fifteen feet off the gravel beach. Beck looked at him and back at the sky. Duncan stared hard at the small man standing on the beach. He looked pale and strangely out of place. As out of place as a human animal could look in what had once been its natural environment.

"You've avoided the subject of my quitting the Hunt Club," Duncan said, fixed on Beck, who looked down now from the sky.

"Because you aren't leaving," he said and turned to look at Duncan. His mouth was closed tight as though his lips were holding back words he might have rather said but thought it better to hold on to.

"And you think you can make me stay in?" Duncan said, still holding the boat in the current out of Beck's reach.

"You *are* the Hunt Club, Jack."

"No, James, you are. I only did it to get out of a financial hole that I've realized was a better place to be than where I'm at."

"There's no getting out, Jack. You're in it until I say you can get out. It's not something you quit or get out of. You're committed. We'll see it to the end."

Beck went back to looking at the sky and the rocky canyon while Duncan held the boat near the shore, and there was a long silence. There was no wind in the canyon. The August heat was mounting, radiating off the sandstone and granite walls, and the only sound was the low roar of the river plunging over the rapid they had just come down. Duncan searched the depths of his brain for something to say, for a compulsion that would trigger Beck to let him out, but there was nothing. As he sat idle in the slack water, he realized that Beck would never let him out, and in fact they were too entangled for either to safely walk away. It would leave each man with an unswept trail— another human with leverage over the other. Duncan was honor-able—he only wished to return to his family—but Beck's honor was skin deep and only for the camera.

Duncan pushed once on the oars, and the raft slid back up on the pea-gravel beach. He tersely said, "Get in."

Beck looked down the beach at him and paused as if Duncan were a small child who had just said, "You can't make me!" Then he slowly walked back to the raft.

It was now silent in the raft. Duncan pushed the nose of the raft up into the bottom of the rapids, and Beck cast his fly into the seam along the edge of the main current. There were no fish to answer his cast, so Duncan eased the raft out into the current again and they continued. Beck hooked a fish that smacked his high-floating dry stonefly imitation as it drifted along only inches from the rock face coming down straight into the water. Beck released the fish, and Duncan broke the silence.

"A friend of mine recently told me that everybody's somebody's bitch," he said, and then paused. "I guess that makes me your bitch then, doesn't it?"

"I like to think of us as partners, Jack. We both have something to bring to the table in this relationship. But due to the insidious nature of the business we conduct together, there's no real way for one of us to walk away. We aren't done yet, young man."

"You mean *you* aren't done yet."

"Yes, which means you aren't done," Beck said and smiled wryly.

"So, I *am* your bitch," Duncan said in a lighter, more playful tone than he'd contrived.

Beck began casting again despite the fact they had drifted out of the fishy water. It amused Duncan that most city folks had no ability to read water or woods.

"So whose bitch are you, James?"

"Nobody's, son—I'm nobody's bitch," Beck said as he continued his ignorantly pointless casting into the fishless water.

He said it without hesitation, and with his back to Duncan. It was the wrong answer, and with that answer, he unknowingly sealed his fate.

The right answer would have been, "Yours, Jack."

But Beck did not know this. Duncan was sure he lacked the ability to empathize, and that his ability to read emotions was entirely superficial. This would make it very easy for Duncan to lead him to believe he was recommitted to the Hunt Club. The truth, however, was that Duncan was only committed to one more hunt—the hunt for Ivan Libor—and that was only to buy enough time to calculate his exit.

At that moment in time, Beck, as usual, was thinking of himself, and Duncan was contemplating the idea of turning the raft over and drowning Beck in the river. Boats sank down there on a regular basis, and swimmers and kayakers had drowned a number of times. If Beck were an average man, nobody would have raised an eyebrow, but because he was nearly famous, there would be media and police. He could probably pull it all off, but he did not want the attention.

They continued down the river, and the mood relaxed. Duncan still had little to say, and Beck did most of the talking. The fishing was good, as it always was in this relatively unfished section of river. The day was hot, and as they neared the spot on the river where Duncan was planning to make camp, he made up his mind that he was not going to give Beck another day on the river. Instead, they floated on, and as they neared the rapid they called the Big Chute, a class five and the largest rapid on that stretch, he considered taking Beck through the whole length of it. His usual practice when guiding was to rope the boat down the first section of the rapid, as it was very rocky and hard to pick through with the oars. However, for the first time, Duncan decided to go from the top. Beck had no opinion of the route, nor was he included in the decision. Duncan was wearing a life vest and Beck was not. If the boat capsized, Beck might be taken care of by the river, and Duncan's problems would be solved.

Duncan lined up at the top of the Big Chute and picked his way left and then right, dodging two rocks, and then he crossed back across the river hard to the left to miss a third, making the raft line up with a large rock right in the tongue of the current. The tongue picked up speed funneling into the chute, and Duncan pretended to miss an oar stroke while dragging the opposing oar to kick the boat sideways right before hitting the rock. They hit it perfectly: the downriver side of the raft kicked up into the air over the rock, and the churning river boiled over the upriver side of the raft, which was sucked down by the current. Beck fell down into the bottom of the raft on the impact and grabbed on to the aluminum tubing that made up the rowing platform, holding on with strength fueled by adrenaline as the water rushed over him. Duncan held firmly to the oars, and the thought flashed through his head that if they had been in a drift boat, they would have already sunk and they would be in the water. The force of the water was so great that Duncan was at its mercy, and he could not have saved them if he was inclined, nor could he affect the boat's sinking.

They hung there momentarily, and then the river kicked them loose, and Beck, who was soaked but unaffected by the cold water in the hot August air, righted himself.

"Shit!" Duncan hissed, but there wasn't time for conversation. The river didn't wait, drawing them ever downward.

From there the float was easy: just stay in the chute and ride the big, rolling white waves to the tail out, and catch your breath. Instead, Duncan positioned the boat to hit a rock they called Saddle Rock, because he remembered that fifteen years ago, a man had fallen into the large boil above the rock while fishing from the bank and drowned. The river gave him back a week later when the man's body washed up on a bank at the top of the lake at the old dam site, and a friend of Duncan's found him while guiding. The river was low that late in the year and the boil was small, spinning the raft off the rock and back into the main tongue, and then rolling them down the balance of the rapid with no ill effects.

When they reached the tail out, Duncan pulled the raft into an eddy and they pulled themselves tighter.

"I've never seen you miss an oar stroke," Beck said.

"I've never rowed that whole stretch before."

Beck looked at him, surprised, as he righted his fly box and gear.

"Usually we portage the boats at the top or rope them down the top half of the rapid. Makes it easier to get lined up in the chute."

"Why today?"

"Thought it might be exciting."

Beck seemed unsuspecting, and Duncan felt relieved at that but disappointed in the outcome. They bailed the raft and continued, now only about three or four miles from the old dam and the take out. Duncan's truck was waiting there, having been shuttled down by some local teenagers who provided the service for fishermen's vehicles during the summer.

"Where are we camping?" Beck asked.

"We aren't."

"Why not?"

"If we're goin' on another hunt, I don't have time."

The last few miles were lighter, and the fishing was good until they reached the small lake left just above the broken dam. They pulled the raft out while admiring the remnants of the broken dam, the last earthen dam built in the United States, just as the sun was setting on the western horizon.

On the two-hour drive back to Ennis, the two men discussed the next hunt. Beck had a client picked out, but he had not finalized the deal with the man. Duncan feigned new interest in the Hunt Club, but not enough to raise suspicion. When Beck pulled out of Duncan's yard to drive the half hour to his own home, it was nearly midnight. Duncan made no offer to accommodate him, but that was normal for their relationship. Duncan promised to study Ivan Libor and talk to his cousin about setting up a deal with one of his men to track his whereabouts and pin down a shot opportunity. Beck would finalize the deal with the client and get back to Duncan, but they were hoping to arrange the hunt in late October or November.

Duncan watched the taillights on Beck's black Escalade fade into the darkness, disappointed, drained, and ready to be home. The lights were on in the kitchen and Erica had left him a plate of leftovers. He barely touched them, preferring instead a shower and a warm place next to her in bed.

SEVEN

T he long, hot, dry days of August turned quickly into September for the Duncans, who were racing the short season on the Upper Madison. It was sunrise to sunset for Duncan at the home site, and the children were kept busy with ranch chores in between helping with the construction project. Erica was running the vet clinic in town, and she was busy with her horses and the ranch stock. There was a feeling of normalcy—or at least it was the normal that Jack Duncan was looking for but had only achieved for a short period of his life, when his kids were very small and he was in the construction business. When Erica was not at the clinic, she and Avery worked to ready the other house to sell. Erica listed it with a local real estate office at a competitive price, wanting to sell it quickly and not too concerned with squeezing every last dollar out of its sale, owing to Duncan's new cash fortune.

They were living on the ranch now. The girls slept in the house with the Bergstroms while Duncan and his boy stayed in the bunkhouse. It had been home to cowboys back when the ranch had required more manpower, and it still served the purpose occasionally. Two of Duncan's friends who were working on the house stayed with them. They labored hard twelve to fourteen hours per day, but the atmosphere was fun. The girls prepared large dinners: elk and beef roasts, chili, and occasional rib eyes on the grill, which they ate as a group late in the evening as the sun set behind the Gravelly Range to the west. At night, Duncan and his friends entertained each other and especially the boy with tall tales of hunts from the past. They slept hard and deep in the cool mountain air after the long days of physical work—at least all of them did except for Duncan.

His mind was restless with unfinished business as he lay in his bunk. He tossed Beck around in his head, and occasionally the faces of the men he had taken part in assassinating crept into his half-sleeping dreams. And sometimes he dreamed of the three Mexicans he shot in the mountains of Baja Sur. In his dreams, they spoke to him, but he could never make out the words, only their mouths moving and their eye sockets alive with maggots and flesh-eating beetles. It was a vision that would wake him with a start, and then he would consciously console himself and lay in his bed, never falling fully back to sleep for fear they would visit him again.

Most of the time he lay awake, however, was spent second-guessing Beck. He spent those dark hours trying to estimate his next move and how he might compel Beck to dissolve the Hunt Club. But he never developed any conclusions, only dark circles under his eyes and the feeling that he was carrying an extra weight on his back as he hustled through his days. Night after night, he circled back over and over his mental trail, but he came up with nothing.

In mid-September, Beck flew in to deliver the documents on Libor for Duncan to study. Beck drove to Ennis, and the men met at a boat landing on the Madison. They walked down to the river with fly rods in hand to discuss the mission briefly. Beck gave Duncan an envelope with an exhaustive stack of documents highlighting not only Libor's current affairs but also his entire life. Much of this information had been gathered by Brett, with some added by Beck. Duncan would study it later, when he was not sleeping in the middle of the night. Beck also informed Duncan of the client he had selected to pull the trigger.

When the name "Tom McCrery" came out of Beck's mouth, Duncan had to resist the urge to show interest. Instead he made another cast, placing the fly behind a rock a third of the way into the river without looking up or raising so much as an eyebrow.

"What's his story?" Duncan asked, as though he had never heard of Tom McCrery, and then he continued to cast his fly out into a seam behind the rock.

Beck went on to describe Tom McCrery as a well-known man in the world of globe-traveling sportsmen. He was, by Beck's description, a business associate of Beck's, but Duncan had learned to take Beck's human interpretations as less than factual. Beck went on to tell Duncan of McCrery's many hunting exploits and of the Safari Club records he held. What he did not tell Duncan was that he and McCrery had a distant, tepid rivalry that had been heating up during the past several years.

McCrery had formed a holding company that had purchased several outdoor magazines and had also more recently started one from the ground up to compete with one segment of Beck's massive media empire. Beck, on the other hand, had been trying for two decades to purchase McCrery's main business. McCrery started and was the major shareholder of a closely held corporation whose business was car washes of several types, including the largest and most technologically advanced automated variety. The corporation had locations in forty-two states and was still growing.

Duncan reeled his fly line onto the reel after biting the small hopper pattern off the tippet as a means of concluding his meeting with Beck.

"I've got to get back to work," he said to Beck, who was still talking but not about much of anything that Duncan needed to hear.

Duncan was very familiar with Tom McCrery. McCrery had completed what was known as the North American Grand Slam of big game hunting: he had successfully taken every species of North American big game, including a polar bear. He had also completed the World Sheep Grand Slam by taking every known species of mountain sheep in the world, as well as the North American Sheep Grand Slam twice, and Duncan had guided him on one of those hunts in Canada. That particular hunt had been a chance pairing. McCrery had a guide that he hunted with regularly under the same outfitter for whom Duncan worked, but that man, a friend and mentor to Duncan, had torn a ligament in his knee just before the hunt, and the much-younger Duncan filled in.

That hunt had gone well, and Duncan had guided McCrery to a trophy stone sheep whose beautiful curled horns taped to just over forty inches. They had gotten along fine, and when McCrery flew out of camp in the Cessna 206, the two men agreed they would like to hunt together again. Duncan respected his client on this hunt, which was not always the case. McCrery had a true love of the wilderness and hunted extensively in his home state of Colorado, where he owned two different ranches: one in the mountains near Gunnison, and one to the east on the plains. He was also an able-bodied man capable of taking care of himself in the woods and a proficient horseman—both traits Duncan considered valuable in a man. Mc-Crery's other interesting attributes were his philosophies on business and the honor and integrity with which he conducted himself in the world.

McCrery was Beck's polar opposite. Human elements entered every business move McCrery made, and he believed in empowering people. He believed that by giving people, including and especially his employees, an interest in their work and some autonomy in making decisions, he would succeed along with them. He was not foolish; he was careful about selecting the right people to work with and making them earn his loyalty and their interest in his closely held yet incredibly lucrative company. But once they proved themselves, McCrery took very good care of them.

The other coincidence was that Duncan had a good friend whose father was also in the car wash business and was, in turn, good friends with Tom McCrery. Duncan's friend was working for McCrery building the car washes, and they had hired Duncan to construct several buildings in Montana, Wyoming, and North Dakota ten years after Duncan and McCrery had hunted together. And while Duncan had traveled to these states for short periods to work on these projects, he had only spoken to McCrery once, when he called Duncan just to catch up, somewhat disappointed that he had left the outfitting business.

Beck seemed to know nothing of the previous connections between Duncan and McCrery, and he went on with making plans for the hunt. Their meeting lasted about an hour, with Beck continuing to fish after they were done talking while Duncan watched impatiently. After an hour or so, they returned to their vehicles and their lives, agreeing they would meet when their intelligence identified an opportunity to intercept Ivan the Terrible. They guessed this would probably come around Halloween.

When Duncan returned to the construction of the new home he had promised Erica since she was a girl, he was distant, preoccupied by his impending engagement with the Hunt Club. He was far less interested in Ivan Libor than he was preoccupied by the fact that McCrery, who he thought was a good and honorable man, was mixed up with Beck and had a desire to hunt men. He was disappointed with McCrery, whom he had held in high regard, but he was more disappointed with himself. And why was he judging McCrery anyway when he, too, was entangled with Beck and was a hunter of men?

He stayed up late that night, long after his friends and his son were fast asleep in the bunkhouse. He studied the information and the photos of Ivan Libor, who was an American but had been born to a pair of Russian immigrants in Portland, Oregon. Libor had learned to speak Russian in his home, and he had family contacts in several of the former Soviet republics, including the Czech Republic, which gave him easy access to his dirty business.

Libor's parents had been raging alcoholics, and they spent all their time either at work in Portland factories and mills or too drunk to notice him. Libor's father had left home when he was about ten, and the man never attempted to contact him again until rumors reached him of his son's amassing wealth. The story went that Libor had met with his father, listened to his plea for a handout, and then slapped him mercilessly and told him that if he ever saw him again, he would kill him.

Libor's mother had died during his teens of alcohol- and drug-related ailments, but he had already been living on his own ever since his father left, learning the ways of the streets. He was cunning and intelligent, with a sociopathic disconnection from every crime he ever committed, from pimping on the streets of Portland and later Seattle to trading young women and girls as slaves. He peddled the same drugs that had caused his own mother's demise with no apparent thought of the users. The more Duncan read, the more he wanted to see the man dead.

Duncan could not, however, answer the question of why McCrery wanted to hunt men. He was neither egotistical nor a megalomaniac like the other men who had participated in the Hunt Club. Duncan had always held McCrery high above most of the men he had worked for. He was, to Duncan, an anomaly, and McCrery gave him back the slightest bit of hope in his fellow man. He gave Duncan the hope that a man could reach success without doing it at the expense of others. The question loomed so heavily in his head that he called his friend with the connection to McCrery and arranged to meet McCrery at his office in Denver. Then, he booked a flight out from Bozeman.

The Hunt Club operated without ever using its own name. The only real members were Duncan, Beck, the pilot, and Brett Duncan, and the name "Jack Duncan" was never said out loud. McCrery, along with the other clients, only knew of him as El Cazador, so when Duncan walked into the man's Denver office, the meeting was at first nothing more than a reunion of old hunting partners. The only party to the arranged execution of Ivan the Terrible who had knowledge of all the players was Duncan. McCrery was happy to see Duncan, but he was adept in human relations, and he knew without a doubt there was another motive for Duncan's visit. The exchange of pleasantries and discussion of adventures both men had been on since their last meeting nearly twenty years earlier was brief, and then McCrery ended it.

"You've come a long way to swap stories."

"You're right. I didn't come to trade hunting stories with you today, but it *is* nice to see you."

"Yes, it is. I was sad to hear you got out of the guide business to get into building. That's a tough gig these days."

"Yeah, it is, and indirectly that's why I'm here today."

"How's that?"

Duncan sat deeper into the leather chair in front of McCrery's large, granite-topped rosewood desk. The desk was the only thing in the office besides the exotic game mounts on the wall that showed any of McCrery's incredible wealth; he was, in fact, a very modest man. There would be no beating around the bush; Duncan would get to the point with only a few games, mostly double-checking that Beck had not lied to him about the identity of his client, or was somehow testing him. Duncan had never taken a client he had known previous to the Hunt Club aside from Beck himself, and he had no contact with any of the clients after their hunts. But this man he knew and respected.

"Have you ever heard the name Ivan Libor?" asked Duncan.

Tom McCrery was a large man only slightly over his ideal weight, with a full head of brown hair with only a little gray. He kept in relatively good shape for the many hunts he did all over the planet. When Duncan brought up the slave trader, his shoulders broadened, and he leaned back, pushing slightly away from the beautiful desk. He very honestly answered, "Yes, Jack, I have. Why do you ask?"

"And have you heard of a man known as El Cazador?"

"I don't know anybody by that name personally," McCrery replied, hedging a little from his usual honest and straightforward approach. He did not want to be tied to an underground organization unnecessarily.

"But you've heard the name, and you know James Beck?"

McCrery paused for a moment. "Why're you asking me all these questions?"

"Why do you want to hunt men? And I need to know if you are a friend of Beck's."

Duncan looked McCrery square in the eyes, demanding the answers he was after, and said no more.

McCrery was quiet for a moment, staring back, not angrily but as a way of sizing up the situation. It occurred to him that Jack Duncan must have some knowledge of the Hunt Club.

"Why do you want to know these things?" he said. "After all, *you* came to see me." McCrery paused for a moment while Duncan sat waiting for the answers to his questions. "And no, I wouldn't say Beck and I are friends. Beck has no friends."

"Then how do you know him, and why are you hunting the slave trader?"

"Beck and I have crossed paths a number of times over the years, in business and at Safari Club and Sheep Foundation functions. We're competitors of sorts. He's been trying to buy my businesses for years. Why?"

"Because I don't trust Beck," Duncan replied.

"Nobody trusts Beck, but what's that got to do with me?"

"What if I told you that I'm still guiding, and you're my next client?"

"You're El Cazador, Jack?" McCrery asked with genuine surprise.

"You had no idea?"

"Beck told me that he'd be traveling with me at the beginning of the trip, and that you'd meet up with us and accompany me alone on the actual hunt. He called you El Cazador. Said your anonymity had to be protected."

"He did, did he?" Duncan said, leaning forward toward the desk, relieved that his identity was probably still not compromised. "But why? Why do you want to shoot a man? I've always held you in the highest regard. Why would you want to be involved with a man like Beck?"

"I could ask you the same questions. You're obviously more involved with Beck than me. Why are *you* hunting men?"

"I'm not; I'm only an escort."

"A whore, no less," McCrery said, playing on Duncan's choice of words. "You're doing it for the money, then."

Duncan thought for a moment about the fact that McCrery had all the same questions for him, and that McCrery's questions were perhaps even more justified in being asked. "In the beginning, I did it for the money, but now I'm stuck. Beck won't let me out. I really don't want to be involved."

McCrery sighed and leaned forward and said, "If it makes a difference, I'll tell you."

"It does make a difference, if you don't mind."

"I have a man that has worked for me for many years, maybe thirty, now. He's a Hispanic fellow and moved to Colorado as a child. I'm very fond of him and his family. Several years ago, his sixteen-year-old granddaughter was kidnapped while visiting family in Mexico and forced into prostitution in a brothel."

"In Mexico?"

"No, here in the good ol' US of A."

"Here in Colorado?"

"No, California, which I guess only resembles the United States these days," McCrery said and laughed.

"Brutal."

"They drugged the poor girl, beat her, and sold her to be raped for money, Jack."

Both men felt anger welling inside them.

"By the grace of God, the brothel was raided only a couple of months after her arrival, and she was freed."

"What about the owners?"

"They were released on bail and skipped."

"Back to Mexico?"

"No, they were Americans—two white and one black."

"Free again on the streets?"

"Yes, until my friend and his sons caught up with them. You know how well the Latin hold on to the nearly lost art of revenge."

"Yes. Dead, all three of them?"

"Yeah, all three plus two of the bouncers that worked at the place."

"And they got away with it?"

"Yes, apparently the authorities weren't too upset about losing these less-than-stellar members of the community."

"Let me guess: Ivan the Terrible was behind it."

"Yes. I felt I could help."

"I've always thought of you as a gentleman. I was just surprised when Beck told me your name."

"Then you'll understand why I'm surprised to find you're my guide. Pleased and disappointed at the same time. I expected a man far more sinister than you, Jack."

"If I were a member of our military's special forces being sent around the world by our entirely corrupt government to shoot 'terrorists,' would you use the word 'sinister' to describe El Cazador?"

"You've made a good point."

"Do you think politicians are more psychologically or intellectually adept at making the decision of life or death than honest, hardworking, God-fearing men like us?"

"Absolutely not. In fact, perhaps we're better for the simple fact we take it on as our own risk, with no veil of legal immunity."

"It's either right or wrong, which doesn't always parallel legality."

"Then I guess we've answered all the questions we have of one another and ourselves, haven't we, Jack?"

Jack Duncan only sighed and shook his head. Even though he agreed logically, he was disappointed in all of it. "Yeah, absolutely." There was a short reflective pause, and Duncan added, "Let's not let Beck in on the fact we know each other. I don't trust him."

"That's probably wise. I don't suppose he deserves anybody's trust."

"Nobody's."

"You understand then why I am going after this monster, right, Jack? Not that I actually owe you an explanation."

"I do, but it really isn't your fight."

"Isn't it? No, I guess it isn't," McCrery said, answering his own question. "I'd be lying I guess if I didn't admit that the proposition excites me a bit. It irks me that monsters like this exist, and I have money—plenty of money. I've helped many people with the money. I've made and donated plenty to charities and conservation groups, but this is different. If I can rid this sort of scum from the earth, I'll feel like I have left a mark. I'm just a regular guy, Jack, and I feel like this is justice for the regular guy."

"Let's not forget that this is illegal as well."

"There are so many laws, Jack. Who do they protect? They didn't protect my good friend's family. Honest men are honest; the laws only protect the jobs of the dishonest."

"Lawyers and politicians."

"Yes, and cops, government employees, and the rest."

"You've grown cynical over the last twenty years. I didn't remember this side of you," Duncan said.

"I'm not saying all these people are bad; many are in fact good people. I'm just saying these people who we pay to protect us failed here, and the laws protect their paychecks. When I fail, I get no paycheck. And now you and I are going to do what the laws and their mediocre enforcers can't."

"Good enough," Duncan said, standing up. Tom McCrery stood up and came from behind the large desk, and the two men shook hands. "We'll get him."

"Thank you, Jack. I'm glad you're going with me."

"As far as Beck is concerned, this meeting never took place. I won't see or speak to you again until we meet on the trip."

Duncan turned and walked toward the door, and McCrery followed him for a couple of steps and stopped. When Duncan reached the closed office door, he stopped before opening it and turned back toward McCrery.

"One more thing," Duncan said.

"What's that?"

"I'm curious," Duncan said. "If you wanted to kill Ivan Libor, how or why did you get involved with Beck to do it?"

"That's a good question."

"Why not just get Libor yourself, and leave Beck out of it?"

"Beck and I see each other several times a year at various functions. About a year and a half ago, we were somewhere—I don't remember where, maybe at the Safari Club Convention—and he hinted about it."

"What did he say?"

"I don't know; it's been a while."

"I'm just curious," Duncan said. "I'm not really involved with that end of it. Beck brings the clients. I'm somewhat involved with selecting the targets, and I take care of the logistics. Mostly, I'm just the guide."

"He asked me where I'd traveled recently and what I'd been hunting. Then he told me he'd gone on a manhunt. A hunt for international criminals, drug runners or something, I don't remember exactly."

Duncan nodded.

"He was pretty wound up about it. Said he could get me in a hunt if I wanted."

"What'd you say?"

"No. I said no. I had no interest in shooting a man. I shot plenty of men in Vietnam. I don't need that kind of excitement. I bumped into him again a few months later and he brought it up again. I pretty much just laughed it off. Then, the situation with my friend's granddaughter came to my attention, and I thought of Beck. I called him, and we arranged a meeting."

"I see," Duncan said.

"After meeting with Beck, I could see he had the infrastructure in place to pull it off. The planes, the pilots, you. I figured it would take all of it to catch up with a criminal who circles the world on a yacht."

"Only you thought I'd be an ex-Seal or CIA guy, didn't ya?"

"Yeah, but I'm good with you."

"No disrespect to our military, but I don't think I'm wired to work for our government," Duncan said. "Working with Beck is bad enough."

"Another reason why I like you," McCrery said and smiled. "And another thing Beck brings to the table is enough money and power to buy his way out of a jam."

"That he does; I was just curious. Thanks," Duncan said and turned back to the door and let himself out.

Duncan left Tom McCrery's office satisfied with their meeting. This would be his fifth mission, and while he desperately wanted out, he felt good about what they were doing. He respected McCrery a great deal, and the personal element to this trip pleased him and injected an energy that previous trips had lacked. He got into a cab and returned to the Denver airport.

Sitting in the lounge in the commuter concourse waiting for his flight back to Bozeman, Duncan drank a little bourbon and watched the people walking through the airport. He wondered about their lives, which made his seem all the more complicated.

Duncan landed in Bozeman in the early evening and drove back to the ranch. There was enough daylight left to allow him to see the progress on the home as he drove in. His crew was making incredible time, and in his one-day absence, his men had finished sheathing the exterior walls and were preparing to start on the roof. Barring an unforeseeable holdup, they would be dried in and finishing the interior by Halloween, meeting his goal and making it easier for him to leave on his next trip with Tom McCrery.

As Duncan drove up the long, dusty road of the bench that took him into the ranch, he could see his daughter riding barrels in the corral with her mother. They were laughing, their blonde ponytails hanging out from under their straw cowboy hats, and the horses were slightly lathered up from being ridden hard in the last of the summer heat. He could see Coulter with Bergstrom up the small coulee behind the ranch one hundred yards from the last outbuilding. They were shooting targets with a .22 rifle. Duncan felt momentarily at ease as he looked around, pleased by what he saw.

He parked his pickup at the Bergstroms' house and did not bother to walk over to his home site. He'd already gotten an update from his men and had the pragmatic mind to know what was done was done, and he was at a stage where he could not do much without his men. Looking at the jobsite would not get any more done for the day, so he would look in the morning. He was more interested in his family, so he walked out behind the old house to the corral where the girls were riding. When he reached the corral, he stood on the bottom rail of the wood fence. When the girls noticed him watching, Erica whispered to Avery. Duncan couldn't hear her words but he could read her lips, even from the side. He loved her lips.

"Show Daddy whatcha got!"

Avery reined the horse around in front of the open gate, which was the starting point when they practiced. The horse was anxious, but she held him back and rode him in a large circle once and then again a second time. Coming out of the second circle, she let him have his head. As they lined out for the first barrel, she heeled the short, blunt spurs into the big quarter horse. Her young legs slapped at the bay horse's flanks in rhythm with his strides, and they rounded the first barrel with a flawless tight turn. They rocked the second barrel and raced for the third. She made it around the third barrel perfectly, and the horse exploded from the turn, lunging into the race to the finish. Duncan loved watching them ride.

Avery turned the horse hard at the corral fence in front of Duncan and came back around to him and reined the horse to a stop. Duncan let go of the fence rail he was standing on and clapped for her.

"You're starting to look like your mom," he said to her.

"In a few years, she'll be better than I ever was," Erica said to them both.

"If she works at it," Duncan said and stepped off the fence. He started a four-wheeler with an arena drag tool attached to the back and entered the corral through the open gate. He dragged the corral, smoothing out their racing surface. He always thought of their safety and that of the horses. While he loved the racing, he had seen enough horse wrecks to make him nervous for his girls. He parked the four-wheeler and then walked out past the barn and up to the open end of the coulee, where Bergstrom and Coulter were shooting.

The grandfather and grandson stood next to one another at a table Duncan had built with an old barn board that rested on two pilasters of stacked granite stones ranging in size between a baseball and a bowling ball. The rocks were squared off naturally and stacked into a tight weave. The old board fit into the weave of the stones, which held it up on either end, and the dry stack continued up on top of and above the surface of the board for roughly a foot. The black granite rocks tapered at the top, and smaller stones and broken slivers of granite were wedged under the board and into crevasses in the bigger rocks to level the board and lock it into its place in the pilasters. A couple of pistols rested on the table, and the boy stood behind it shooting a lever-action .22 rifle while Bergstrom stood next to him loading a clip for another rifle that rested on the table between him and Coulter.

The little rifle made a snapping crack that echoed back at them off the walls of the long canyon they shot up. With each report of the gun, Duncan could see cans jump up into the air off a dirt berm in front of the boy.

"Good shootin," Duncan said as he walked up to the two at the table.

"Yeah, Dad, I shoot low under the cans. Makes 'em jump up into the air. It's cooler than just puttin' holes in them."

"Grandpa teach you that trick?" Duncan asked and looked at Bergstrom, who was smiling.

"Yep," Coulter said.

"It's a good one."

"Can I shoot one of your big guns, Dad?" Coulter asked.

"Might as well check one. Make sure it's on in case we get a chance to hunt this fall."

The boy smiled, excited at the opportunity.

"Why don't you bring up my .270? That'd be a good gun for you to hunt with."

"All right," the boy said and jumped on the four-wheeler to ride to the house to get the rifle.

"Grab a box of shells and a big target, too," Duncan said to the boy as he raced off. Then he turned back to his father-in-law.

"So you met with the client for your next trip?" Bergstrom asked.

"Yes, he's a good man. I guided him almost twenty years ago in Canada."

"So you already know him?" Bergstrom asked. His curiosity was growing, but he knew better than to ask the client's identity.

"Kind of, but that's just a coincidence."

"Life is just a coincidence."

"You think life all boils down to fate?"

"I think fate is the rope that entangles humans in relationships."

Duncan looked at Bergstrom as though he were seeing him for the first time. "I've always thought of you as too pragmatic for fate."

"Did you choose to be born without a father?" Bergstrom asked.

"No."

"Of course not; fate stole him from you before you hit the ground. I had no more choice in the matter of being born into this ranch. It was purely fate. And it was fate that I met Erica's mother. Barb walked into our law office in Helena to apply for an administrative position, and I was so enamored with her I could hardly interview her."

Bergstrom paused for a moment, looking to the Gravelly Range, but Duncan knew he was watching reruns of his life in his head.

"She was so beautiful," he said and smiled. "Where do you think Erica gets it?"

"So you hired her at your law office—that's how you met?"

"No, the partners didn't want her for some reason, I don't remember why. So I looked at her résumé and figured out where she lived. I jogged by her house every morning for a month until I bumped into her leaving. I acted as though it were an accident and asked her to coffee. It worked."

"So it wasn't fate that got you together—it was that you stalked her for a month," Duncan said and laughed.

"It was fate that brought her into my office to steal my heart," he replied with a smug look. "Just like you and Erica. Fate. Neither one of you chose to fall in love, it just happened."

"I guess," Duncan said reluctantly.

"She still loves you. She can't help it. And you're no different. But at the moment, she's having a hard time living with you and your lifestyle."

Duncan looked at the ground and rolled a rock around in the dust with the tip of his boot. He felt as though he'd failed them all: Erica, Bergstrom, his kids, and himself. He struggled in his head with how to fix it.

"It's no different with you and Beck. It was fate that paired you on that first sheep hunt in Mexico that got you into this tangled mess."

"I need fate to get me out of it," Duncan said, looking up at his father-in-law. "I want out of this so bad."

Bergstrom shook his head. He looked at Duncan, and he could see the strain in his eyes. There was a short pause. Then Bergstrom said, "The fault, dear Jack, is not in our stars, but in ourselves, that we are underlings."

Duncan pulled back for a moment and thought about the line from Shakespeare. He knew Julius Caesar. And he knew how the story ended.

After a long moment of silence, Duncan said, "First you sell me on fate, and now this."

"Fate brought you and Beck together, but it's a conscious decision to act that will get you out of the mess."

"I don't know what to do."

"You mean you haven't figured out how to get out without getting your hands dirty."

"What do you think I should do?"

"I think if you're finally wise enough to ask what I think, you have the wisdom to answer your own question," Bergstrom said and set the rifle he'd reloaded for Coulter on the plank table.

"I'm sick of it all: the killing, Beck, the fear of getting caught, and the pressure to get out. The lack of control, I guess. I can't just put a closed sign on the door."

"Hmm," Bergstrom said and rubbed his clean-shaven chin.

"It keeps me up at night. I see their faces sometimes, and then I can't go back to sleep 'cause my brain won't shut off. I just keep going over it all in my head."

"You know my brother Dan, right?"

"Yes, I like Dan."

"You know Dan was in Vietnam, right?"

"That's what Erica told me."

"He was a ranger and was in some serious firefights. Some real shit," Bergstrom said and paused for a moment. "He shot a twelve-year-old Vietnamese girl."

"What?"

"Yeah, he and another fella. The girl tried to run into the middle of a dozen or so unsuspecting army rangers with a picnic basket full of bombs."

"A twelve-year-old suicide bomber?"

"Yeah, horrific, huh?"

"Beyond words."

"Dan ordered the girl to stop—he knows some Vietnamese—but she kept comin'. Then she started to run. The fella next to him was a buddy. I forget the guy's name, but he was from Wyoming, so they had a lot in common. There were two other men in position to shoot, but they couldn't pull the trigger. When she didn't stop, Dan and his buddy lit her up. He told me the story once, and we've never spoken about it again. He said there's nothing so horrifyingly unnatural as the sight of a twelve-year-old girl riddled with bullet holes. The basket was full of explosives and they saved at least ten of their buddies, but the army doesn't hand out medals for shooting women and children. All they got was the lasting image of the girl's broken and mangled body."

"That's terrible. Poor Dan."

"It was hard for him to live with."

"I'm sure."

"He told me that after a couple of years he put it away in his head. He decided he didn't kill the girl; he saved his buddies. It was fate, and he did the best he could do with what fate gave him. And he's OK now."

"What about his buddy from Wyoming?"

"Dan tried to help him. Went down there a lot for a number of years. Even had him up to his home in Billings, where he put him to work, but the poor guy couldn't deal with it. He drank too much and then he drank more, and about ten years after the war ended, Dan got a call from the fella's brother. Said they found him hanging from a noose in the barn on their family ranch."

"Brutal."

"He saddled his favorite horse, threw the noose over a rafter in the barn, put the noose around his own neck, and kicked the horse out from under himself. The horse was standing next to him when they found him."

The men heard the four-wheeler start up and looked toward the house, knowing Coulter was on his way back. Then they looked back at each other, and Bergstrom said, "You have to stop Beck before he takes Rome." Duncan just looked at him. "Then you have to put it away in your own secret place, and get on with your life. Get on with raising your family."

Bergstrom turned toward the house and toward Coulter, who had just pulled up on the four-wheeler.

"Where ya goin', Grandpa?" Coulter asked as he climbed off the machine.

"I've got some work to do, so your dad's gonna shoot with you for a while."

"You want to take the four-wheeler?" the boy offered.

"No, I need the walk."

Duncan watched Bergstrom for a moment as he walked back toward the house. He shuffled his feet a little as he went, and at one point he took the old gray Stetson off, pushed his hair back with his hand, and then put the hat back on his head. Duncan turned and looked up the draw and beyond the eyebrow of the little coulee where they were shooting. He looked at the Gravelly Range and then north to the Tobacco Roots, where he could see the front edge of an approaching storm that would bring the first snows to the high country. He knew that when the storm passed it would take the warm air with it, and the first freeze would touch off the aspen into their golden autumn colors, signaling the beginning of the end of summer.

EIGHT

F all was Jack Duncan's time. It was the time when he was most alive and most productive, and he loved this time of year so much he chased it. However, this fall was slipping away from him. The last week of October came far too soon, arriving at the incredible speed with which Duncan was beginning to realize life got away. It was that dead time of autumn when the aspens and cottonwoods were stripped to the bare skeletal remains of the brilliant golden foliage they had possessed only a few weeks earlier. A little snow was showing on the north slopes of the highest peaks and would be there from then until spring. The valley grasses had turned a wilted brown, bitten by the freezing mornings and waiting for the cleansing winter snow, which would hide their austere testament to the bleak end of summer.

Duncan had not made his usual trip into the mountains with Bergstrom and whichever gentlemen were lucky enough to be invited to chase elk with the two modern mountain men. He was hoping to hunt with his boy later in November, depending on how his trip with McCrery went. He was simply too busy building and preparing, if nothing more than mentally, for the trip to eliminate Ivan Libor and for getting away from the Hunt Club. It was the last week of

October. The house was dried in on the exterior, and the crew had moved indoors and was finishing the interior when the call came from Brett letting Duncan know that Ivan the Terrible was to be in port for a shot.

Duncan left his family at the ranch with both Erica and Avery in tears. His son had disappointment in his eyes, but he was too proud to cry at his age. Erica had never cried before when he left, but she knew now what he was doing, and his little girl teared up every time he left for more than a day or two. Bergstrom shook his hand with a reassuring nod and said nothing.

Duncan had his crew lined out to finish the home, and the work would continue in his absence. He boarded a commercial flight in Bozeman and got a connection in Colorado to Dallas. There, one of the resident employees of Beck's Texas ranches picked him up in a white Hummer and delivered him to the ranch where Beck and McCrery were waiting.

Duncan opened the front door without knocking and passed through a grand entrance rising three stories high before reaching the ceiling. The main floor of the house was a combination of cool terra-cotta Mexican tile and matching patina-acid-stained concrete. There were zebra and gemsbok rugs on the floor between the large leather sectional sofas, one covered by the tanned hide of a kudu and the other by the tanned hide of an axis deer taken on the ranch grounds. The walls were adorned with trophy mounts, mostly from Africa, but on one wall, perched on a faux rock outcropping, stood the mounted desert sheep he and Beck had taken the day they were accosted by the three Mexicans—the day when the Hunt Club had truly begun.

Every time Duncan came to the Texas ranch, he was overwhelmed by the gaudiness of the place. He continued through the house, passing the kitchen where a chef and two helpers were preparing a feast of several varieties of game with vegetables from the ranch garden. The scene gave the place a lodge-like atmosphere, a warm feeling Duncan kept in his memory from past trips around the globe but had never felt in Beck's presence.

Duncan knew the men would be on the back lanai. It was partially covered for shade and looked out over a spectacular stone pool with a waterfall and the green, manicured grounds that framed the estate from the arid hill country surrounding it. It was an oasis of sorts. He walked through the wood-and-glass French doors, which were open, and saw Beck and McCrery sitting at a table holding cocktail glasses that were sweating from the ice melting in them against the hot Texas evening. Nearby at another table were two other men, who looked to be in their early thirties and whom Duncan did not recognize. Neither of them held a cocktail glass. Beck and McCrery stood while the other two men remained seated.

"You must be Tom McCrery," Duncan said, extending a hand.

"It's a pleasure to meet you. I've heard so much about you."

"Jack, good to see you," Beck said, shaking Duncan's hand after McCrery.

"Who are these other two gentlemen, James?" Duncan asked, nodding in the direction of the other two men sitting at another patio table somewhat removed from the conversation.

"They're friends of mine, Jack, joining us for a drink."

The two men rose, and Beck introduced them. All shook hands, and the two new men went back to their drinkless table.

Duncan sat at the table glaring at Beck. There was an awkward silence. There had never been anybody else present at these meetings in the past except the clients and the pilot, who was Duncan's personal friend. The deviation angered Duncan, and Beck sensed it. The two strange men wore light over-jackets, which Duncan knew concealed handguns, and they had the intent look of men who were on duty. They were no doubt bodyguards, and Duncan wondered whom they were protecting Beck from.

"Let's go for a ride and look at the ranch, shall we?" asked Beck, who was rising from his patio chair.

Beck, Duncan, and McCrery loaded into a four-seater Polaris Ranger, and the two bodyguards followed them in a jeep. Now that the three were alone, Beck confessed that the two men were bodyguards, and that he'd had some threats made against his life, but he went into no further detail.

"If they go on this trip, I stay home," Duncan demanded the instant the last word of explanation rolled off Beck's lips.

Beck agreed, and the three discussed plans for the trip and details of their engagement. Ivan Libor lived on a one-hundred-and-thirty-foot yacht, and while the home port written across its transom was Seattle, Washington, the ship rarely spent time in Elliott Bay. Libor lived primarily on the ship, moving from one port to another and transporting his human contraband. He never spent too much time in any one location. It was part of the overall plan, and while the stolen young ladies had it relatively easy on the yacht other than perhaps satisfying Libor's own personal desires, they were made to look like—and documented as though they were—passengers or part of the crew. This arrangement was perfect cover for the rare occasion on which any sort of authorities inspected the vessel.

Libor's living arrangement made the task of hunting this criminal a bit of a challenge: the only possible opportunity for a shot would be while he was in port picking up or delivering contraband or sup-plies. The only predictable way to catch him in port was by knowing when he was delivering his hostages to a buyer, and Brett's people had obtained that knowledge. Libor had purchased or stolen a load of girls in El Salvador, and he was ready to bring them up the coast in his decadent ship to deliver them in Acapulco, from where they would be sent to brothels in Guadalajara and Mexico City. The would-be purchasers included a high-ranking police officer from Mexico City and a political figure.

Under aliases, Duncan and McCrery would check into a hotel room with a view overlooking the harbor and bay where the mod-ern-day slave ship would moor or dock. They would use the same modus operandi that had worked for them in the past: shooting from the back of the room, hidden from sight, and using a suppressor to quiet the report of the rifle, which would already be muffled by the room. There would only be one shot, and they would leave the room immediately after firing it. They traveled with one small carry-on bag. Duncan would carry a second rifle in his bag and a Beretta .9mm with a silencer, and McCrery would have a rifle and a silenced .9mm as well. It promised to go as smoothly as their previous operations had, and in the end, the world would be rid of one more monster.

After touring the grounds, the men returned to the ranch home, where they were served a spectacular meal of axis deer medallions grilled with a sweetened chili-lime marinade made from limes off the trees of the well-manicured grounds. There were also whitetail venison loin chops crusted in pecans, fresh baby yellow squash, bourbon mashed sweet potatoes, salad, pecan pie, and ample supplies of French Bordeaux to wash it all down. The two older men traded stories while the bodyguards seemed to show what Duncan thought was a little too much interest in him. Duncan sat mostly quiet, thinking of something his father-in-law had told him as a boy: "There's a real good reason why God gave us the ability to shut our mouths but not our ears."

Duncan had only one glass of wine with the meal, which was difficult because the wine was wonderful and a meal like this deserved it, but he felt uneasy. Duncan was always a little nervous and uneasy on these trips, which made it hard to tell if this one really was different. Either way, he would not dull his senses with alcohol.

The next morning, they woke with the sun and enjoyed a leisurely breakfast on the patio, which was already warming. It was a contrast to the weather back home, where Erica was probably driving the kids to school on Halloween in a snowstorm. It was hard for Duncan to enjoy the sunshine. After breakfast, the men went for a short quail hunt while they waited for Duncan's pilot friend to arrive. He did so around lunchtime, when he landed on the airstrip located on the ranch. They ate a quick lunch of leftovers from the previous night's dinner, and then they left for the Dallas/Fort Worth Airport and Beck's Gulfstream.

Beck had a private room in the back of his plane with a bed and lounge area, and he typically remained there during the flights. This left Duncan alone with the flight staff and clients, which was an arrangement he actually preferred. This flight was no different, until Beck came into the general seating area and asked Duncan to join him in the back. When Duncan was seated in one of the lounge seats, Beck informed him that he had picked the next target. Duncan felt his face flush with anger. They had not even finished this operation, and Beck was already pushing for another. But Beck assured him that this target would be of great interest to him, as it was an old friend of his. For a moment, Duncan wondered whom he meant, but he realized quickly the only person Beck could be referring to.

"In fact, Jack, he's an old friend of both of ours," he said.

"Who're you talking about, James?" Duncan said, although he knew already the name that he was going to hear when Beck's response came.

"Your sheep-hunting friend in Baja, Mr. Vasquez."

Duncan sat speechless for several seconds, which felt like an eternity. He wanted to force the silence on Beck and make him speak first, but he could not wait. He had not spoken to Joaquin Vasquez in nearly twenty years, but he would not help take part in killing him, nor did he believe he was guilty of any sort of crimes. At least nothing that would put him on the Hunt Club's list.

"I won't be a part of that."

"I was afraid you'd say that, Jack. Don't be so naive! He tried to kill you. He sent those Mexicans up the mountain to kill you."

"No, he didn't! You don't know that, goddamn it."

"I do know it; I know it for sure. He'd had enough of you screwing his daughter. He had other plans for her, Jack. He had a husband picked for her. You just don't understand decisions made at this level. You don't understand that there was a marriage that made a better business alignment for Señor Vasquez—and you were getting in the way."

"Bullshit. I don't believe it, and I won't do it."

"I think you'd better let it soak in, Jack. Sleep on it, and we'll talk about it tomorrow."

"What do you say he did to deserve to be shot?"

"He's running drugs. He's just a regular Mexican drug runner. He uses his charter boats—those big fishing yachts—to move drugs up and down the coast, even into the States."

Beck handed Duncan a folder containing information on Vasquez and his alleged crimes against humanity, but this packet had been compiled entirely by Beck or his people.

"Whatever, Beck," Duncan said angrily. "When I knew him, he didn't even step on those boats but twice a year for the marlin tournaments in Cabo and Loreto, and the one year he won it, he donated the prize to a charity of his daughter's choice."

"Don't be a fool, Jack. Think about it."

"I'd like you to find a different target," Duncan added as he stood and returned to McCrery in the other section of the plane. He knew it was best to go along with Beck for now, and he *was* going to think about Beck's plan: he would think about how to stop it, as he was fairly confident Vasquez was not involved with any drug business.

They landed in Guatemala City that evening shortly after dark. The men returned to Brett's estate in the hills on the edge of the capital city, where they ate dinner and retired early after the meal. They would be on their way to Acapulco in the morning. Beck would typically have stayed behind with Brett to monitor the operation, but this time, he would be returning to the States in the morning, as he said he had business to attend to. This change did not bother any of the men involved, as Beck really was not needed during the operation itself, and his absence would be a pleasantly welcome change. He assured the group he would be in constant contact with them; they all had radio equipment and a remedial code system as well as cell phones.

In the morning, Duncan and McCrery left for Puerto Quetzal, where they boarded a forty-five-foot Bertram fishing yacht owned by Brett's family. They started up the coast for Acapulco under the guise of being big game fishermen. They were two days ahead of the slave ship, which was sailing from a port about one hundred miles to the south. The trip would take them about two and a half days. It was pleasant: the Pacific was calm, and they trolled tuna feathers behind the boat in the warm blue water, occasionally hooking dorado, which they ate on the way. The captain, who was a Mexican national and a close member of Brett's family, would deviate his course slightly if birds or flotsam were spotted to increase the odds of hooking fish, but the goal of staying well ahead of Libor's slave ship was never compromised. Once, the captain spotted a sailfish leaping into the air. Duncan changed the rigging slightly, and they hooked the fish for McCrery to land. Despite taking nearly every big game animal of significance on the planet, he had never landed a billfish.

The large sail took the trolled mackerel, and McCrery fought it to the boat with the captain doing no more than idling the engines for twenty minutes to land the fish and then taking some photos. Other than the single sailfish, they avoided hooking any large billfish. Unlike the dorado, the billfish could not be horsed to the boat without slowing their progress. They arrived in Acapulco in midmorning on the third day of travel. The men felt somewhat refreshed by their fishing cruise, but they were anxious to get on with their order of business.

The captain moored the Bertram in a portion of the bay where the larger ships and yachts moored so they could see the slave ship when it came in. Duncan and McCrery took the inflatable Zodiac dinghy to shore and spent the day surveying the strip on the waterfront, looking for shooting positions and wandering through hotels, getting a feel for how it would all go down.

One hotel in particular caught Duncan's attention for the odd fact that it had a waterslide that dropped eight stories from the top floor. Late in the evening of the next day, the large yacht came in and anchored a few hundred yards from the Bertram. This gave the men a good look at the boat, but not at the people on board. The only real good shot opportunity would come when the slave trader boarded the shore boat, a twenty-one-foot Boston Whaler. There would be a few moments during boarding before the hydraulic sling hoist lowered the boat to the water when the target would be stationary and in plain view. The Alta Vista Hotel, with its waterslide from the eighth floor, would have a perfect angle from which to view the Boston Whaler in the sling.

Duncan called the hotel and made a reservation for three nights starting with that night. The captain ran the men to shore, where they were met by one of Brett's men. The man had been flown in by Duncan's pilot to a private dirt airstrip on an *estancia* in a mountain valley east of the city. The Guatemalan handed the men duffels containing rifles, spotting scopes, range finders, first aid kits, and a small amount of bivouac gear should things go badly and they need to make a run for it.

The Guatemalan was in a Honda when they met, and he would also be their driver after the shot was fired. He would be waiting a block from the hotel rather than right in front. Duncan and McCrery would slip out of the hotel with the carry-on bags that contained the equipment, including the guns. Brett had taken care of the paperwork for all the guns. The paperwork listed the registered owners as guests of a hunting lodge two hours away. This was in case they were stopped with the weapons, in which case they would say they had been separated from their guide in Acapulco. Beck had no knowledge of this portion of the plan, but this wasn't unusual; Duncan and Brett always kept a certain number of details from him for their own protection.

Duncan and McCrery checked into the hotel under their aliases. They had selected the eighth-floor room on the end that was nearest the entrance to the waterslide. They settled in and found the yacht with night-vision binoculars. They also pinpointed the Boston Whaler and began to position the room. They made a shooting bench out of a desk for the shot, which at twelve hundred yards would be the longest any of Duncan's clients had ever made. It was a shot Duncan would not have wanted to make, but it would be a cinch for McCrery, who had a two-thousand-yard range on one of his ranches, where he practiced regularly with a half-dozen different rifles, including the same model .338 Winchester he would be shooting from the hotel. They had measured the wind from the yacht for two evenings to learn its direction: downslope at that time of year, with no onshore flow. They took readings from several hotels, including the Alta Vista, to compare direction and speed and to correlate them with the target location and the computer-reported wind conditions. They fortified the shooting bench they'd built from the desk with pillows and one small bag of sand until McCrery felt he could not miss.

The captain would stay in the yacht and watch from the wheelhouse and bridge, and then he would call them when he saw movement. He had repositioned his mooring in the night so he could see into the aft deck of the large yacht, where the Boston Whaler was hanging in the sling. The captain would call the shooters in the hotel room when he saw the crew ready the shore boat if they had not seen it already. The information they had was that Libor would be leaving the ship for a meeting with the buyers of a load of teenage girls on the boat the following evening at about five o'clock. They settled in to wait.

The two men were as comfortable as two honest men could be in a foreign country with hellish prisons while doing something completely moral yet completely illegal. At that point in time, the weight of taking Libor's life did not press on them at all; they only felt the pressure to save their own lives once the shot or shots were fired.

The night was warm and humid, and Duncan purchased a bucket of Coronas on ice. They ate shrimp in their room while drinking the beer and began their wait.

Duncan's cell phone rang. It was Beck on the other end, which promised to ruin what was turning into a pleasant evening.

"Where are you staying?" Beck asked.

"The Alta Vista," Duncan replied and then had the sinking thought he should have lied.

"Will that work for the shot?"

"Probably. Won't know for sure till the yacht anchors."

"I'm making arrangements for the next hunt."

Duncan listened but said nothing.

"I made a reservation at the hacienda in Baja to hunt sheep."

"I told you I wanted a different target."

"Too late. The wheels are already in motion," came the words over Duncan's cell phone, which he'd switched to the speaker setting so McCrery could listen in. "I'm as excited to harvest a ram as I am to harvest your friend."

Duncan thought it was strange that Beck referred to Vasquez as "your friend," as he hadn't seen the man in almost twenty years.

"I've got to go," Duncan said.

"I think I'll use a black powder rifle for this hunt. Make it a challenge."

"Whatever," Duncan said and then ended the call. He'd agreed with Beck in words, but there was anger and frustration written clearly across his face.

"He's a piece of work, isn't he?" McCrery said from across the hotel room after he saw the frustration in Duncan's eyes.

"He's no better than any of the sons of bitches we've killed. He's one of them—just slightly more polished."

"I know, Jack, I know."

"Then why're you friends with him, Tom?"

"Who said we're friends? It's like that old saying:'Hold your friends close and your enemies closer.' He's been trying to take my businesses for years; I just don't let him."

"But now he'll have this to hold over you."

"It's a wash. I have the same over him; he wouldn't turn me in. He might kill me, but he wouldn't turn me in to any authorities. He thinks the law is for common folks like you and me. Everybody but him, really."

Tom McCrery's words touched off a chain of thoughts in Duncan's head that snowballed into the darkness of the unknown. Duncan was nothing more to Beck than a servant—a commoner who might use the law against him—and the only way for Beck to leave the slate clean was to eliminate him. McCrery was a bonus. With him gone, Beck had a better shot at taking his businesses. It was nothing more than a twisted game for Beck—all of it.

"He asked where we're staying," Duncan said.

The two men sat in the hotel room staring at each other, and the thought occurred to each of them that this could be a trap.

"What do you think? Is it a setup?" McCrery asked.

"I think we'd better be ready."

Duncan texted Brett: *Heads up. Think Beck may be double-crossing us.*

OK. Keep in touch, was Brett's reply.

Duncan and McCrery began to fear that Beck was arranging something to go wrong, so Duncan had the captain of the Bertram come ashore and check into the room next door. Duncan paid a Mexican woman and her two kids to pose as the man's family for cover while he checked in at the front desk. When this was done, the captain went up to the room, opened it, left the keys, and returned to the yacht while Duncan and McCrery moved in. Next, they hid a tiny camera in a tropical plant in the hallway. The camera was positioned to catch the door to their first room as well as the door of the room next to it, which they had relocated to. The tiny camera delivered a real-time feed wirelessly to a computer in the room with Duncan. All they could do was wait and watch.

The two men watched the aft deck of the slave trader's yacht while at the same time watching the computer screen, but all was quiet. The sockets of their eyes became bruised from the binoculars that were constantly being pressed against them, and except for an occasional tourist passing down the hall, the video feed on the computer screen remained empty. The hours went by slowly, the sun eventually set, and they switched to their night-vision optics.

After many uneventful hours, Duncan saw something.

"Did you see that?" he said to McCrery, who was looking more at the computer screen than at the bay where the boats sat on anchor.

"See what?"

"A light from the yacht. Like a spotlight, maybe."

McCrery got up from his chair at the table where the computer rested and picked up his regular binoculars. He stayed behind the table, however, so movement on the screen could still grab his attention away from the binoculars.

"There it is again!" Duncan said as the light bounced around the blackened water of the bay, lighting up one boat and then another and then another. The two watched as the beam of light coming from the yacht danced its way around the moored boats until it landed on their Bertram, and then moved on.

"That was our boat," Duncan said.

"I know."

"Did they linger on it?"

"I don't know. Couldn't tell for sure."

"Probably just seemed like it 'cause it's our boat."

"Maybe."

The light was now shining out the other side of the yacht, and they couldn't see its beam, but occasionally they could see a boat visible from their angle spotlighted by the light coming from the slave trader's yacht. Again, the light worked around to their side, and again it fell on their Bertram.

"It lingered on our boat, didn't it?" Duncan said.

"I think so, but still can't say for sure."

"I think we've got to get the boat outta here."

"Yeah, we've got the plane waiting."

Duncan called his cousin from a cell phone secure from Beck, and they conferenced the captain of the yacht on.

"Did you see the lights on you?" Duncan asked the captain over the phone.

"Yes, a spotlight," he said in heavily accented English. "They seemed to be looking at boats around them."

"Yes, they looked at yours twice."

"But they looked at others, too."

"I still think you should pull anchor and head back toward Puerto Quetzal," Duncan said.

"I think it's a good call," Brett added.

The captain agreed.

"Wait a couple of hours before you go," Duncan said. "Just so it's not obvious."

"OK."

"If anything approaches, we'll take them out."

"OK."

"If you're sure nobody is following you, linger for a day or two offshore around the border."

The shooters waited and watched for the target or for any movement from the yacht, but nothing happened. A couple of hours passed, and the Bertram slipped out without turning on its running lights for the first few hundred yards toward the open ocean. They watched the boat until it disappeared, swallowed by the darkened nighttime ocean.

After a sleepless night and a long day waiting for the slave trader to present a shot while boarding the Boston Whaler to come to shore, neither Duncan nor McCrery was surprised when the camera footage streaming on their computer screen revealed three men at their original hotel room's door. The air was heavy. It was hot and humid and hard to breathe in, despite the salty sweetness of the ocean lingering in it. The difficulty came from the pressure on the chest that Duncan and McCrery felt from the anxiety of what was about to happen. Nobody wanted to go to a Mexican jail, and if Beck had blown their anonymity, there was no way to know who would be after them. Duncan and McCrery were ready for the trap; over the previous twenty-four hours, they had come to expect it. They had considered abandoning the mission, but that inexplicable urge to finish things that lived inside of men like them compelled them to stay.

The three men who showed up at their door while they watched the computer screen were obviously not with the welcome wagon: one wore a suit and tie while the other two wore *federali* uniforms. All three men had pistols drawn and stood in a stack outside the door, with the dapper man in the back. One of the three men knocked and listened for noise inside the room, and then knocked again as Duncan and McCrery watched on the computer screen from the adjacent room. Duncan wondered if they should have stepped into the doorway as the three Mexicans ransacked the room for clues of the two gringos' business and shot the intruders dead, but he did not do it. He figured it would only add complications to their predicament, so he just hoped they would go away instead.

There was no sign of Ivan Libor, and now that the federalis were searching the room they'd checked into, Duncan and McCrery knew without a doubt they had been double-crossed.

Duncan was sure the lobby was being watched, so they broke the rifles and other equipment down, packed it all into their duffels, stepped out onto the lanai, and walked to the waterslide. With the .9mm Berettas tucked into the waistlines of their quick-dry pants and covered by long Hawaiian shirts, the two very grown men climbed into the tube of the waterslide.

They hit the pool below, holding their bags over their heads to keep the gear dry and checking immediately to make sure the pistols hadn't come loose. They stood up in the water and waded to the edge of the not-too-deep swimming pool, only attracting the surprise of a few kids and onlookers.

"We had to try it once," Duncan said, grinning slyly at a pretty, young American-looking mother whose elementary-school-age children were playing in the water.

"That's funny," the pretty woman said with a surprised tone.

They walked up the steps out of the pool and stepped off the terraced landscaping that the hotel was built upon, slightly above the beach. It was nearly dark, and Duncan wondered what would happen next. Their driver should be waiting for them in the burgundy Honda Accord a few blocks down the street from their hotel. Duncan never left the car and driver too close to the location they shot from. He wondered over and over in his head if they should have shot the man in the suit and the other two in the sloppy local official uniforms. McCrery followed him silently, not altogether nervous about their situation but feeling the false sense of security that comes over a man who has a guide.

It was nearly dark, and lights were twinkling down the beach. There were people strolling along and enjoying the evening, and it was a challenge for the two men to walk calmly, as though they were no more than tourists enjoying the tropical evening. After walking for what Duncan figured was a block or so, he turned up toward the hotels and the road that fronted them. They could see the Honda parked on the curb, and Duncan felt a sense of relief. He knew his pilot friend would be waiting a short drive from the private airstrip, and that they would soon be back in Guatemala, safe with his cousin, or at least safe until they figured out what to do about Beck.

The driver greeted them in Spanish with a simple instruction: "Get in!"

Both men put their packs in the backseat. Duncan sat in the back next to the packs and McCrery sat in the front next to the driver. They eased out into the light traffic and started down the Avenida Costera Miguel Alemán. Duncan watched the mirrors to see if anyone was following them, but the gathering darkness and the headlights made it difficult to tell. They traveled several blocks and started to turn away from the bay, but then the driver turned again as though they were headed south. Duncan estimated that they should have been heading in more of a northerly direction and inland on the highway toward Amatillo and La Concepción, where they were to meet Duncan's pilot and fly out of the private airstrip. Duncan could sense they were going the wrong way, and the GPS on his phone confirmed his instinct when he discreetly checked it. They continued out of the city, and though Duncan was beginning to get a bad feeling, he decided he would rather get out of town and deal with things in the woods than in the city.

In the meantime, he began to wonder if the driver was really the same man who had met them when they checked into the hotel. It was the same car, but he wasn't sure about the driver, so he texted his cousin his doubts, keeping his phone near his lap.

We're in the car but think driver is an imposter, Duncan texted.

I'll call driver for mission password, Brett replied.

A word was chosen for each mission as a pass code, known only by the parties involved, to identify imposters in the event of kidnapping or some other breach of their secret circle. The most inner circle, which did not include Beck.

Seconds later, the driver's cell phone rang. "Quién es?" he said, and then promptly hung up.

Imposter. Driver hung up when asked for password, Brett texted Duncan.

Thx, Duncan replied.

Duncan knew now their driver was a kidnapper. He knew that they were being taken somewhere they didn't want to go and that their original driver had been abducted and likely murdered, so he texted his pilot, who was waiting at the private dirt airstrip near La Concepción.

Are you well?

I'm fine. Why?

Return home immediately!!!!

Without you?

Yes. We have been compromised. Take off now!

OK.

There was no way to know at this point how much of the Hunt Club Beck had betrayed. Brett had always gone by an alias in Beck's presence, but who knew how much research Beck had done? If he knew Brett's true identity, it would be easy to ferret out his in-laws, who were deeply involved with the operation. There was just no way to know what, where, or who was safe.

Duncan texted the captain of the yacht.

Mission compromised.

What about you?

We are good. Stay within 30 miles of shore. Head south and wait near border.

OK.

Will be in touch for a possible pickup.

K.

Then Duncan turned his attentions to the problem at hand: technically, they had been abducted. Duncan held his phone low behind the back of McCrery's seat so their assailant could not see that he was using it. Duncan had no way to convey the information about their fraudulent driver to McCrery. He would just have to act. He also knew that McCrery had served in a special ops unit in Vietnam, and that he'd do fine under pressure. The only advantage they had at the moment was that their kidnapper seemed to have no idea they knew he was a kidnapper. What they did not have going for them was that they were being followed, but Duncan was now aware of that as well. He had watched a single set of headlights from the time they pulled away from the curb. The lights weaved in and out of traffic, catching them and then falling back.

Duncan located their coordinates on his GPS as the road they were on turned into Mexico Highway 200. They were nearing the southern end of Acapulco, and fifteen miles or so farther south, when the highway began to run along beautiful beaches that alternated between polished rock and white sand, they would arrive at a bridge that crossed a deep ravine and a significant river. This would be the place to ditch the vehicle and the followers. It was time to act.

Duncan thought about sparing the driver, but he could see a bulge in the man's shirt where the butt of an automatic pistol of some make protruded from the top of his jeans. It was too risky, and why bother? This guy was not going to do him or McCrery any favors. He also thought about letting the situation develop, but he had no idea where they were being taken, and in a split second, he had another thought.

With the explosiveness of a cougar pouncing on a deer, he pulled the pistol from under his shirt and bashed the butt of it across the driver's temple, which split his head open and knocked him immediately unconscious.

"Take the wheel!" Duncan yelled to McCrery. McCrery grabbed the wheel with his right hand and pulled the pistol from the driver's waistband with his left, taking Duncan's lead although he had no actual knowledge yet of the breach.

The impact to his skull had caused the driver to stiffen and push on the accelerator, and the car was careening onto the shoulder of the road. McCrery overcorrected as he tried to keep control of the speeding car.

"Damn it! I gotta get 'im into the back!" Duncan grunted as he pulled on the man's rigid body.

Duncan tugged and struggled as McCrery steered the vehicle. McCrery managed to kick the unconscious driver's foot from the gas pedal with his own left foot, and then he slid over the man's body to pull the seat release, which made it easier for Duncan to drag the limp body into the back.

McCrery sidled into the driver's seat and took control of the vehicle, continuing south on Highway 200.

"They kidnapped our driver!" Duncan grunted as he manipulated the man's limp body until it was facedown across the backseat.

"I figured. How'd you know?"

"I had a hunch, then I texted Brett."

"Take his shoes off and use the laces to tie his hands behind his back!" McCrery said.

"OK."

"Tie them as tight as you can! Tight enough to stop the circulation."

"Like this?" Duncan asked as he cinched a knot down tight on the driver's hands, which were crossed behind his back. He kneeled on the driver while he worked. Then he pulled the man's feet up behind him and tied his feet to his hands. When the man regained consciousness, he'd find himself completely neutralized.

"Yeah, good. I don't care if his goddamned hands fall off."

Duncan finished binding the man while he filled McCrery in on his plan. They were on their own for a stretch, and they had to get rid of whoever was following them—presumably, the suited fellow and his two federali officers.

They continued on to the southern edge of the city where the highway followed the coastline and fantastic hotel resorts lined the blue ocean, whose peaceful edge lapped at white-sand shores. There was only the faintest sliver of light on the Pacific horizon, and none but the tallest coconut palms showed silhouetted against the thin orange glow in the seemingly infinite distance. The traffic had thinned significantly and they were mostly alone on the road, which made it easy to see the headlights following them, speeding up and slowing down whenever McCrery did. They even stopped once on the side of the road, just to see how the followers would react. They stopped as well at a good distance and continued when McCrery pulled the car back onto the road, which caused him to laugh out loud.

"These guys are idiots," Duncan said to McCrery, who was sweating but alert and ready for action. "We're almost out of this, but I'm gonna need your help."

Duncan got out the rifle with the night-vision scope, put it together, and slid a loaded clip into the open port in the bottom. Then, he screwed the large cylindrical silencer onto the threaded muzzle.

The driver, who had a great bleeding lump on his head, had come to, and Duncan was speaking to him in Spanish. The beaten Mexican man said nothing but nodded in agreement.

"What'd you tell him?" asked McCrery.

Duncan looked at McCrery and listened to his words, looking for signs of fear, but if there were any, the man was hiding it well.

"I told him we're gonna dump him in the center of the highway at the start of the bridge, and that if he stays down, he'll be alive when the shooting stops. I told him he'd be the only living witness, and that he should tell whoever he works for that we're dead, killed in the shoot-out that is about to happen. If he's the only witness and we're presumed dead, he will have done his job and earned his safety. If not, I told him, I'm El Cazador, and I'll hunt him down. I'll kill his wife, his mistress, and his children, one at a time so that he has to watch. And when I've killed everything he ever loved, I'll kill him, too."

"Jesus, Jack," McCrery said, snickering.

When they reached the bridge, the tailing vehicle was at least one hundred yards behind them. McCrery stopped the car, quartering it diagonally in the highway so Duncan could slip out the driver's side rear door undetected. Duncan pulled the bound driver's legs until his body fell from the backseat, and he made no attempt to soften the blow. With his hands tied to his legs behind his back, the man hit his knees and then his face when he landed on the asphalt. He winced on the impact.

After the man fell onto the center lane of the highway, he was instructed to stay there. McCrery then turned all the Honda's lights off, and Duncan slipped away from the car and off the side of the highway. He hid in some brush and palmetto plants and waited. McCrery drove the car across the bridge and turned sideways just past the end of the bridge. Then, he got out of the car and set up quickly on the opposite shoulder with his night-vision-scoped rifle. When the other car pulled up to the body in the middle of the road, the men began shooting at the Honda. They unloaded a clip apiece from their silenced pistols, and then a man stepped from the backseat. It was the dapper man in the suit from the hotel. He approached the beaten driver lying in the road, and when he stooped to check him, his body suddenly jolted back, rolled over backward, and piled up in a limp heap in the road, struck by a bullet from McCrery's rifle. At that cue, Duncan slipped from the tropical brush and fired multiple shots into the two uniformed men in the front of the car. Both men slumped over dead with bullets in their heads. Duncan hurried around the front of the car to where the suited man lay, took a photo with his phone, and then shot him once more in the head without giving the action a second thought. There was no time.

He cut the shoelaces that bound the driver's hands and feet and then picked him up. The man was still dazed by the head wound Duncan had given him, and he struggled to get to his feet. Duncan threw the suited man's pistol off the bridge into the river as he helped the driver to the shoulder of the road.

He made the man repeat what he would tell whomever he worked for and the authorities. Then Duncan told him that if he failed to keep his cover, his family would look like the men in the street. A few onlookers who had come up from the adjacent beach had started to gather, but they were relatively unalarmed, as all the guns in the melee had silencers, even the big rifle McCrery had shot. Duncan released the man's arm and started across the bridge. He walked calmly but without loafing, his back to the Mexican driver he had pistol-whipped with a vengeance. Duncan never looked back.

He was sorting the events out in his head, and he felt a momentary release from the adrenaline high, but the feeling was fleeting. They still had to escape the scene and then the country, which would be crawling with federalis looking for the two gringos by morning. There was no wave of emotion for Duncan this time: no regret, no remorse, nothing but willful intent to save his own hide.

Meanwhile, McCrery watched the Mexican driver on the shoulder of the highway through the scope with the crosshairs leveled on his chest. If he made a move for the vehicle in which the dead federalis' weapons lay, Tom McCrery was ready to punch his tag as Duncan had instructed him.

When Duncan reached the end of the bridge, he positioned the car so it pointed down the ravine on an open path that ran parallel with the bridge. He summoned McCrery to help him. Duncan placed the car in neutral, and the two men pushed until it started to roll, sending it off into the thick tropical foliage that lined the river and then down into the turbid, rolling water at the bottom.

There was no time to talk at this point; they had to hoof it on foot through the woods a half mile to the beach, from which point they could follow the water south. Once they arrived at the water's edge, they began walking in the tranquil surf only as deep as they had to in order to hide their tracks and cover their scent should anybody try to track them with dogs. They covered several miles in the first couple of hours, with Duncan pushing the aging McCrery, who was doing very well at keeping up. They hadn't slept or eaten much for nearly twelve hours, and the heat and humidity were hard on two men from a cooler part of the world. After a few hours, Duncan allowed them a momentary break. They ate Clif bars from their packs and drank a sip of water, but then he pushed them on.

Using his phone, Duncan had located a small, rustic palapa hut resort on a secluded beach. He figured they could reach it during the night if they pressed on, but the going was tough. The beach turned rocky, and impassable cliffs that came all the way to the water forced them into wooded hills for a mile at one point. They moved on with little rest, and at around three in the morning, they rounded a rocky peninsula and saw the lights of the rustic resort. To Duncan's great relief, a large fleet of fishing pangas lined the edge of the small bay, beached for the night.

It was too late in the evening to approach the resort or any of the local fishermen, so they hunkered down in some banana trees and palms up the beach from the water, where they were hidden and momentarily safe. Duncan could see the fatigue in McCrery's eyes, and he himself was tired. He was young compared to McCrery, but old enough to realize that he hurt more than he would have twenty years earlier after such a journey.

The two men hunkered down in the sand and foliage, back to back, leaning against their packs between them. They would rest until the sun rose enough to stir the fishermen, and then Duncan would make arrangements, as he knew the road would be dangerous. There would be roadblocks, both police and military, but he and McCrery would not be on the roads.

"You sleep; I'll watch out for us," Duncan offered.

"You need to rest, too."

"It's OK, you go ahead. I can't sleep now, anyway. I'll rest tomorrow when we get on one of these pangas." Duncan was tired but still keyed up on adrenaline. His sweat-soaked clothes stuck to his skin, and leaves and twigs were stuck to his hair.

"Do you regret getting involved with this one, Duncan?"

"Which one?"

"This trip with me to shoot the slave trader," he said with a slight grin that Duncan could hear in his voice. McCrery was worn out. His clothes were torn, and he had several bloody scratches on his forehead and face from when he'd fallen once in the rush through the brush.

"I've regretted every one of them from the beginning, but this one the least."

They did not talk about the events of the day as they might have recapped a hunt for big game; neither man made mention of the shootings or the chase or any of it.

"I'm glad to have you watching my back," Duncan said.

"What do you mean? I thought you were watching mine," McCrery replied, smiling again.

"Go to sleep, get some rest."

After a few minutes of quiet, McCrery's breathing became heavier and then a bit nasal, coming close to a light snore. Duncan was wide awake. He was thinking, sorting out the events of the past days in his head. He did miss home, but he would not allow himself that, at least not until he and McCrery were safe. He had to stay focused on the situation at hand. But it was difficult. He could not keep himself from coming back to the same thought, again and again: one of the richest men in the world wanted him dead.

When the sun started to rise, lights began to show inside the palm-thatched huts that were tucked into the palms and the jungle-like forest at the edge of the white-sand beach. They were perfectly organic, and Duncan thought about how they mimicked the landscape so well—like a log home in his mountains back in Montana, and very unlike a high-rise in the city. The fishermen seemed none too eager to leave early, which was a relief to Duncan, who did not want to approach them in the dark with an air of desperation, but in the daylight, relaxed, as if he were a tourist.

When the sun peeked over the ridge above the rustic village and resort, Duncan told McCrery to wait for him at their spartan camp, and he walked by himself down to where the men were readying their boats. He looked the men and their boats over as they readied rods and reels, handlines, and gill nets, and he was drawn to a man a little younger than he was who had a boat that was around twenty feet in length with twin seventy-five-horse Yamaha four-stroke outboards. It looked fuel efficient and relatively fast, which would help them make the trip in a day.

He approached the man, who was tying monofilament leaders, and said, "Hola."

"Buenos días," the man said back, hardly looking up from his task.

"Se habla inglés?" Duncan asked, hoping the man spoke English, as his Spanish had atrophied over the years.

"No."

"I want to rent you and your boat," Duncan said, pulling for the Spanish stored in the back of his head.

"For fishing?" the Mexican man said, wrapping the leader around a Styrofoam block and sticking the point of the hook into it when it was tight.

"No, for a ride down the coast for my father and me. I will pay you a lot of money."

"How much?"

"Two thousand dollars, plus I'll cover the expenses."

This number got the man's attention, and he looked up from the new leader he had started tying. He looked Duncan up and down. While Duncan had replaced the previous day's shirt with a fresh one from his pack, he was still wearing the pants he'd had on during their flight from the federalis. They were torn and stained. They were not the pants of a tourist.

"Where do you want to go?"

"Escondido."

"Too far," the man said, and his eyes returned to the hook and line.

"Three thousand dollars, and I still cover the costs."

The man finished the leader and wrapped it on the foam block next to the others without saying a word. Duncan let the silence build, saying nothing. The man shook his head slightly from side to side as if to say no, but still there were no words. Duncan knew he was thinking about the proposition, and that the reluctance was probably more about the length of the journey than anything else.

"My father is sick, and this is the last time we will be able to make a trip like this," Duncan said, hoping to play on the man's emotions a little.

"OK, we can go tomorrow," the man said, and looked at Duncan for a reaction.

"Four thousand and we leave right now," Duncan said to him and pulled a wad of hundreds from his pocket. They were folded over and wrapped tight with a piece of black electrical tape.

"OK," he said in English, looking up at Duncan and raising an eyebrow.

Duncan handed the man $500 in $100 bills and told him they would need food and fresh water and extra fuel cans so they wouldn't have to stop as frequently. The man hurried off, saying they would leave in about an hour.

Duncan purchased some beans, tortillas, and tamales off a woman who was selling lunches to the fishermen on the beach, and then he returned to McCrery, who was watching from the woods with binoculars. He had one of the big rifles out and was ready for action, should it be required. They were so far in now that surrender was not an option. McCrery would have shot any man who molested Duncan, as surrender would only have landed them in a Mexican jail and spelled a brutal end for both men.

They ate the food, both feeling somewhat relaxed, and when they were done, they took their packs down to the boats. Most of the fishermen had left, and they waited for the man who called himself Ignacio.

When Ignacio returned, he loaded the extra fuel tanks and a cooler with food and water into the boat, and they pushed into the gentle waves.

The trip was long, and in the face of its length, Duncan nodded off almost immediately. He lay on a small amount of fishing net piled in the middle of the boat while McCrery, who had slept some in the early morning darkness, stayed awake. The new outboards droned on, and Duncan felt the vibration in the hull of the boat. It lulled him into a deep sleep for a couple of hours, and he woke when the midmorning sun started to heat his face.

They were lucky that the ocean was very calm, as this time of year it could be quite different. Duncan remembered a hurricane that had destroyed Acapulco at about the same time of year when he was living with his cousin nearly twenty years earlier. He remembered going to the salinas that weekend with his cousin and looking at the angry sea, how the pangas were pulled far up the beach out of reach of the incredibly tall, frothy brown waves, and how the locals had left the beach palapas and moved inland to wait out the storm. And they had been two hundred miles south of the center of the storm.

Duncan called the captain of the Bertram and verified that he was still lingering around the Guatemala border. Duncan let him know they would be around Escondido that evening. The captain agreed to meet them roughly fifteen miles southwest of Escondido after he had fueled the Bertram in port. Then Duncan called Brett.

"Jack!" Brett said on the other end of the line, anxious to hear from his cousin. "Are you all right?"

"We're fine."

"Thank God. We've been worried about you."

"Does 'we' include Beck?"

"No, I haven't heard from him since the day before you were scheduled to connect with the target."

"Good."

"He's set you up."

"Yes."

"Where are you?"

"In a boat headed south, somewhere north of the border. We should make Puerto Quetzal tomorrow afternoon."

"Great! I'll be there to pick you up myself."

"Thanks. And in the meantime, call Beck and tell him you haven't heard from us in two days and you fear the worst."

"Done."

"We will now have the element of total surprise," Duncan told Brett. "Do nothing until we meet tomorrow."

Duncan settled in for the long boat ride, but he never fell back asleep. McCrery slept on and off, and once, they hid under the nets when a small plane passed over them. Ignacio noticed, but he never asked any questions. Duncan talked fishing with him a little, but most of the trip was quiet and uneventful, with only one stop for fuel in an unnamed fishing village north of Escondido, Oaxaca. Some local boys greeted them on the beach, and Ignacio handed them money. The boys took the empty fuel cans up the brown-sand beach and disappeared into the palms. They returned in a half hour with full cans of fuel, and the men resumed their trip. Duncan was sure that Ignacio sensed there was more to his story than a trip of nostalgia with his father, but he pressed on without questioning.

Duncan offered him a $2,000 bonus if he would deliver them to the Bertram offshore of Escondido that night in the dark, and he agreed graciously. The captain of the yacht gave Duncan coordinates to a waypoint where they would meet in the dark Pacific. Duncan plugged them into his GPS on his phone, and they headed in that direction, passing Escondido in the dark. They nearly ran into the Bertram, which was idling in the darkness with no running or moorage lights, completely blackened from any eyes that did not need to see it. The captain briefly shined a spotlight on them, and Ignacio pulled up alongside the much larger boat. Duncan and McCrery shook hands with Ignacio and climbed into the Bertram. Duncan gave him the remaining money: the $2,000 bonus, plus another $1,000, which Duncan told him to use to spend the night in Escondido, get a good meal, and have his motors serviced for the hours they had put on them. Ignacio thanked them, and they disappeared into the darkness.

The two men lay down in the berth, and Duncan felt a release as he came off the adrenaline high. He fell deeply asleep and slept until the sun began to rise the following morning. There were no thoughts, no ghosts, no regrets: just regenerating sleep so deep that dreams were not remembered. Killing people was becoming easier.

NINE

D uncan awakened in the predawn light and entered the wheel-house, where he found the captain sleeping and autopilot running the boat. Duncan examined the chart plotter GPS and re-alized their position was ten miles offshore of Brett's sea salt facility on the northern Guatemalan coast, and that they would be back to Puerto Quetzal in the afternoon. The captain awoke despite Duncan's efforts to move quietly in the wheelhouse, and he rose to check the electronics as well. Duncan and the captain exchanged pleasantries as though they were on nothing more than a fishing trip.

Duncan went out into the warm morning air, and on the deck, he began putting tackle into the water. He lowered the outriggers and rubber-band-clipped a line to each, sending them out to the ends of the long poles that swayed ever so slightly in the calm morning seas. They had nothing to do but fish for the balance of the trip.

McCrery joined Duncan on the deck, and the men watched the feathered clones drag far behind the boat, leaving a jet of bubbles behind each lure in the glassy, calm water. The sky was brilliantly clear, and a sliver of the sun peeked over the rim of the volcanic mountain range to the east.

"That was more excitement than I bargained for,'" McCrery finally said, breaking the silence.

"With me dead, Beck can do whatever he wants with the Hunt Club."

"And with me dead, he'll have a crack at stealing my businesses."

"The funny thing is, if he'd just let me out of it, he could have done what he wanted with it. I don't give a shit. I never had an interest in it. I just wanted out of a bad financial situation. Just wanted enough to set my family up."

"That isn't OK with Beck," McCrery interjected. "He wants control of everything: you, me, and everyone else around him. He's like a real-life comic-strip villain, and he has enough money to pull it off."

"He isn't bulletproof."

"You've never been especially impressed with men of wealth and status, have you, Jack?"

"Not so much," Duncan replied. "But then again, I haven't been much impressed by mankind in general."

"We are a bad lot, aren't we, us humans?"

"We all fail at times, but most of us are just plain failures."

The two men sat quietly for a few moments, absorbing the therapy of the morning water and the lures being dragged behind them. They bubbled and occasionally skipped across the surface in their attempt to entice a fish to strike. The dull rumbling of the diesel engine in the bilge added to the lull, and McCrery and Duncan were at ease for the moment.

"We have to kill him, Jack."

"I'm gonna!" Duncan said.

He was angry now. Calm, but angry at the same time, and in survival mode. He was thinking of his family, and of the rumors of his demise that would get back to them. He had to warn his wife and

Bergstrom. At some point, there would be some news or some contact with them from Beck, and they would think he was dead. He could not bear the thought of his family in mourning.

"As long as Beck thinks we're dead, we're miles ahead of him."

"It'll be tough."

"He tried to kill me, too, Jack."

"Killing him will be easy; it's the waiting that'll be hard."

"Yeah."

"He has to continue thinking we are dead, though. We have to hide out."

"That won't be hard for me, my kids are all grown, but what about you?"

"I've got a plan. I've thought about this a lot. In fact, I haven't stopped thinking about it for months. I know his next target. He's an old friend of mine."

"Who's that?"

"Joaquin Vasquez."

"Why would Beck want to shoot him?"

"You know him?"

"I know who he is."

"For the same reason one male dog mounts another male dog, I guess."

McCrery chuckled.

"I'd like your help getting Beck," Duncan said, looking at McCrery for a response.

"I'm in," McCrery said without pause. He reached out, and the two men shook hands.

"He'll be at Vasquez's hacienda in Baja in January for that, and we'll get him then."

Duncan caught movement out of the corner of his eye. The line on the outrigger to his right snapped the rubber band holding it to the cable. Then it fell through the air from the end of the long, straight pole into the sea, where it disappeared into the water. There was a moment in which Duncan knew they had a fish even before the clicker went off on the reel's drag and announced it to the world. Duncan looked over at McCrery as he took the rod with the drag buzzing from the rod holder.

"I'm glad to have you on my side, Tom," he said as he handed the fish-loaded rod to McCrery. "You are an exception to the human race."

Then a second and a third rod went off with fish stripping line from the reels. They horsed the acrobatic dorado into the boat. The fish jumped in the morning sun, which spotlighted their fantastic golden-yellow and green-blue iridescent-spotted bodies. The fishing continued for an hour and then fell off, but by then they had plenty of fresh fillets to bring to Brett and his family.

The yacht reached Puerto Quetzal in midafternoon. Duncan could see his cousin drinking a bottle of Cerveza Gallo under the shade of an umbrella near the exit of the dock in the very small marina. He greeted them at the boat, tying the lines off to the dock cleats. They wheeled a cooler full of fish up the dock. There, they put fresh ice on the bagged fillets and loaded the fish into the back of the car along with the packs with the guns, which had different paperwork for Guatemala. Then, they headed back to Brett's family compound near the capital city.

On the drive, they discussed the events of the trip and laid out the groundwork for killing Beck. They would try to get him back to Guatemala City. If they succeeded, one of the cousin's men would pick him up at the airport and drive him to a location on the outskirts of the city. The place was called Acantilado del Muerto, or "Cliff of the Dead," and there they would execute him. The location was where a bridge crossed a canyon so vertically steep that if Duncan and Mc-Crery shot Beck, his body would tip over the guardrail and the vultures would have time to eat him in the air on his way to the bottom.

In the meantime, Duncan and McCrery lay low, living between Brett's house in the capital city and a mission-style family home that his in-laws kept in Antigua. They also penned notes to their wives to let them know they were safe and to give them instructions for how to deal with whatever came up.

Duncan's note to his wife was simple and straightforward; he was never much for writing anything long or drawn out:

Dear Erica,

In the coming days, you may or may not hear that I am dead. I've been double-crossed, and an attempt was made on my life, but I prevailed unscathed. I am very much alive and well, but I must hide out, as those who would like me dead think I already am. The opportunity to end this predicament I'm in will come at the end of January, and then I will come home to Montana and won't have to look over my shoulder. In the mean-time, I have to hide out to keep the element of surprise, and the only unpleasant part is missing you and the kids.

It is possible that Beck may contact you about my death or some rumor may reach you. I don't want the kids to hear this, so take them out of school until I'm home. Have your mom and dad help them keep up with their studies. You should cut back at the clinic to just a couple days a week. Give my absence as the reason, and if anybody should ask, I'm on an extended trip to South America and the South Pacific. Beck will likely send somebody snooping, so watch your back. Stay close to your dad. He will take care of you and the kids until I'm home.

Hug the kids for me as well as yourself. I am sorry to put you through this.

Love, Jack

He printed some pictures of Beck's two Texan bodyguards to include with the letter. He also included photos of a few other people who might show up in Montana.

When they reached Brett's estate in the hills above the capital city, Duncan felt very relaxed. His cousin played with vineyards and raspberries and blackberries and wine making, and he always had a business project he was working on. After greeting Brett's family, the three men slipped into his office and Brett made a call to Beck, on speakerphone so Duncan and McCrery could listen in.

"Yes," Beck said, answering the call.

"James, it's me."

"What do you know?"

"The information our people are getting is that my cousin and McCrery are dead."

"That's unfortunate."

"Unfortunate? That's all you have to say about this?"

"Are there bodies?"

"No. The word is that federalis shot them and threw them off a bridge into a river south of Acapulco."

"Any chance of recovering them?"

"Slim, but we'd like you to come down here and help us."

"I don't have time."

"That's it?" Brett asked, shaking his head with an angry look in his eyes. Duncan and McCrery just smiled. They knew James Beck.

"I liked Jack, but there's nothing I can do."

"So you're just done? Not your problem anymore?"

"Let me know if you need money," Beck said and ended the call.

When Beck hung up and the phone line was cleared, the three men looked at each other, grinning. They knew now, without a doubt, that Beck had set them up. The men agreed that his tone was emotionless, and there was no surprise in it, as though he'd heard what he was expecting to hear.

"Fine, we'll hunt Beck," Duncan said, pouring some scotch into a glass from a decanter that sat on a beautiful handcrafted madrone hutch and cigar humidor. Brett offered both men a cigar, and the rest of the evening was nothing but pleasant. They tried some of Brett's wines and enjoyed the fresh fish, both turned into ceviche and grilled with lemon and sea salt. It was simple but perfect.

The next day, Brett took a commercial flight to Los Angeles and then on to Denver, where he took a rental car from the airport to McCrery's residence. There, he knocked on the large wooden doors. Mrs. McCrery opened them and stood in the threshold, wondering who the handsome younger man at her door was.

"I'm Brett Duncan. I've been helping on your husband's extended trip."

"Oh, is everything all right?" she asked, and then a worried look came over her face.

"Everything is very well," Brett said, handing her the note McCrery had written for her and then starting back down the steps. "Your husband is doing great and having fun. It's all in the note."

Brett waited a moment while Mrs. McCrery opened the note and started reading it in the doorway, and then he headed down the steps to the car. She looked up from the note and waved to Brett as he backed the rental car down the driveway.

He then caught a connection to Bozeman. When he landed in the evening, he rented a car and drove all the way to the ranch in Ennis, where he arrived late that night. It was nearly ten thirty when he pulled into the ranch, and Bergstrom greeted him in the driveway with a pump shotgun.

"Sorry it's so late, Mr. Bergstrom," Brett Duncan said as he stepped from the rented car. "I'm Jack's cousin Brett." Bergstrom recognized him, as he and his wife and kids had been to Ennis on several occasions over the years.

"Sorry, Brett. You're obviously unexpected," Bergstrom said as his heart jumped into his throat, nearly closing it to the point where his mouth was moving but the words coming out were losing strength.

"Again, I apologize."

"My god, what's gone wrong?" Bergstrom said.

"Nothing. Jack's fine. I mean, things have gone a little sideways, but Jack is fine."

Bergstrom felt the tightness in his throat and chest ease, and he slid the forearm back on the shotgun with a snap, ejecting the shell up in the air in front of him and catching it with his right hand. Then he pushed the shell back into the magazine.

"Come inside, let's get out of the cold," Bergstrom said and motioned to him with the shotgun toward his house.

"I came to see Erica," Brett said. "I've got a note for her from Jack."

The two men could see that the lights were still on in the Duncans' home.

"Looks like she's up."

"That's the new house?"

"Yes."

"Get in, and I'll drive you over there," Brett said to Bergstrom, who put the shotgun muzzle down and leaned the gun against the front seat between him and Brett. A couple of inches of light, dry snow covered the ground, and it squeaked under the tires as Brett eased the car to a stop in the Duncans' driveway.

Brett knocked on the front door of the new house, and Bergstrom stood on the porch a couple of steps behind him. Erica opened the door almost immediately, as she'd seen the headlights come down her drive. The two men saw the smile evaporate from her whitening face when she saw her husband's cousin standing on the cedar deck of her new home at that late of an hour.

"Jack is fine," Brett said quickly.

Erica stepped forward and hugged him tightly. It felt good to her. Brett was a very handsome man, and from behind you couldn't tell him from Duncan. It was almost like hugging Duncan himself.

"I'm sorry," she said. "It's that when I saw you I thought—"

"I know what you thought, and he's fine."

"Where is he?" she asked as the three of them walked into her house and out of the cold.

"He's at my house in Guatemala."

"When is he coming home?"

"We aren't sure yet," he said, handing her Duncan's note. "But when he does, he'll be through with Beck."

"What's going on?"

"Beck tried to have Duncan killed in Mexico."

"And?" Erica just shook her head and tried to get her mind around the situation. It was surreal. She felt as though she had a ghost for a husband, but he wasn't even dead.

"Beck thinks he's dead. As long as he continues to think Jack is dead, we have the upper hand."

Erica read the note, and then let her father read it. Bergstrom nodded, agreeing with the plan. But Erica took the note back, holding it and looking out the darkened window as though it were daylight and she could see the view that was behind the curtain of night.

"He wanted to call you, but I wouldn't let him," Brett said. "There are obviously no bodies, since Duncan and his partner are still alive, so we're sure Beck is watching your place. And probably listening to your phones. And if he isn't already, he will be."

"Who's his partner?" Bergstrom asked.

"Tom McCrery. He's a client, really, but since Beck tried to kill them both, they've teamed up."

Bergstrom made a mental note of the name with the intention of looking into Tom McCrery after Brett had left.

"When do you think this'll be over?" Erica asked.

"We don't know. January. Maybe February?" Brett said. "He wants to come home for Christmas. He misses you and the kids, but I told him it's too risky."

"Tell him not to come home till it's all over," she said, then took the note and walked into her bedroom.

"This is a lot for her to handle," Bergstrom said to Brett.

"It's gotten out of hand."

Brett stayed in the Duncans' new guest room. The next morning, Erica rose at 4:00 a.m. to make him coffee and a quick breakfast before he returned to Bozeman for an early flight back to Guatemala.

"By the way," Brett said between sips of coffee. "Jack asked me to bring a pair of pistols back. They're antique-type revolvers. Do you know where they are?"

"I think so," she said, and retrieved the pistols from Duncan's office.

"What does he want these for?" Erica asked as she set the two pistols down on the kitchen table in front of Brett.

"Don't know. Said he'd explain when I got back."

After Brett's taillights disappeared at the place where the Bergstroms' driveway dropped off the bench and descended into the valley below, Erica sat alone in the kitchen with a cup of coffee. It was too late to return to bed and too early to do much else. After reading for a while, she walked out to the barn, where she brushed and curry-combed a couple of her horses, just to keep herself busy.

Bergstrom had awakened at the sound of the car leaving, and when he saw the light on in the barn, he went outside to join his daughter.

"Can't sleep, either?" he asked, looking over the top of a stall gate at her brushing a large bay quarter horse.

"No," she said and continued brushing the large horse. It was a cold morning, and the sun was rising to its low winter place in the sky outside the barn, but the air was yet to hold the effects of its solar warming.

"At least we know Jack's all right," Bergstrom said, knowing what was on his daughter's mind.

"I just want him to come home, Dad," she said. "I want him to be home."

"Me too, honey, me too."

"I just don't understand why he thought he had to do all this.

Why he thinks he had to have the money to be a success." There were circles under her eyes, but she stood tall and unbeaten in a wool overcoat with a black silk scarf around her neck and face. Her long blonde hair was down, keeping her warm.

Bergstrom looked at his daughter and saw that her eyes were glassy, filled with tears that she refused to let flow down her face.

"You're angry," he said.

"I guess," she said, and looked back at the brush in her hand as she ran it over the horse's wooly winter coat. "Shouldn't I be?"

"He's a man. A good one who wants the best for you and the kids. Don't take this wrong, but you're a woman and probably wouldn't understand why a man does what he does. No more than we understand you girls."

"I guess," she said, walking out of the stall gate and hanging the brushes up on nails on the post on the outside of the stall.

"If it makes you feel better, I understand why he's done what he's done. I might have done the same thing in his shoes."

"I don't know, Dad. I wonder sometimes why I married him."

"You're not the first woman to wonder that about a man."

"I don't know, Dad. I just don't know."

"What don't you know?"

"I think back to when we were kids and how innocent it all was. How happy we were, you know?"

"Yeah, I know."

"I think I would have chosen differently if I knew things would go this way."

"I don't think you can choose who you fall in love with," Bergstrom said in a country-slow but wise way. "Do you?"

"I guess you're right. Or who you were born to," she said as she hugged the old cowboy and smiled at him. "At least I got lucky there."

"He is a wild one, though, isn't he? Even as a boy, wandering all over these mountains and most of the time alone."

"Immutably wild," she said.

"You wouldn't have it any other way."

"Wouldn't I?"

"I don't think so."

———

Brett returned to find Duncan and McCrery already growing bored with reading and drinking whiskey in the shade while they watched hummingbirds, parrots, parakeets, and the many other tropical birds that were abundant around Brett's lush mountain estate.

Duncan was growing restless in Guatemala, but McCrery was aged enough to have learned to take things as they come, and he'd appreciated their break. They inspected Brett's berry plants and studied his wine-making room, which was attached to a well-manicured stucco barn that held several custom cars Brett had finished or was in the process of refinishing. All the architecture of the compound owed itself to the Spanish influence in the country and his wife's family's ancestry. Duncan loved the architecture and enjoyed studying it and the different building methods.

When Brett arrived home, he took the two men to the family house in Antigua. The mission-style walls of the property's exterior hid a fantastic courtyard with a pool and croquet course in a beautifully manicured, parklike setting with a mix of native flora from palms to oaks and pines. They spent a week there while Brett's people went to work making arrangements for Duncan and McCrery to go to Loreto. There, they would get a feeling for the hacienda, Vasquez's habits, and the surrounding area so they could plan a trap for Beck. Brett was working on renting a small casita within range of the Vasquez hacienda, which would allow them to study the facility with high-powered optics. They would go by yacht to Cabo and pick up a car that would be waiting for them upon their arrival.

Duncan and McCrery swam and read and cooked elaborate meals for themselves, all of which helped to pass their time in seclusion. They donned long, ponytailed wigs and hats, and they'd grown beards to add to their disguise on daily trips to the market, where they purchased fresh fish, fruits, vegetables, and meats.

Looking in the mirror at the wigs one day, McCrery said, "I feel like a goddamned idiot in this costume."

"Don't be so hard on yourself," Duncan said to him, laughing. "You make a great hippie."

"I never had a ponytail in the sixties or seventies; I was too busy getting shot at," McCrery said, uncomfortable in his disguise.

The city of Antigua had a strong European influence and population, as well as a fantastic European meat shop with locally cured delicacies like pancetta, prosciutto, salami, hams, and smoked fish. The markets were full of ripe-on-the-vine produce, which they combined for fabulous meals, and they were often joined by Brett and his family, but after a week and a half, the two sequestered men were becoming restless, and even the large amounts of fantastic Chilean, Spanish, French, and Italian wines could not keep them sedated.

Brett's father-in-law, Tomás, picked them up in the dark one morning and took them into the mountains of the Petén in the northeastern part of the country. When they passed through police and military checkpoints, the two gringos were never required to produce documentation, as they were guests of Tomás.

They arrived at a log cabin with a banana-leaf-thatched roof, which was interesting to Duncan and McCrery. They spent three nights at the cabin, where they hunted with the bodyguards and Tomás for a variety of game neither gringo had ever dreamed of hunting. They took a strange variety of wild turkey and some very interesting long-tailed birds, which the locals called grouse but which resembled nothing the Americans had seen. The birds looked to be relatives of the barnyard chicken, the pheasant, and the magpie. On the second day, Tomás shot a white-tailed deer, and they ate the liver with onions for dinner on their last night together. At the end of the three-day trip, they returned to the home in Antigua and said good-bye to their friend. The following morning, Feliciano drove them to Puerto Quetzal, where they boarded the yacht again for the long trip to Cabo.

In the meantime, Erica and her folks kept things going in Montana. The kids were doing their schooling at home, and they also had ranch chores such as feeding the horses and helping with the cattle, which were down for the winter from the high country. The kids missed their father, but not as much as he missed them. None of the locals questioned Duncan's absence, as he had been gone as often as not since he was a teenager, and Erica spent more time in town than he ever had anyway. She did, however, notice that a gray Ford SUV was following her at a distance whenever she was in town.

The SUV caught her attention largely because she did not recognize the vehicle. In a town the size of Ennis, a person grew familiar with the people and the vehicles they drove, and this one did not fit into her mental catalog. Bergstrom went into town late one night and promptly found the gray Ford parked in the back of a local hotel.

He contacted his nephew, who was a Madison County sheriff's deputy, and had him run the plates. They were Montana plates, but the registered owner was a corporation headquartered in Texas, which they eventually connected to Beck.

Two days later, Erica waited for the men outside the hotel. When they walked out the back to cross the deserted street, she pulled her truck in between the men and their gray SUV. Both men had brown hair, were clean cut, and looked to be in their early to mid-thirties. One looked to be slightly over six feet tall, and the other slightly under. They wore mid-length wool overcoats that would normally be worn over a suit, which made them stand out against the locals, who were typically the only ones left in Ennis by winter. She looked at the photos Duncan had sent and clearly recognized one of the men as one of Beck's Texan bodyguards.

"You two fools have been following me for a while now," she said from the open window of her truck. "Is there something I can help you with?"

The two men were caught slightly off guard, and both said, "No."

Erica calmly pointed the muzzle of a short, double-barreled shotgun at their faces, resting it on the open window.

"If I see you following me again, I will kill you rapists, is that clear?"

"Clear enough," one of the men said. The other, whom Erica had recognized from Duncan's photos, said nothing but nodded.

Erica drove off and went about her day at the clinic. She did not see the gray SUV again, but Bergstrom knew the men would not leave altogether. They were there because there were no bodies, or at least none that Beck knew of, and he wanted to ease his own doubt. He wanted to know if Duncan and McCrery were really dead.

The two men simply kept watch from a greater distance, and Bergstrom soon found that they were hiding the SUV about fifteen miles south of town and east of the river from the ranch. From there, they would walk out onto a rimrock and glass the ranch day and night, watching for a sign of Duncan.

Bergstrom waited for a night when the thermometer dipped below zero, and then he slipped into their hiding spot and disabled the vehicle in the dark. He also wired a pound-and-a-half package of cocaine to the frame of the SUV under the hood. He had acquired the bundle unwontedly many years before, but he had held on to it for reasons even he didn't know until then.

When the men returned to the vehicle at around eleven at night, they were nearly frozen already, and they expected to get in and warm up. Instead they had to walk three miles through the dark, frozen sagebrush to the highway, and five more miles back toward Ennis before somebody picked them up and gave them a ride into town. By then, their toes were frostbitten, and their fingers were not far from it.

In the morning, Bergstrom placed an anonymous call to the local sheriff, who used a contraband-sniffing dog to help him find the package. He promptly arrested the two men, who were still at the local hospital having their toes attended to. This kept them occupied for nearly a month and out of Erica's way.

Duncan and McCrery spent a week on the yacht as they fished their way to Cabo San Lucas at a leisurely pace. They carried enough extra fuel cans in the fish hold to fuel at sea, and they had also pre-arranged a fuel stop at a small fishing village along the way. The village wasn't on the tourist maps, and the men did not stay any longer than it took for them to fill the diesel tank. The trip's highlight came when they got into an amazing school of yellowfin tuna. The spot was boiling on the surface with frigate birds and albatross pounding a school of small mackerel pushed to the surface by the tuna. They put a couple of one-hundred-and-fifty-pound fish into ice, and they ate sashimi and seared tuna the rest of the trip. When they arrived in Cabo, they picked up the waiting car and made their way to the small, adobe-looking block-stucco house they would live in until their intended mission was complete.

They set up a bedroom that looked down on the Vasquez hacienda with a spotting scope and small telescope. This would enable them to watch the comings and goings of Señor Vasquez, a man whose life they were attempting to save but only in a peripheral effort to saving their own. Feliciano had been with them on the trip by boat and would remain with them for assistance until the trip was through. The monotony set in.

They watched the compound day and night and directed little effort toward anything else. They had yellowfin and dorado fillets in the freezer of their stucco house, and every two or three days, Feliciano went out to a local market for tortillas, beans, limes, and some fresh vegetables. They gave him money for Coronas, and once a bottle of tequila, which they used to make margaritas.

A week before Christmas, Duncan gave in to McCrery's urging not to return to Montana to see his family at the holiday. It was too risky, and both men knew it. As badly as Duncan missed his wife and kids, as badly as he wanted to be there, he knew it would put their anonymity at risk. He was sure Beck would have somebody watching the ranch and his family, and it would put the whole operation at stake. This was his chance to get out without a scratch, and he couldn't risk it.

Duncan dictated a note for Erica over the phone to Brett, who sent it overnight from Guatemala to a mailbox store in Bozeman. Brett had it picked up by private courier and delivered to the ranch. Bergstrom came out of his house and took the note addressed to him and Erica from the courier, but he didn't open it.

Erica had come out of the barn when she heard the crunching of the crusted snow under the tires of the courier's car, and she walked to her dad, who was standing in the driveway. He handed her the note, which she opened eagerly.

Erica,

I am sorry, but I can't come home for Christmas. It would be too risky for all of us. But when I am done here, I will be done…

Bergstrom could see the tears beginning to fill up his daughter's eyes as she looked up at him and dropped the note without reading the rest.

"He isn't coming for Christmas, is he?" Bergstrom asked.

"No. Damn it, the kids will be crushed."

"It's better that he doesn't."

"Is it?"

"It's too risky if he comes. He just needs to get this done and get out."

Erica looked back at the note in her hand but didn't read any of the words.

"I'm just pissed," she said. "And I can't even tell him."

"I understand. I'm disappointed too, but you do realize it's best this way?"

"I don't know what I realize anymore," Erica said and turned to walk back to her own house. She kicked at a frozen clod of snow left from when Bergstrom had last plowed the driveway.

Bergstrom watched her walk toward the house, which twinkled in the late afternoon shadows where he and the kids had hung Christmas lights across the front porch. Inside, he could see the kids hanging ornaments on the spruce tree they had cut on a snow machine trip into the mountains above the ranch. He watched his daughter until she reached the porch, wishing he could do more for her but knowing he was really only a spectator.

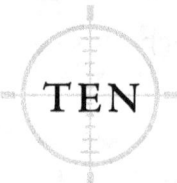

TEN

Duncan could feel the warmth of the Baja sun touching his face through the curtainless bedroom window. He could feel its light through his closed eyelids as though they were dark shades drawn over windows lit by a sun that wanted in from behind.

He had dreamed one of those dreams from which you wake relieved you were only dreaming. He dreamed he was hunting elk with two men in the northern Rockies, but after several days of hunting, the trip ended with no success. The elk they were pursuing had never materialized, and at the closing of the hunt, one of his hunting partners—nobody he actually knew, but a faceless dream character—simply shot the third hunter in their party as the man walked on the opposite side of a creek. He'd done it for lack of an elk—an act committed purely in cold blood—and there had been no time for Duncan to stop him. In his dream, he felt panic at the thought that the murdered man had done nothing to deserve being shot. He'd also felt an intense desire to turn back time for an instant and to reverse the outcome. And panic that he would be implicated in the crime. But lying there in the simple single bed and feeling the warm sun's caress, he did not want to open his eyes from the safety of sleep; his current reality was no escape from the nightmare.

Duncan lay there awhile, pondering the dream's meaning and knowing that his competent partner, who had stayed up taking the late-night shift, was glassing the hacienda. He was getting edgy.

Duncan had never been especially patient about things, and he had been holed up now for too long in the little casita on the hill, removed from his family, from his life, and even from the resort atmosphere of the community on the beach below them. He had no great interest in joining the tourists and expats who frequented the area south of Loreto closer to Puerto Escondido; he was just plain tired of waiting.

They were comfortable in the hand-stuccoed block casita, which had a thatched palm-leaf roof and a healthy population of geckos that liked to race upside down across the ceiling while the men stared up at it. Duncan and McCrery had little information other than knowing that Beck had said he would be there at the end of January with a client. He had never said with whom, or the exact date. Brett had tried to get info out of Beck without alarming him, but Beck had never admitted to his intention to assassinate Señor Vasquez. They were without a formal plan, but Duncan was letting things develop and toying with several options.

With no knowledge of Beck's travel dates, they could not simply snipe him from long range, as it would be impossible to arrange immediate escape plans. And besides, if they did, it would be news all over the globe: a murder exploitable by the media, as it would provide dirty laundry to sell to the mass of dumbfounded dipshits drooling in front of their televisions. This would ultimately increase the men's likelihood of being caught. Duncan knew that Beck's demise had to be an accident, and they had to execute their initiative before Beck had his opportunity to kill Vasquez.

Duncan rehashed all the possibilities in his head until he had to get out of bed. He joined McCrery in the other bedroom.

"Good morning, Jack," McCrery said from behind the spotting scope.

"What do you see this morning?" Duncan asked. "No, let me guess: the same nothing as we've seen for the last month?"

In the back of Duncan's mind, however, he did know Beck. He knew Beck wanted to harvest another desert bighorn, and he could safely assume he would come to the hacienda and stay long enough to take his ram before executing Vasquez. He was also sure Beck lacked the intelligence and assistance he would normally receive from Brett, as Beck had dropped contact with him, so his stay at the hacienda would be his reconnaissance. He was probably not even planning to shoot Vasquez on this trip. Beck would either return, or leave the client behind to snipe Vasquez from the back of a room in a hotel within rifle range of the hacienda. Or perhaps even from one of the brushy ridgetops running down from the mountains to the west of the hacienda that ended at the shores of the typically tranquil Sea of Cortez. Duncan knew there would be time to react once Beck arrived, but pinpointing his arrival was important, as that was when the clock would start ticking.

The two men looked down the long, wide arroyo, which opened up below them to a sweeping crescent-shaped beach with a rocky point on the north end where the hacienda sat majestically in the tan desert setting, surrounded by tall palms. The casita they were in sat on the hilltop opposite the ridge running out to the hacienda. The tan, low-brushed landscape was broken by palo verde trees in the bottom, an occasional palm, and then homes along the beach. The beach itself was mostly visible from the casita's elevation, and there were typically more people on it closest to their end and fewer near the hacienda, except guests who were using the hacienda pangas, which were tied to a floating dock that could be brought ashore in sections in foul weather.

"The scenery is better than it was a minute ago, Jack," McCrery said. "You should see this woman! Take a look."

He moved away from the scope so Duncan could approach the eyepiece.

"This is the third day straight she's come from the hacienda and gone for a run on the beach."

Duncan looked through the spotting scope quietly. Then he moved for the telescope and focused it on the beautiful brown-haired woman with the body of a swimmer running down the water's edge toward their end of the beach.

"Marialena," Duncan whispered under his breath while he watched through the glass.

"You know her, Jack?" McCrery asked.

"Very well, or at least I did almost twenty years ago."

"I suppose it would surprise me the people you know, huh, Jack?"

"I don't really want to know anybody anymore. I reckon I know all the folks I'll ever really need to know already. But I did know this girl quite well."

"And are you going to let me in on who she is?"

"She is Señor Vasquez's daughter."

There was a long silence in the corner bedroom of the casita while Duncan studied the grown-up version of the girl he had loved at one point in his young life. McCrery watched Duncan, captivated by his rapt study of the beautiful woman. McCrery also watched a green gecko climb along a crack in the tan stucco wall of the bedroom, which showed only the slightest trowel marks. He listened to the whistle of California quail in the scrub above the little house and watched a buzzard as it circled below in the morning thermals, climbing as the air rose from the protected sea at the bottom of the arroyo. He could hear Feliciano stirring in the kitchen, heating refried beans and tortillas for his breakfast. And he watched Duncan follow the woman down the beach through their high-dollar optics and waited without saying anything.

After at least ten minutes had passed, McCrery finally interrupted the otherwise peaceful morning and Duncan's study of the girl by asking, "What are you going to do?"

"What do you mean what am I going to do?" Duncan replied.

"She would know, or could find out, when Beck arrives at the lodge."

"When I left here nearly twenty years ago, it was in haste in the middle of the night," Duncan said, and paused as he looked through the scope again. "Just gone in the middle of the night—no good-bye."

"So what does that mean?"

"She might rather slap me than look at me?"

Duncan sighed and sat back in the chair, taking his eye away from the optics in a brief moment of reflective melancholy. He did not regret the outcome of his life; he had married the right woman and had the family he knew he was supposed to have, but that entire period of his life had left him with an empty feeling of unfinished business. Duncan was an honorable man, and he conducted his personal life and business without exception in that manner. Slipping away in the middle of the night without a good-bye was not his way, and even though Señor Vasquez had been driving a wedge between him and Marialena, he regretted the ending. And he regretted the unknowns that remained between him and her father.

"Seriously, Jack, we have no information, nothing to go on. What if he isn't coming? How long can we hide out playing dead?" McCrery pressed.

"What if she's angry and blows the whole thing for us?"

"We don't have to tell her why we're here; we don't have to even ask about Beck specifically. Just ask her who's coming and find out when."

"I'll think about it."

"Please think about it."

Duncan and McCrery joined Feliciano in the kitchen. The three men sat quietly, spreading the black-bean paste onto the freshly fried tortillas and dousing them liberally with lime, picante, and white Mexican feta cheese. After eating two of them, Duncan asked Feliciano to go to a stable in Puerto Escondido to inquire about renting some horses and tack for a couple of weeks. The casita had a yard with nothing appealing for a horse to eat. It also had a fence that had at one time kept horses or burros or some other stock. Feliciano would say he was visiting with his family from Belize, a country with which he was familiar, and he would use his own credit card. He would not give the address of the casita, nor any more detail than the stables needed.

When Feliciano left in the car, McCrery asked, "Why do you want the horses?"

"The truth is, I don't really know," Duncan said as he watched the car wind down the dusty road toward town. "I'm bored and homesick, and for some reason I think the horses will make me feel more at home."

"I guess that's reason enough."

"It'll give us something to do. We can ride them up the hill behind us or down to the beach. Besides, I think we may use them to get Beck."

The hacienda had horses of its own ridden by the guests in addition to stables in Puerto Escondido. Locals traveled on them as well, so they were very common on the beach. Besides, the men needed a distraction.

By the time Feliciano returned, he had made the arrangements for the horses despite resistance from the men at the stables. He kept offering them more money until the fee was so high it would have replaced the horses and saddles outright, and they ran his credit card, promising to charge it exorbitantly if he did not return the horses weekly for an inspection of their health. The three men drove back to the stables in the car, and when Feliciano led the two Aztecas out of sight of the stable employees, Duncan and McCrery mounted them and rode them back to the casita.

For two days, Duncan took his turn glassing and riding close to the casita, pondering how he would deal with Marialena. In between these activities, he would groom the horses and clean and oil the saddles. After two days of this and two mornings of studying Marialena in the scopes, as they ate fish tacos prepared with dorado fillets and chilies he'd picked in the yard, Duncan decided he would ride down to the beach and at least have a close-up look at the woman.

"I'll go check her out," Duncan said to McCrery, who washed down a bite of food with a gulp of Negra Modelo beer.

"Good."

"You're right—we need whatever info we can get."

"Yes, we do."

"I'll make sure she's the right daughter—Vasquez has two."

"Do you know them both?"

"Only the one, but I'm pretty sure it's Marialena."

"You're nervous about it, aren't you?"

"A little," Duncan said, and then got up and began clearing the table and washing dishes.

Duncan felt nervous in his belly for many reasons, not the least of which was his apprehension about blowing their cover by showing himself to her. He lay awake, even after his late shift with the night-vision scope, through which they had seen nothing of more interest than the beautiful woman.

Duncan woke up early the next morning, as the woman rose early for her beach runs. He saddled the gray-black gelded Azteca, which stood fifteen-and-a-half hands—the high side of average for the breed—but not before he groomed him until he shined. If his daughter were there, he would have had her put braids down his long black mane.

He mounted the horse wearing his brown no-frills bullhide cowboy boots and jeans long enough to cover their tops, even with his feet in the stirrups. He rode the dark horse down the dirt road, which took them to the beach and past the houses that lined it, slowly so as not to lather him up. Most of the tourists were not out yet, and the morning had a chill in the air that made Jack Duncan comfortable in his jeans and long-sleeved button-down shirt. He wore the tightly woven straw cowboy hat he'd had custom made when they arrived in Cabo to protect him from the sun. Around his neck and lower face he wore a bone-colored silk scarf with a gray plaid design, which he could hide behind. It provided some anonymity, but a touch of theatrics as well.

He rode past the houses and onto the beach, heading north toward the hacienda, and when he did not see any sign of the woman, he turned the horse around and rode south toward Escondido for fifteen minutes or so before turning around and heading back toward the hacienda. As he got closer to the south end of the beach where the tan rocky ridge ended at the Sea of Cortez and formed the backdrop for the Vasquez place, he spotted the woman on the beach, now running in his direction. He trotted the horse for a moment and then slowed him down to a walk again, not wanting to meet the woman too close to the hacienda.

As they neared each other, she looked at him and smiled politely as he passed her with the brim of his hat pulled down, shadowing his face. He was at a safe distance, but he was close enough to look into the woman's eyes and see that it was, indeed, Marialena.

He watched her as they passed each other traveling in opposite directions. She could feel his eyes on her, but she paid little attention, as she was used to being gazed upon by men. Duncan shortened up the rein on her side, pulling the proud horse's head down slightly and around while digging his offside heel into his flanks and snapping the athletic beast around on a tight one-hundred-and-eighty-degree turn as he trotted him up alongside her.

She continued jogging but glanced at him and said, "He's a beautiful horse."

"Yes, he is," Duncan replied with a feeling stirring in the pit of his belly that was familiar but nearly forgotten. "And you are a beautiful woman," he said back.

She continued running, and he continued to trot the horse alongside her, but there was something distantly familiar about his voice.

"Are you always this forward with strangers?" she asked.

"No, in fact, never, with the exception of the exceedingly rare case I'm forced to look into the face of breathtaking beauty," he said, still mounted, walking the horse next to her.

"Do I know you?" she asked.

"Yes, or should I say, you knew me at one time," he said, pulling the scarf down a little, exposing more of his face.

She slowed her run to a walk and then stopped to look up at him. He swung off the saddle and landed in front of the beautiful woman with his hat in his hand, the scarf now sagging down his chest and exposing his whole face.

"*Jack Duncan,*" she said.

"Hello, Marialena."

"I don't know whether to slap your face or kiss it," she said, looking him over.

Duncan gazed back at her. She looked slightly stunned at his surprising and somewhat dramatic appearance after a nearly twenty-year absence.

"Could we compromise with a hug?"

She grabbed him and pulled him close—closer than platonic—and Duncan felt her hands cupping the back of his head and her fingers running through his hair as though she were positioning his head to kiss his face, but there was no kiss. They embraced even tighter with no words.

Marialena released him. They stepped back from each other, but she held on to both of his hands and leaned back, looking him in the eyes invitingly. Duncan felt the tension and anxiety, and then they separated.

"May I walk with you for a while?" Duncan asked her.

"I'd love that," she replied.

"You aren't mad at me? I never had the chance to say good-bye."

"I was at first, but I'm not anymore. It does no good, you know."

"What's that?"

"Anger; it does no good. Especially to be angry at a man," she said and smiled.

"Your father—" Duncan started in on what was going to be an explanation as to why he left in the middle of the night never to return, but she intervened.

"I know, Jack," she said, truncating the explanation before it began. "Please tell me about your life. Tell me, do you have a family?"

"Yes, but your father can't know I'm here!"

"He's not here right now; he won't be here until the end of the month. I run the hacienda now, and he really only comes when he has hunters."

Duncan was relieved to hear her say this, as it meant Beck was probably still coming.

"You can't tell your father I'm here; nobody can know, Marialena. I'm here in hiding. There are some men who need me dead, and until I can straighten it all out, not one person can know," he said to her very seriously.

"OK, Jack, you're safe with me. I won't tell my father or anyone. There's really no one to tell."

"Good. If anybody knows I'm here, it'd be the end of me."

"What sort of trouble are you in?"

"No trouble, really. I think the men who want me dead are probably in more trouble than I am." Duncan watched her pretty olive-skinned face tense up. "You don't have to worry. The men who want me dead already think I am."

"Do I look worried?"

Duncan looked at Marialena. Her furrowed brow had relaxed, and her face was content and wrinkleless.

"I have too much to worry about to worry about anything," she said.

They walked on the beach for an hour in one direction and then an hour and a half in the other direction back toward the hacienda while Duncan led the horse. Back at the house, McCrery watched them both through the optics.

Marialena had married a man that her father had secretly provided for her and endorsed. It was an arrangement she hadn't found out about until her mother told her ten years into the marriage. In that same conversation, her mother also revealed that her father had sent Duncan home in the middle of the night and told him not to return for his own safety. Her mother said that it was because of a mishap in the mountains, and that Duncan had no choice but to leave without saying good-bye, and that while her father liked Duncan, he had wanted her to marry a man from the right Mexican family.

Marialena now had two teenage children with that man, who spent most of his time, and more recently all of his time, in the States and in various parts of Mexico, mostly Mexico City, Guadalajara, and Puerto Vallarta, where he had business interests. The two children lived at a prep school in the States and were home for three months in the summer and a month at Christmas. They had just returned to school several days earlier, and she was lonely.

She loved Baja, however, and the hacienda. It was the place she felt most at home, and now running it was what kept her busy. Marialena enjoyed the guests, most of whom were not sportsmen, as they were in her father's day. She liked visiting with them and she loved children, so she had begun marketing to families. She loved taking them on horse rides on the trails up the ridge and on the mostly secluded beaches to the north toward Loreto, and at night she typically dined with them at a large, sit-down, family-style Mexican dinner. The hacienda's sporting activities were still running, including fishing from the pangas and her father's large fishing yachts, which operated most of the year out of Cabo San Lucas. Vasquez also kept his bird dogs—three English pointers that stayed with Marialena in her room at night—and a guide or two who could work them in the brushy arroyos. The hacienda typically booked three sheep hunters each winter and early spring, and Vasquez resided at the hacienda at these times to host the hunting gentlemen, although he rarely joined any of the big game hunts. He often led quail hunts and occasionally joined a group on a fishing excursion, but he was getting older and slowing down a bit.

Duncan could see that this striking woman he'd had such an intense relationship with was lonely, and this put him in a dangerous place. She was so incredibly beautiful with her long light-brown hair that showed no gray; her jade-green eyes, just as striking twenty years later; and her curvaceous body, hardened by the hours of swimming. Marialena was very intelligent, and Duncan felt a slight pity that she had been left alone, with nearly grown children and a husband who was probably spending more time with a mistress or whores than with her. She had probably never really loved her husband in the first place. She was proud and not beaten, still in control, but she seemed to be living with the arrangement because untangling it would be more complicated than living with it. To Duncan's mind, it did not seem a dignified life for such a noble and splendid woman.

His life was so different from hers—at least when he was not hunting men. He told her about Erica and his two kids and the ranch.

He was proud of his wife and kids, and while he felt as though he had failed at a lot in life, his family was his success. He told her his only intent was to sort out his issues with the men who were trying to kill him so he could get home to his family.

She asked him to dinner at the hacienda. He declined, saying that it was too risky, as one of the old employees might recognize him, but Marialena assured him that none of the current employees had been there when Duncan guided for her father. Again, Duncan politely declined, but he asked if she would instead accompany him on a dinner picnic. She accepted this plan, but insisted on putting together the food.

Duncan returned to the casita, where he found McCrery sitting in a wicker chair drinking coffee.

"You look like you're on vacation," Duncan said with a smile.

"You look like you were on a romantic stroll on the beach."

"You're the one who pushed me to go talk to her," Duncan said in defense.

McCrery laughed. "I'm just jackin' with ya, Jack."

Duncan smiled and hung his hat on the wooden peg of a coatrack that hung on the wall just inside the door.

"What'd you find out?"

"Nothing, but I'm having dinner with her tonight, and I'll get it all."

"Oh," McCrery said with a big smile spreading across his face. "A date."

"You're the one who pushed me to do this," Duncan repeated as he felt his cheeks get warm.

"No, that's good."

"I'll get details from her then."

Duncan and McCrery discussed their options now that they had Marialena as a resource. They concluded that it was OK for Duncan to go to the hacienda. It would be safe enough; nobody would recognize him, and it was better than being seen in town with her, as the locals would undoubtedly know her and would wonder about the gringo who was with her.

That evening, Duncan and Marialena ate their picnic on the beach below the hacienda as they listened to the waves lap gently at the shore. Marialena had packed a Caesar salad, shrimp gazpacho, tortillas, cold black beans, guacamole, and sliced tri-tip rubbed with a sweet-and-spicy rub and grilled. She'd also brought a delightful Argentine malbec and a chilled sauvignon blanc that Duncan did not pay much attention to. They laughed and talked, mostly of their children and a little of Señor Vasquez.

Marialena sat next to him on the blanket they had spread, which made Duncan nervous. She touched his hand and his knee a couple of times, saying, "Try this," and putting a combination of foods in his mouth with her slender, manicured fingers. The air was perfectly warm but not hot. Lights twinkled off the water and shined from the homes that lined the beach to the south of them, which illuminated the curved and drooping underside of the fronds on the tall palms lining the beach. And she was stunning, which reminded Duncan of another night nearly twenty years earlier.

It was right before he'd left Baja and the hacienda after the shootout in the mountains. Vasquez had been at the hacienda for a week and a half and had been an effective barrier to Duncan and Marialena's intimacy. They were still in the early phase of falling in love, when the physiological fireworks driving their passion were hot and blinding, and after a week of separation, they were desperate for a sensual interlude. Marialena packed a picnic in a cooler, and they snuck out well after dark for a prearranged rendezvous on the beach near the pangas. They loaded the smallest of the boats, and Duncan rowed it out a couple hundred yards away from shore and started the outboard. The lovers ran across the flat water to Isla Carmen. Duncan ran the boat right up onto the sandy beach, and they leapt from it, falling to the sand and spreading a blanket all in one entangled act. Duncan cut his foot on a shell while disembarking, but he paid no attention to the bleeding, putting all his energy into making love to the beautiful, sun-kissed girl. Following the impassioned romp, they ate the picnic and rested, and then drank some wine and repeated it all. Tired and spent, they snuck home across the water an hour or two before sunup.

That evening was on Duncan's mind as they sat eating on the beach in the sultry night air. He still managed to focus enough to confirm that Beck was, indeed, the client coming to the hacienda in ten days to hunt sheep. Marialena also told him that Beck was bringing a guest, whom they would be accommodating but did not yet know the identity of. The evening was enjoyable, and Duncan could feel the tension growing.

"We should probably get going," he said as he started picking up their food.

"I suppose it's getting late," Marialena said.

They packed the food into the canvas bag Marialena had brought the meal in and folded the blanket and placed it on top in the same bag.

"Will you walk me home?" she said, smiling at him.

"No, I can do better than that."

He had ridden down the mountain on the dark horse, and instead of walking, he mounted the horse and pulled her onto the haunches of the animal behind him so that she could ride up the trail to the edge of the hacienda grounds, where he would deliver her. He balanced the canvas bag on the horn and the back of the horse's neck while she wrapped her arms tightly around his stomach and laid her cheek against his back. He was sure she could feel his heart pounding in his chest.

When they reached the edge of the hacienda grounds, he swung off the horse and lifted her down.

"Would you like to come up?" she asked.

"Yes…No…I mean, I'd like to, but I can't," Duncan said and swung back up into the saddle.

"You know you could stay here at the hacienda until my father gets back. He shows up now a day or so before the sheep hunters."

"Thank you, but I can't."

"Can't or won't?" she said and smiled again.

"I don't know; both, I guess?"

"Then have dinner with me tomorrow night," she said as she turned to walk away.

"OK."

From his seat on the horse's back, he watched her walk that last little distance to the hacienda, which was lit by the lights in Vasquez's trophy room—the one that held the .36 Colt revolvers in the teakwood case. The view was sensual and tempting.

For seven days, Duncan dined with Marialena at the hacienda and then rode the almost-black horse leisurely back to the casita on the hill after dark. He studied the grounds, and he more than enjoyed her company. They mostly rode the trails north of the hacienda, and in the evenings, they dined together in the private dining room, separate from the guests. They enjoyed the meals she cooked in the private kitchen, which kept Duncan's identity away from the staff. He felt slightly guilty that McCrery was stuck at the casita dining with Feliciano, but with no need to watch the hacienda, they were free to recreate a little. One day, Duncan and Marialena took one of the pangas out and fly-fished, landing a half-dozen sierra mackerel and one yellowtail. Duncan caught the yellowtail with live bait, which he said was "cheating," but he wanted Hamachi. Marialena had hoped for more, but she did not get it.

On the eighth night after dinner, Marialena walked Duncan out to the horse stables to collect his horse for the ride back to the casita. In the darkness of the stable, where the horse was waiting in a stall, she stepped in front of him, and, grabbing his hands in hers, she kissed him gently on the lips.

"Stay with me tonight," she said. "My father will be here tomorrow and then you will disappear from me again, but stay with me tonight."

Duncan had thought long and hard about the proposition for the last week, as he knew it was coming, and he answered her immediately.

"I'd like nothing more, Marialena, but I have to meet somebody tonight who's helping me with the trouble I'm in. I'm nearly late as it is. I'd love to, but I can't." He'd rehearsed the response many times, fearing that the proposition would come.

The truth was that he had loved Erica since he was a small boy, and he had rushed to tell her of any accomplishment of which he was proud. She would not have taken this one lightly. He did, however, care for this beautiful woman who had unknowingly helped him with his troubles, and he wanted the best for her. He wanted to do the right thing without hurting her.

He kissed her again, briefly. She smiled and looked at him with disappointed eyes. Duncan wondered if she knew he was lying, that he really did want to stay, but that he couldn't for more noble reasons. He'd been away from home for months and his own wife had been less than affectionate to him for years, and there was the thought that perhaps Erica had had enough of him and the trouble he was in. But the answer was no, if for nothing more than to maintain one layer of himself that Beck and the world couldn't strip from him. He was fatally loyal and honest. If he had stayed, nobody would know but him and Marialena, but that was one too many people.

She led the horse out of the stall and stables and held the reins while Duncan swung up into the saddle. He looked down at her and smiled gratefully.

"It's been wonderful," he said.

She let him go, again, and Duncan spurred the horse firmly with the heels of his boots and trotted off into the darkness.

Duncan slept well that night, but he and McCrery were up early the following morning; there would be little time to rest for the next couple of days. They saddled the horses, which were now part of the mission, and the two men rode down into the arroyo and up the other side until they were on the ridge above the hacienda. From there, they followed the spine of the ridge for a mile until they dropped off and headed into the brushy, flat country to the north of the hacienda. Duncan had ridden the trails with Marialena, and he had decided that they would ambush Beck in this isolated country privately owned by Vasquez, where he conducted his quail hunts. Marialena had told him that Beck was scheduled to arrive in the evening. During the first full day of his stay, Beck and the client would hunt quail in the morning and sight in rifles in the afternoon, which would provide Duncan and McCrery with their opportunity.

They picked the location for the ambush, and they also chose the location from which McCrery would cover him with the big rifle from a safe distance of three hundred yards. They had discussed a dozen different scenarios for ridding the world of Beck, but the men determined the ambush in the desert to be the best option. It would also leave Vasquez in the position of having to dispose of the bodies.

They returned to the casita and again to waiting—now for the opportunity to move on with their lives without looking over their shoulders and wondering when Beck would catch up to them. They went through the equipment, and McCrery shot the big rifle with the silencer to check and confirm its accuracy. They double- and triple-checked the rest of their weapons and equipment, including the horses and tack, in preparation. In the evening, they confirmed Vasquez's arrival when they got a glimpse of the man in the spotting scope.

"There's Vasquez," Duncan said.

"Are you sure?"

"It's him, all right. Beck should be here tomorrow." Vasquez was hard to miss with his full head of silver hair, which stood out against his tan skin. Duncan watched him in the scope, and while he couldn't mistake the man he'd been friends with years ago, he could see that age had begun to erode the man he'd known. He did not stand quite as tall, and while he had always been a lean man, he looked slightly atrophied by the inescapable effects of age.

Duncan contacted the captain of Brett's fishing boat, which was waiting for them in Cabo, and he told the captain to come up the inside to Puerto Escondido. The following day—the day of Beck's arrival—Duncan and McCrery met the yacht in the marina. There, the captain rented a transient slip, filled the Bertram's large diesel fuel tank, and put on board some ice and a large supply of bait. They loaded the small amount of baggage onto the boat, minus what they would need to dispatch Beck, and then they returned to the casita, where Duncan sorted through a delivery he'd received from his cousin a week earlier containing all the info his people had reconnoitered on Vasquez.

It was a packet of photos, documents, and printed information on Vasquez: all his holdings, his associations, and any bit of dirt the cousin and his men could uncover on him, which was very little. There was a small handful of men gone missing who had worked for or had been associated with Vasquez over the previous fifty years, but most of them were of suspicious character and had probably been killed for crimes they had committed that had nothing to do with Vasquez. There were references to a handful of connections to dubious political figures, but Duncan was convinced that the number of politicians and government leaders in the world who possessed even the slightest shred of honor, integrity, or compassion could be counted on one hand. He also felt that having those connections was sometimes necessary for a man, but it did not mean they shared the same character deficiencies. Much like McCrery's connection to Beck, or for that matter, his own. Vasquez owned a number of lucrative hotels and resorts, plus a large distillery that sold mostly in Mexico, Central America, and South America, and had a small distribution in the States. And there were his charter boats, which took fishermen out on short- and long-range trips out of San Diego, Cabo San Lucas, and Puerto Escondido. The boats were first purchased for Vasquez's own use, but gradually they'd begun to make a small amount of money. These boats provided the only possible connection to a crime of any sort.

One of the charter captains, an American, was using one of the boats to move drugs up and down the Pacific, but there was nothing to link Vasquez to the operation. Brett and his men were sure that Vasquez had no knowledge of, or at least no involvement in, the trafficking. The packet of information Beck had given to him on Vasquez en route to Guatemala on the ill-fated trip to Acapulco to execute Ivan Libor had been almost entirely fabricated. Brett's research uncovered the likely reason for Beck's motive, and Duncan was relieved to see the proof that Vasquez was the man he thought he was.

The research also uncovered that Beck had been involved in a plan to buy out or take over the hacienda and its grounds from Vasquez, either by negotiation or by force, but Vasquez had thwarted all his efforts for nearly thirty years. Vasquez was more familiar with James Beck than Duncan had realized.

Duncan had McCrery call Marialena using an alias and book the fishing charter captained by the drug-running American. Unsuspecting, she accommodated his request and contacted the captain, ordering him to ready the boat for a three-day trip and bring it to Puerto Escondido.

The men ate dinner as the sun sank lower and slipped behind the Sierra de la Giganta. The mood was a little heavy, and all three men were eager to finish what they had started and go home.

After a restlessness night of sleep, the men rose well in advance of the sun. They saddled the horses in silence and rode them in the dark across the arroyo and down the ridge above the hacienda. They tied the horses to a palo verde tree in the bottom of a wash and climbed on foot with their gear to the top of the small knoll from which McCrery would cover Duncan. The horses were out of sight from the dirt road four hundred yards below, at the place where the small entourage, including Beck and Vasquez and the bird dogs, would pass on its way to the quail-hunting area to the north. The two men cleared the low brush and built up an area from which McCrery could shoot in a prone position, right next to a stand of stunted pipe organ cacti.

The sun was beginning to illuminate the eastern horizon and the mountains on the far side of the Sea of Cortez, and soon there was enough sun peeking over the distant skyline to cause a shimmer on the tranquil water. Duncan admired the view and entertained the thought that one day he would again like to watch the sun rise over the Sea of Cortez for no other reason than to enjoy the view. The air was comfortable and the winds were light and down the mountain, but by the time the quail hunters had returned and they had positioned themselves for the ambush, those winds would be traveling up the drainage with the warming thermals. The world of Baja began to come to life before them.

There were two vultures circling the ridge above them in search of some unfortunate creature that had met its end in the night and would make a buzzard meal. There were three burros working their way through the low prickly pear and brush of the desert floor. On the water, fishing pangas were beginning to depart for their favorite fishing holes, and as the sun rose just high enough to light the slightest warmth on the two men's faces, the three Polaris Rangers, loaded with men, passed below them on the road.

McCrery tracked them in the scope. He held the crosshairs just in front of Beck, who was riding in the second vehicle, following him in the scope as the Ranger rolled down the dusty road. Moving the scope, he worked his way around the rest of the vehicles' occupants, studying them. In the first Ranger, two Mexican men bounced out to lead the small convoy with an English pointer leashed into the bed on the back of their vehicle. The silver-haired Vasquez drove the vehicle in which Beck rode. In the Ranger behind Vasquez and Beck, which was the last in the group, a white man drove with another very overweight gringo seated next to him. The fat white man looked out of place in the austere, sunbaked desert environment. A second English pointer bounced around in the back of the last Ranger.

When they passed and all signs of the men had disappeared into the low desert except for the faint plume of dust that followed them, Duncan mounted the dark horse and rode down the mountain to wait for them on their return trip to the hacienda.

When he reached the road the entourage had just passed and would be returning on, he crossed it and tied the horse to a palo verde tree. Then he went back and brushed his trail out of the dust with a branch off one of the shrubs that dotted the desert landscape. He wanted to cover his tracks should somebody follow them out later. He then slipped into a brushy draw out of sight from the road, where he was hidden by some palo verde and brush that surrounded a water hole. He set in to wait.

He lay in the shade of a steep canyon wall and gazed up at the sky. He knew he would have several hours or more of waiting while the men hunted quail, and his thoughts wandered, first to Marialena. He was excited that such a beautiful woman was attracted to him. At the same time, he felt guilt. Guilt that he disappointed her and guilt that he considered a betrayal of his wife. But he placated his conscience by congratulating himself for resisting a nearly impossible opportunity, and for the fact that not only was his bond to Erica still intact, but so, too, was his integrity.

He thought of the fun he and Erica had as kids, and the times they'd met in the middle of the night surrounded by sagebrush after he swam his horse across the Madison River. They had kissed under the moon like their young lives depended on it. He thought about the time they skinny-dipped and made love on the bank above the cold river, and about the inquisitive buck antelope that had been lured in by his curious white ass protruding from the green prairie grass. They laughed when they realized the antelope was watching. A lot of their laughter had faded with the struggles of life, and lying there under the Baja sky, Duncan began to make deals with himself and with God should he get through the day unscathed and free. Then, his thoughts became muddled and dreamlike as he slipped into a light sleep.

The sound of a rock tumbling down the canyon wall jolted him from his dozing, and when he became fully aware, he realized he was sitting up with the pistol in his hand pointed in the direction of the sound. He released the air he was holding in his chest and began breathing again, but harder, and the thought occurred to him that maybe he was a little scared.

He looked at his phone. It was almost ten o'clock. He figured he still had an hour or two, so he called McCrery on his cell.

"Are you awake?" Duncan asked when McCrery picked up on the other end.

"Yeah, you?"

"Yeah," Duncan said, but didn't admit to having nodded off.

"I couldn't sleep if I wanted to."

"That's good. No sign of them?"

"Only some occasional distant shotgun blasts when they get into a patch of quail."

Duncan couldn't hear the distant shots from his hiding place in the canyon.

"Are you still OK with this, Tom?"

"I'm good with it. I don't see any other way."

"If we prevail, I'll be free by the end of the day."

"Freedom is always worth fighting for."

"Call me when you see something."

"Will do," McCrery said and ended the call.

Duncan looked at the antique pistol in his hand and at the initials "T. V." carved into the metal butt frame. He thought of the man who had originally owned it and of the men who might have died by it. He thought of freedom, and that he'd heard it said many times that freedom wasn't free, but the thought occurred to him that only a small few actually paid for it. *Today*, Duncan thought, *Beck will pay for mine.*

He lay back against a rock and closed his eyes. He thought about his kids and his dad and his grandfather and his old Labs that were gone. He'd never been afraid to die until his children were born, and if it weren't for them, he thought, he'd have no reservations about what he was about to do. But he couldn't leave his children behind, and while he wasn't especially religious, the sudden urge to pray came over him. He laughed out loud at the thought of asking God to help him see his impending task through, so instead, he simply asked him to guide him home safely to his wife and kids. He apologized to God for even praying, as he'd made a deal with him when his daughter was born that he'd never ask him for anything again if he would see to it that his children stayed healthy and grew old and happy. And until that day, he hadn't asked God for anything else. But he rationalized his new request as being part of his prayer for his children's happiness and health. He felt they needed him for that. And when he was done, he relaxed a little and thought about the mountains and the hunts he'd been on, and he thought about how he'd lost his passion for things he'd once loved. He again promised himself some changes if he got to the end of this day. Then his head started wandering off to a light sleep again. Duncan was dozing when the cell phone vibrated in his pocket, and he answered McCrery's call.

"They're on their way back; I can see the cloud of dust," McCrery said.

"How far out?" Duncan asked as he got up out of the dirt.

"Based on timing them on the trip out, they should be in your canyon in about six minutes, unless they stop."

"OK, I'll be ready," Duncan said, untying the horse's reins from the palo verde tree. "Stay on the phone and talk them in to me."

"You got it, Jack," McCrery replied.

Duncan mounted the horse and slowly walked him out to the edge of the road, where he waited the last few minutes in the desert sun. McCrery looked at Duncan through his binoculars and thought he could have passed for one of the local desert inhabitants who often traveled on horse or donkey. Duncan could have also passed for one of his own ancestors who rode the plains of Texas and Montana with his wide-brimmed cowboy hat and large, sweeping scarf, which was again pulled up to cover much of his face. He looked as though he were about to rob a train in another century.

Duncan wore a light coat that was split in the back so that it would still hang low enough while he was in the saddle to conceal the two pistols hung around his waist in a leather double-holster rig he'd had made in Loreto. The two pistols were, in fact, from another century, and while they were technological relics, they were still deadly in the hands of a man like Duncan.

They were also Duncan's key to involving Vasquez. He had taken the pistols from their teak-and-glass case at the hacienda one night while Marialena was tending to some business, and he'd replaced them with his own replicas, which Brett had brought back from his trip to deliver the note to Erica. He wore the two pistols proudly and sat tall in the saddle.

"They'll be coming around the point of rocks in less than a minute," McCrery said.

"Watch the bodyguard close; he'll be the first to go for his gun," Duncan said with the cell phone in his left hand and the reins in the other.

"Roger."

"Shoot straight, Tom. My life may depend on it."

"Good luck!"

"You, too," Duncan said and slipped the phone into his coat pocket.

In addition to the good line of fire it offered McCrery from above, Duncan had chosen this spot for the ambush because when the ATVs came around the point of the rocks that the road curved around, they would be too close to him to back out. They would be inside thirty yards—long pistol range—with no option to get around him.

Duncan moved out into the middle of the road now and stood facing the direction from which the men would be coming. He could feel his pulse quickening. He heard the churning of the motors of the Polaris Rangers. He felt tightness in his chest and a shortness of breath, but he shut his eyes for the briefest second, then took a deep breath and exhaled, consciously slowing his racing heart as the air left his body. And then they were there, coming to a dusty stop in the middle of the road, with each vehicle pulling up to the left side of the vehicle it had been following, until all three were lined up side by side in front of Jack Duncan.

"Qué pasa, amigo?" said Señor Vasquez from the passenger seat of the Ranger on Duncan's far left. One of his men was at the wheel.

"I'm an old sheep-hunting friend here to protect you from the man you're quail hunting with," Duncan replied in bad Spanish that was unrecognizable to Beck.

"Cómo?" asked Vasquez, slightly confused.

"This man is here to kill you," Duncan said in Spanish again while holding up an envelope with all the documents Beck had falsified about Vasquez in it. "Walk with me, and I'll show you the proof."

Señor Vasquez told the gentlemen to wait where they were, as the *vaquero* had a gift for him, and he would be right back.

Duncan backed the horse up in the road to give the two men more distance so they would not be heard. Beck waited impatiently, still unaware of the identity of the vaquero under the large hat, while the other men sat calmly, blissfully ignorant of what was about to happen.

Vasquez approached Duncan, who leaned down from the saddle and allowed the scarf to fall from his face as he handed the packet of lies to the old man.

Vasquez was still striking, with his silver-white hair and moustache standing out against his very tan skin. Duncan looked the old man in the eyes, and those eyes now recognized the gringo under the hat and behind the scarf.

"Don't say my name out loud," Duncan whispered as he leaned

in toward him to hand him the packet. "Beck is here to kill you, Señor Vasquez. I know because he wanted me to help him do it."

Vasquez took the packet of papers and photos and studied them for a minute or less, but it felt like an hour to Duncan as well as to McCrery, who was watching the bodyguard through the riflescope.

"Lies, all of it!" Vasquez said, looking up at Duncan.

"Yes, I know, and when I refused to help him, he had me killed."

"You don't look that dead to me," the old man said, smiling for the first time.

"Come on, Vasquez, let's get going," Beck yelled rudely from the seat of his Ranger.

"No, I'm quite alive, but if you will excuse me I have to tend to some business, or else you and I are both going to be very dead men," Duncan said, smiling back.

"I can help," said Vasquez, reaching out and shaking Duncan's hand.

"No, sir, I've got this one," he said.

"You know his guest is a US congressman?"

"Really?" Duncan hesitated. He stopped his horse for a moment and then said, "There's no bigger criminal that exists, is there?"

"I can't think of any."

He smiled at the old man in the khaki bird vest and rode past him, approaching the three Rangers. The congressman had traded places with Vasquez and was driving the Ranger he and Beck were in. The two Mexican men looked at Señor Vasquez for a sign as to what to do, and he motioned at them to do nothing. As Duncan approached the middle car with Beck and the congressman sitting in it, he let the scarf fall from his face again. Beck turned ghastly white, as though he were looking at a ghost.

Then he regained his arrogance. The color came back to his face, and he said, "Who do you think you are playing games with me, Jack Duncan?"

"These are pretty high stakes for a game, Beck," he said as he swung out of the saddle and landed ten feet in front of Beck and the fat congressman, who was sweating profusely next to Beck in the direct sun from behind the wheel of the middle Ranger.

"Do you know who we are, son?" the congressman said to Duncan. Duncan laughed directly at his jowly, round face.

"The question is, fat man, do I give a shit who you are?" Duncan stared down Beck, anger festering in him, growing, making it easier to do what he was about to.

"You stand aside, young man. I am a US congressman," the man demanded, wiping sweat from his brow with his forearm.

"In the end, you're worm shit like the rest of us," said Duncan calmly, still fixed on Beck but taking in the entire scene.

Suddenly, Beck's bodyguard, who sat in the vehicle to the far right, reached into his vest for the pistol hidden in his shoulder holster. At the same moment, Duncan drew the pair of antique .36 Navy Colts that had belonged to Vasquez's infamous gunslinger grandfather. The bodyguard jumped backward in the seat as McCrery's bullet struck his chest from the ridge above and Duncan put a .36 caliber ball next to it only a fraction of a second behind McCrery's well-placed shot.

"There's no need for this, Jack," Beck said. "I can give you millions to walk." He spoke with an anxious tone uncustomary for the man who usually controlled everything.

"You don't want to shoot an old congressman, do you, now, son?" the fat man said from behind the wheel of the Ranger as he looked down the barrel of the pistol in Duncan's right hand while Beck looked down the one in his left.

Duncan said nothing. He just glared at Beck.

"Really, Jack, how much do you need to walk away?"

"How much is your life worth?"

"I can buy you freedom," Beck said, shifting slowly in the seat of the Ranger to reach a shotgun that lay against the seat, muzzle down.

"Freedom isn't free, Beck. Somebody's got to pay for it."

"Yes, I'll pay for yours. Name the amount."

"You don't have enough to buy your way out of this payment."

"Sure I do," Beck said.

"You tried to kill me a few months ago, and now you want to give me money?"

"I didn't try to kill you."

"No, you don't have the balls."

"Come on—be reasonable."

"Is selling your soul being reasonable?" Duncan asked as he slowly nudged the horse to his left, which opened up Beck's body from behind the front roll bar of the Ranger for a clear shot. "You sent a couple Mexicans to do your dirty work, just like the rest of your life—built on the backs of real men."

The congressman looked at Beck and Duncan, then at Vasquez and the Mexicans in the Rangers on either side of him. "Aren't you going to do something?" he said, but nobody acknowledged him.

"You're no different from me, Jack Duncan," Beck shouted.

"Oh, I'm very different from you."

Suddenly, Beck swung his shotgun from under the dash of the Ranger in a last attempt to defend his miserable existence, but a ball from the pistol in Duncan's left hand hit him square in the chest.

The force knocked him from the seat of the vehicle as the congressman stomped on the accelerator and came directly for Duncan. Duncan instantly fired the right pistol into the fat body of the congressman and dived out of the way, rolling once in the dirt and coming up grasping for the reins of the spooked horse with a pistol still in each hand.

The congressman sped down the road, forcing Vasquez to jump quickly off to the side while Duncan jumped back into the spooked horse's saddle and gathered the reins. Duncan spurred him hard and whipped him with the end of one of the reins as he raced the horse up alongside the Ranger. He leaned out with the pistol and fired a ball into the congressman's side.

The horse jumped sideways at the gunshot, away from the scary noise and the plume of white black-powder smoke, throwing Duncan into the dirt and leaving him with what felt like a broken rib or two. Duncan gathered himself, spit from his mouth the dust he'd eaten during his fall, and winced at the pain in his right side. He was dazed, but he collected his senses. The fat man lay still and lifeless in a heap over the wheel of the Ranger, which had stopped suddenly against a large tan boulder. Duncan had a nasty cut on the left side of his forehead and could feel the blood mixed with sweat running down his crow's foot and into the corner of his left eye. He wiped the blood from his eye, making it worse with the grit stuck to the back of his sweaty hand. Then he clutched the right side of his ribs with his left hand for support and began to limp slowly back toward Beck.

Vasquez and his men, who had gotten out of their Rangers, stood silently and watched Duncan. One of them had kicked the shotgun away from Beck's reach, somehow understanding that Duncan was a friend of their boss.

Beck lay on his back. His right leg pulled up and then dropped, and his right foot rolled back and forth nervously. Then the right leg pushed at the ground as if to move the dying body away from Duncan's approach.

When Duncan reached Beck, he clutched a blood-soaked patch of clothing on the right side of his chest. Frothy red lung blood bubbled at the edge of his lips.

"I don't deserve this," Beck said with a gurgling cough.

Duncan stood over him, the pistol in his right hand bouncing uncharacteristically out of control around Beck's flushed face. Duncan's vision was blurred with blood and dirt in his left eye, and by the tears that were filling both. Duncan looked down the barrel of the pistol, then he took a breath and let the air out, and the little brass front sight found a place to stop in the middle of Beck's forehead. He steadied the pistol.

"Maybe not, but you certainly earned it."

Duncan touched the trigger, and the antique pistol spit fire and smoke and jumped in his hand.

When the white smoke cleared, Beck was staring blankly at the sky, his mouth agape. Black burn marks and spent black powder speckled his lifeless face, and a neat round hole in the center of his forehead punctuated his life.

Duncan pried the percussion caps off the nipples of the remaining loaded cylinders as he walked slowly to Vasquez. He reached for the pistol that should have been in the left side of his holster, but it wasn't there. When he reached him, he handed the pistol butt-first to Vasquez so the man could see his great-grandfather's initials engraved into the frames of the grips. "The other one must have fallen from the holster when I got thrown," Duncan said.

"I guess this makes me an accomplice," Vasquez said, taking the pistol and seeing his great-grandfather's initials.

"That's better than a victim."

"Yes, it is," Vasquez said and smiled a thin smile.

"This was entirely self-defense, but there's no shortage of folks in the States who would see it different," Duncan said.

"I'm sure you're right about that."

"I tried to reason with him, but he wouldn't have it. He tried to kill me instead."

"He was a piece of shit," Vasquez said and smiled.

"Nonetheless, I needed your help to get rid of the bodies, so I used your guns."

"Stop talking, son, I'll take care of it. Let's call things even."

"Good. Thank you, Jack," Duncan said to the old man.

A puff of white smoke and the crack of a pistol fractured the moment. Vasquez lurched and then clutched his belly just under his last rib as if to prevent precious life from escaping from the hole that had just been punched through his body. He staggered forward, falling to his hands and knees while Duncan instinctively reached for the pistols that were no longer in his belt. Then Duncan lunged for his wounded friend and they stumbled for the cover of the Ranger. Another crack, and Duncan heard the ball whistle over his head. He saw the two Mexican guides dive for cover, one behind a large boulder, and the second behind one of the other Rangers. He glanced over his shoulder as he ran with Vasquez in his grasp and saw the congressman staggering toward them with the missing pistol in his hand and blood covering his pressed white shirt and khaki canvas hunting pants.

Again the pistol barked and shattered the windshield of the

Ranger they were hiding behind. Then, from up on the mountain near the base of the pipe organ, came the muffled metallic snap of McCrery's big rifle, and the congressman folded into a fat, dead heap in the road.

"Where did that come from?" Vasquez asked with weakness entering his voice.

"A friend of mine who was watching over us." Duncan stood up and then stooped over Vasquez. "Where'd you get hit?"

"It doesn't matter, Jack. I'm old and used up."

"It does matter," Duncan said. He pulled Vasquez's bird vest back and ripped open his button-down shirt. "Shit," Duncan said in a controlled tone when he saw the location of the wound.

Vasquez's two men rushed up to his aid when they saw the shooter go down. The older of the two grabbed Vasquez's hand and held it tightly.

"Está mal," the man said.

"Está bien," Vasquez said back to him. "Duncan es cómo un hijo. Ayúdale a cualquier manera podría necesitar." *Duncan is like a son to me. Help him in any way he needs.*

"OK," one of the men said.

"Ya saben…qué hacer con los cuerpos," he said, struggling to finish the sentence. *You know what to do with the bodies.*

"Sí, pues," the two men said. They got up from Vasquez and went immediately to work.

Vasquez's men dragged the bodies into the brush near the water hole, and Duncan—dirty, bleeding, and holding his broken ribs—limped after the horse, which was standing there looking at the men as though he were the intelligent one. He grabbed the horse by the reins and led him back to Vasquez, who was still lying behind the

Ranger. Duncan tied one of the reins to the front bumper of the off-road vehicle and pulled out some medical supplies from the saddlebags. He walked back around to Vasquez and knelt over him, hastily spilling clotting powder from a packet he'd taken from his saddlebags. He covered the wound with a bandage, which he taped to Vasquez with athletic tape.

"You need to know something, Jack," Vasquez said quietly as Duncan worked on him.

"What's that?"

"The three *campesinos* you shot in the mountains years ago were not after you. They were after Beck. But you were too good, too quick for those men…too deadly."

"Oh," Duncan said as he finished up his bandaging.

"I am an old man now…I see the past more clearly than the present…I don't bother looking at the future." Vasquez paused to muster more strength to finish. "I regret that I sent you away…I should have brought you back. Not for you, but for Marialena…and me."

Duncan leaned down and reached out, slowly and painfully, to shake Vasquez's hand. He looked him in his eyes, and those eyes seemed less strained now.

"Go now," Vasquez said.

"I can't leave you like this," Duncan said through the tightening of his throat. He felt tears starting to fill his eyes, but he gritted his teeth and willed them not to fall.

"Get outta here," Vasquez said and closed his eyes. "There's nothing you can do for me. Now go."

One of his men had retrieved the pistol from the dead congressman and returned it to Duncan, who handed it to Vasquez. He looked at the pistol for a moment, then laid it next to the other one, which rested in the dirt by his side. "Shot by my own great-grandfather's gun," he said. "Maybe they're more cursed than haunted."

"They're neither," Duncan said. Then he untied the horse and climbed slowly into the saddle and looked down at the man he'd known so long ago. He tried to think of something more to say. He could see the old man's face relax. He looked strangely younger than he had when they'd met minutes earlier, only paler. He closed his eyes again for a moment.

"You've turned into a fine man, Jack Duncan."

"So have you."

"I hope…you accept my apology."

"If you'll accept mine," Duncan said.

"I'd like you to come hunt with me next winter…here at the hacienda," Vasquez said in a quiet, fading voice.

"I'll be here," Duncan said, but he knew it was the last time he would see his old friend.

Then, he turned the horse away from Vasquez. He let the tears roll out of his eyes and down his cheeks as he walked the horse away from the scene, and he never looked back. He slapped the horse's flanks with his heels, the horse jumped forward, and they clambered painfully up the hill, riding at a canter to the pipe organ cacti, back toward the casita.

EPILOGUE

Duncan and McCrery stepped onto the yacht no less than an hour after Duncan left Vasquez. At the same moment, Vasquez's men booked Beck and the congressman on Vasquez's fishing charter for a two-day tuna-fishing trip with the drug-running captain in Vasquez's employ.

Later that evening, after the sun had set, his two men took the bodies down to the panga and then ran them out to a five-hundred-foot-deep underwater canyon. The men wrapped the bodies in chains to keep them on the bottom and dumped them in. The following day, three hundred miles south and west of the men's watery grave, the charter yacht sent out a distress call that was picked up by the Mexican and American Coast Guards. Vasquez's men sank the yacht before help could arrive. They'd knocked the captain in the head and stored him on ice in the fish hold, where he went down with his ship for betraying Vasquez. Then, they returned to shore in a panga they'd towed out with them.

That evening, it was reported all over television, on the Internet, and in newspapers that two well-known Americans had been declared lost at sea along with the captain, and that it was unlikely the bodies would ever be recovered.

Erica and Bergstrom saw the story on the evening news in Montana as the family ate dinner in the Bergstroms' dining room. Erica rose from the table and walked to the television to get the details, but there were not many.

Bergstrom winked at his daughter and said, "Kids, I think your daddy will be home any day now."

The kids cheered.

Brett had booked Duncan and McCrery on extended hunting and fishing trips in Central and South America and had their real passports stamped accordingly. There were flight records and lodge reservations for alibis, and when they returned to Puerto Quetzal, Brett took them to the airport, where they did actually fly to Argentina and hunt ducks and perdiz for a few days before flying home.

The trip to Argentina was made not out of the men's desire to hunt, as both were eager to get home to family and business, but to allow a little more time to pass to see if any officials would come to ask questions. None did.

There were so few people who knew of Jack Duncan's connection to James Beck that there really was nobody to ask questions. One of Beck's bodyguards was with him at the bottom of the ocean, and the other was now unemployed. All those with intimate knowledge of the relationship who were still upright were honest, loyal friends and family to Duncan, and while his tracks were covered, there were never any questions to answer.

It was two days before Valentine's Day when Jack Duncan walked through the large custom wood door of his new home back on the ranch overlooking the Madison River. Chinooks had blown warm air down the mountains, and most of the winter snow was melted around the ranch houses except for where it had slid from the roofs and piled up on the north sides of buildings. The warm air had turned cold again, but the sun was shining. The high country was still painted white by winter's brush, and with the afternoon sun just behind the Gravelly Range to the west, the alpenglow was heavenly on the Madison Range, which they looked at to the east. It was framed by the bluest sky anywhere on earth.

The kids mobbed Duncan upon his entrance into the family home, inundating him with stories of all they had done, were doing, and were making plans to do in his absence. Erica stood off to the side, watching her completed family, and let the kids have their moment with their dad. Duncan rose from the kids and looked at Erica.

"And you? Are you happy I'm home?" Duncan looked at Erica, and they stared at each other, saying nothing. Then she hugged him and kissed his lips. To Duncan, it felt like an embrace from deep in their past, and the kiss—the kiss was real. For a moment, he felt that they themselves were kids again.

She pulled away from him but kept her arms wrapped around his head. She leaned back with a big smile and looked him in the eyes and said, "How can a girl love somebody and hate them so much at the same time?"

"Hate's a pretty strong word."

"Of course I'm happy you're home. But this is it. No more, right?"

"No more," Duncan said and kissed her again.

They saw Bergstrom and his wife out the front window walking from their home across the field between the houses to greet him. The women went to work preparing a celebratory dinner, and Duncan, Bergstrom, and the two kids went to the corral and barn to feed horses.

The two men had a drink together, and Bergstrom never asked Duncan about what had gone on. He just let him have his moment. The kids showed him a new foal, and his daughter showed off a new saddle she had earned working for her grandfather. Soon, Erica joined them.

When the kids were on the other end of the corral forking hay, her smiling face turned serious for a moment. She asked with concern, "You killed him, didn't you, Jack?"

"No, hon, greed and an overestimated self-worth killed him," Duncan replied. He looked her in her sky-blue eyes, and she smiled. There was nothing more to say.

"I'm just happy you're home," she said.

"Me, too," Duncan replied, and he admired her walking away to rejoin her mother in the house.

He looked back at Bergstrom, who was standing at the other end of the barn with the kids and looking out over his family's lands, beyond the corral and beyond the sagebrush coulee to the deep purple mountains and the coming darkness.

After some time had passed and Bergstrom knew his daughter would be back to the house, he looked at Duncan, who was staring out at the mountain view now, too.

"It's a helluva thing, killin' a man, Pop," Duncan said to Bergstrom.

"Yes, it is," Bergstrom said, smiling at him.

"One day, I'll tell you the story."

ACKNOWLEDGEMENTS

Writing a book is no small task. It takes more than just one crazed person holed up in a hotel room, cabin in the woods, or a quiet back corner of a house banging away on a keyboard to produce a book. It is a group effort, and there are a few people that I need to thank. First, my editor, Erin Bernard. Beyond being great to work with, you did so much to polish the rough spots and turn this into a complete package. I learned so much from you about writing along the way, and most amazingly, you are the only person I have ever known that meets every one of your own deadlines. Bobbi Benson, thank you for your encouragement and help with the entire process and your awesome cover art and design. Thanks also to Jeff Campbell, Donna Zattau, and Darrin Thornton for your help and suggestions. And most importantly I have to say thanks to my family. Merissa, Cole, and Lauren, you really are my inspiration. Thanks for giving me so many hours in the semi-quiet back corner of our house to bang away on my keyboard when I probably should have been playing with you or remodeling the kitchen.

www.ingramcontent.com/pod-product-compliance
Lightning Source LLC
Chambersburg PA
CBHW070918260626
47162CB00007B/2721